The Dark Beyond the Bridge

"It's a starting point," I said. "What happened in southeastern Michigan in September of 1998?"

I could hardly wait to get home and turn on my computer.

"Your catastrophic event," Lucy murmured.

"The alien invasion," Annica said.

"It may not be easy. Suppose there's no record of any unusual happening?"

"Then we're back to Square One. The ghost town keeps its secrets."

"Is it getting darker or am I imagining it?" Lucy asked.

I looked around, glanced at the sky. The sun was still visible, burning down on the town, and the clouds were puffy. I saw blue and white... and shadows. "No, but it's getting windier."

"I can feel the darkness," Lucy said. "It's the town, and I hear something."

"Voices?" Annica asked. "What are they saying?"

"It's more like a hum."

I shivered. Lucy saw a different kind of darkness, one that wrapped itself around the town, and, in a sense, isolated it from the rest of the world.

Why had the town allowed us to breach its defenses?

As we neared the Focus, an apple flew past us, like a red bird flying close to the earth. Misty launched herself at it. I gave the leash a tug, and she gave me a whine of protest.

The apple?

I kicked it and breathed a sigh of relief when I saw the chunk bitten off.

It was *the* apple.

"Let's get out of here," Annica said.

The Dark Beyond the Bridge

Dorothy Bodoin

A Wings ePress, Inc.

Cozy Mystery

Wings ePress, Inc.

Edited by: Jeanne Smith
Copy Edited by: Joan C. Powell
Executive Editor: Jeanne Smith
Cover Artist: Trisha FitzGerald

Wings ePress Books
www.books-by-wings-epress.com

Copyright © 2017 by Dorothy Bodoin
ISBN 978-1-61309-671-0

Published In the United States Of America

Wings ePress Inc.
3000 N. Rock Road
Newton, KS   67114

Dedication

To Aaron Richards, whose generosity with his time and computer expertise has been invaluable in the production of my Foxglove Corners series.

One

The first warning of a ripple on our carefree afternoon was a disturbance in the air, a sudden wind that came out of nowhere and whipped the tall grasses along the roadside into wild motion.

"What on earth?"

Annica let the map of Michigan fall into her lap and slid forward on the seat. "Where did that come from?"

Before I could reply, lightning crackled across the sky which had grown perceptibly darker in the last few minutes.

"It wasn't supposed to storm," she said. "Where are we, Jennet?"

"The middle of nowhere."

In other words, about two hours out of Foxglove Corners, heading north to pick up a rescue collie and transport her to Sue Appleton, the president of our rescue league. Female, sable and white, one year old. Her name was Echo.

I had volunteered for this mission, and Annica, freed for the day from her waitressing job at Clovers and her class at Oakland University, had begged to join me.

"It'll be like a holiday," she'd said. "The last one of summer."

I was grateful for her company. In truth, I wouldn't have undertaken the day-long trip alone, even with the company of a dog on the way home.

The rain began with a splattering on the windshield and a crash of thunder directly overhead. I held onto the steering wheel while the wind threatened to send the Focus careening into the woods. With lights on and windshield wipers swishing back and forth, I drove until heavy sheets of rain pummeled the window, creating an instant white-out. If that was the correct term. I only knew that all I could see was water.

"There should be a town... out there somewhere." Annica picked up the map and the flashlight I kept in the glove compartment. "But I don't see one. If only we could find a nice restaurant or even a gas station, we could wait out the storm out in comfort."

Alarmed, I glanced at the gas gauge. With over a half tank of gas, we should be all right.

"Maybe we'll be lucky," I said.

We had been traveling through a never-ending wilderness. Tall fir trees encroached on the narrow road. When had we passed the last house, that imposing white Victorian on the hill top? It was a magnificent structure but a solitary one. All right, when had we passed the last town?

We'd left the freeway miles back to avoid detours caused by the interminable roadwork. I was happy to be driving on a country road as here, in Nowhere, we wouldn't be likely to collide with another vehicle.

Still, this was no place to be driving in a storm.

"This reminds me of a Nancy Drew book," Annica said. "Nancy and her chums are caught in a storm and they end up having tea in a mysterious inn."

"*The Sign of the Twisted Candles*?" I said. "I have it in my collection. Well, this is life, not a girls' mystery. Jennet and Annica are caught in a thunderstorm, and Jennet decides to pull off by the side of the road."

Once we were safely parked and enclosed in our own little world, Annica reached over to the backseat into a box packed with sandwiches and treats from Clovers, along with bottled water.

"Have an oatmeal cookie?" she asked. "Or an apple?"

"A cookie," I said.

She brought out a bottle of water for each of us.

It felt good to let my shoulders and hands relax and to listen to the rain beating against the windws, good to bite into the crisp raisin-studded cookie.

"Tell me again," Annica said. "Why is this collie so special?"

"Sue's younger sister, Serena, found her in a high-kill shelter. She took her out of there, but she can't keep her. Serena already has a female, and the two dogs don't get along. Echo is supposed to be gorgeous, and Sue thinks she can easily place her in Foxglove Corners."

"If she's so gorgeous, why couldn't Serena find her a home up north?" Annica asked.

"That's a mystery," I said.

I had wondered why Serena hadn't tried to find the dog a new owner in the area, perhaps someone who owned acreage. Surely a collie would be a boon to any farmer.

"Anyway, I'm going to be extra careful with Echo," I said. "The last time I drove a collie across the state, I lost her at the end of the trip."

Annica gasped. "How did you do that?"

"I had the idea to stop at Rosalyn Everett's kennel, River Rose, just to look around. Leonora was with me that time. She left the car door opened and the dog escaped."

"She must have been really stressed out, poor baby." Annica moved listlessly in her seat. "I wish I could see something. The rain isn't letting up a bit."

"It will," I said.

If we were delayed, however, we might not be able to drive home with the dog today. We'd have to find a motel, a dog friendly one. Maybe I should have stayed on the freeway.

Don't look for trouble, I told myself. *No rain lasts forever.*

~ * ~

When the storm dwindled down to a half-hearted patter and it was possible to see clearly again, I steered out to the road. The surface was slippery, but the wind had diminished. As I drove through the wild stretch, the countryside looked the same: woods washed clean with rain under a gradually lightening sky. But I sensed that something was different.

"We're on the same road, aren't we?" I asked. "I didn't make a turn?"

"Only when the road twisted," Annica said, adding after a moment, "We aren't lost?"

It sounded like a question.

"I don't see how we can be. Would you check the map, Annica? Where can we get back to the freeway?"

She aimed the flashlight on the map. "Not for a while. It would help if we knew where we are."

"The last town where we gassed up was called something Branch. Green Branch? Gray Branch?"

"I don't see it," she said. "I need a magnifying glass."

"What I don't see is the name of this road. It seems to go on forever."

"It's like that up north."

Comforting words, but at that moment I would have given anything to be on the freeway, speeding up north to our destination. Or to have a GPS. Oh, for a sight of Lake Huron's waters!

As the miles and the minutes flew by, I began to worry. No 'I-75 North' sign pointed the way to a freeway entrance. The scenery underwent a subtle change. The woods thinned, and blue-green water sparkled behind the trees.

It wasn't a glimpse of Lake Huron.

By then an hour had gone by, and my anxiety increased with every added mile.

"Serena's phone number is in the glove compartment, Annica," I said. "We'd better let her know we'll be later than we thought."

Annica nodded and pulled her cell phone out of her purse. "Uh-oh," she said. "No signal. So much for our call."

That meant I couldn't talk to Crane either, not from this road. My husband would worry when I didn't call him at the designated time as I'd promised. He would be certain I'd met with a mishap on the way north. Well, I could still place that call as soon as I had a signal.

I wondered if we were on the same road we'd traveled before the storm. Although I didn't remember making a turn, I could have done so when it first began raining, thinking I was following a curve.

That sense of something different grew stronger.

Annica dropped the phone back into her purse. "Is anything else going to go wrong?"

In answer, thunder rolled over the sky. The storm had skipped ahead of us, waiting in our path to throw one more delay our way.

Two

I had to get back on the freeway before the storm trapped us on a country road again.

Bringing the car to a stop on the shoulder, I reached for the map. I was so close to the woods' edge that pine branches brushed against the passenger side. Their spicy fragrance stole in through the window, mixing with the smell of wet earth. It was too strong to be pleasant and made me feel a trifle unwell.

Annica pulled a sketch pad and pen from her purse. "We were blown off our course. Let's figure out a new one."

"We must be about here." I pointed to a space on the map, and together we plotted what appeared to be a straightforward route to the freeway.

Left at the next turning... wherever that was. About a mile west, then north. West again...

Thunder rumbled, a fearsome monster stirring in its sky lair. Crane had cautioned me never to drive in an electrical storm. I, of course, would never do that, except in an emergency.

"Let's hurry," Annica said. "We don't want to get stuck in this backwater."

"Not if we can help it."

It seemed, though, that we were never going to emerge from the woods. We passed acres and acres of trees, some of which had lost their branches in the wind. I steered warily around them and various other obstacles in the road. Finally we came to a crossroad, and I turned left.

"So far, so good," Annica said. "Now we go west for about a mile. Then turn again."

What had seemed like a short distance on the map felt like several miles. The twisting road distorted my sense of direction. Was I going west or north? Gradually the tightness in my arms travelled down to my chest.

Wrong, wrong, wrong. What was wrong?

Suppose we were driving around in circles? What if we ended up back at the Victorian on the hill and lost more time? And still were nowhere near the freeway?

The rain began as it had before, a light splattering on the windows. I turned the lights and the windshield wipers on and hoped I was heading in the right direction.

I had to be. Maps don't lie.

Annica powered up the windows and stared out into the rain. Presently she leaned forward. "Hey, Jennet. Look. Ahead."

I saw it, through a rainwater blur in the distance, a rustic covered bridge spanning a wide stream and beyond it…

"A town!" Annica cried. "Thank God. We can stretch our legs and ask directions. Maybe have a cup of coffee."

I couldn't imagine a more welcome sight. It was small like many towns in Michigan. Blink and you pass them by. Try to remember their names, and you find that you can't. In fact, viewing the buildings and houses from this vantage point, I was reminded of a child's play town carefully arranged on an upward sloping green cloth.

Squinting through the rain, I saw it all in one quick glance. A main street lined with stores, about two dozen houses, most of them white, built in rows that bracketed the street and branched out to a lake in the distance, and, best of all, what appeared to be a restaurant.

There would be someone to ask if we were heading in the right direction to enter the freeway. Annica could have her coffee. I'd order a glass of iced tea, and we could go on our way, rested and refreshed, to complete the rest of the trip.

The rain increased. It pounded the bridge as I drove over it. On the other side, the diner beckoned. It was an odd color for a restaurant, pale lavender with purple trim, subdued colors that managed to shine through the rain. But what did appearance matter? It was shelter. Any port in a storm.

As we parked, I noticed that it had a strange name: the Forever Diner.

I had an umbrella in the trunk, but Annica said, "Let's make a dash for it."

Four steps, perhaps five, brought us to the door. I pushed it open and Annica dashed in ahead of me, only to come to an abrupt stop in the entrance. I nearly ran into her. The jingle of her silver shell earrings sounded unnaturally loud.

"What…?" She turned to me. "It's closed. There's nobody here."

"It can't be. The door was open."

"I don't see anyone," she said.

Neither did I. It looked as if the diner had just opened for the day. And the wait staff had retreated to the kitchen?

Small tables covered with faded gingham-checkered cloths in all colors waited for customers who hadn't yet arrived. The grill was bare, as was the counter without a single loaf of bread or kitchen utensil in sight. I couldn't see any dishes or glasses or cups. No serving trays. The clock on the wall had stopped at three o'clock. Most telling, there was no enticing smell of coffee brewing or good food cooking. And the floor was dusty.

"Ugh," Annica said. "It isn't clean. We wouldn't want to eat here anyway. I don't even want to sit on these chairs. Shall we try to find another place?"

"We could, but how many restaurants will a town this size have?"

"Let's drive down Main Street and see."

Bracing for an onslaught of rain, we hurried back outside. I sat behind the wheel, shivering in my damp blouse, but didn't start the engine. As I stared at the street in front of me, a thought hit me with the force of a heavy rock.

It appeared to be true. But could I believe it?

"Do you notice anything strange about this town?" I asked Annica.

She shrugged. "It's small. One of those one-horse towns."

"Something else?"

"I give up. What?"

I said, "Where are the other cars?"

"They have to be here," Annica said.

"Where? Do you see any?"

She hesitated. "Drive down the street a little way. The people who live here have to have vehicles. How else would they get around?"

How else indeed, living in the middle of nowhere?

Where are the people? I thought.

Main Street was deserted. No cars were parked in front of the stores, no people holding umbrellas rushed to destinations where they could escape the rain.

We were alone, Annica and I, the only humans in miles, or so it seemed.

I drove slowly past a pharmacy, a small grocery, a barber shop, a dime store… Yes, dime, not dollar, store. There were no other restaurants. As for the houses beyond the street, from what I could see, they looked deserted with weeds grown to astounding heights in the front yards, empty driveways, and shuttered windows.

"I see a car," Annica said.

An older model Volkswagen whose robin's egg blue paint was speckled with rust, whose tires were flat. A single car in an entire town, and no one could drive it.

"It's a ghost town," I said, bringing the Focus to a stop in front of a handsome gabled house with a wide veranda. A lawn chair had fallen over, and a swing hung from the ceiling by one chain. A 'For Sale' sign had fallen over on the front steps. "I'd love to get out and explore."

"Let's do it," Annica said.

"Except..." I remembered why we were here, miles from home. We had a rescue collie to pick up, and, before we could do that, a freeway entrance to find.

"But not today. It's a temptation, though."

Making a U-turn, I drove back to Main Street, noting the stores on the other side, none of which was a restaurant.

"It's just as well," Annica said. "This place is creepy. I wonder why everybody bailed out."

I couldn't imagine. It was like a scene from a science-fiction novel. The entire population of a small town loading their possessions onto trucks and cars, driving away from houses that looked as if they were frozen in time. Everyone in town running away. From what? And how long ago had this happened? Over a span of time or all at once?

The houses appeared to be in good condition in spite of peeling paint, broken fences, and an occasional missing window. In a true ghost town, the structures would be weathered and falling apart.

I had an almost irresistible urge to browse in the dime store. Would it be stripped bare of merchandise or would the counters still hold paper and costume jewelry, inexpensive make-up and toys? Would it perhaps have a lunch counter?

Unlikely. The dime store would be a ghost like the Forever Diner. Obviously no one lived in the houses and no one frequented the businesses. But a strange aura seemed to hang over the town, like the dark clouds that still filled the sky. The town was alive and waiting.

Not warning us to get away, because it wanted company.

"We need to get back on the right road," Annica said. "Maybe we can come again another day and do some exploring. I wonder what the town's name was."

I knew the answer immediately and without reflection.

"Forever," I said.

Three

In spite of a rocky beginning, the rest of the trip proceeded smoothly and without incident. Annica took over the driving while I ate a ham sandwich, and we entered the freeway where we'd guessed it would be. The rain had ceased, as had the roadwork, and I was able to place my call to Crane.

"It's getting late," he said. "If you run into a storm on the way back, don't keep driving. Find a good motel."

"We'll have a dog with us."

"Look for one that accepts pets."

Nothing easier. I decided that, barring a flash flood, I would drive through to Foxglove Corners. I missed my home and my own collies, not to mention my handsome deputy sheriff husband.

"I'll see you soon, honey," Crane said. "Drive carefully."

I didn't anticipate further trouble. We still had three hours of daylight left, which should give us ample time to pick up Echo and be on our way home.

Sue's sister, Serena, lived in a small lakeside town. This one bustled with color and life. Unlike Forever, Shoretown had a theater, a dress shop, an antique shop, and a restaurant specializing in fresh-caught fish.

The tree-bordered streets were neat, and the flowerboxes in the houses overflowed with bright blooms. Best of all, there were people and cars.

By then, our brief stopover in Forever had acquired an air of unreality. Had we really stumbled onto a ghost town in the middle of Michigan's Lower Peninsula? It seemed like a dream or a scene from a Beverly Gray adventure come to life.

I wouldn't mention the ghost town to Serena.

She lived in an elegant Victorian house similar to those in and around Foxglove Corners. Climbing red roses brightened its soft beige façade. She sat on her porch waiting for us. Beside her lay a collie who watched our approach quietly with alert eyes. Apparently we weren't to have a rambunctious tail-wagging collie welcome.

I parked in front of the house, and we got out of the car. The air was hot and humid, which was unusual, considering how far north we were. It was certainly a marked contrast from the air-cooled Focus.

"If that's our collie, she *is* gorgeous," Annica murmured.

Serena rose and descended the six steps to meet us. She resembled Sue slightly, a younger version of her in jeans and a white blouse. She had long dark hair held back by a large barrette that looked as if it were made of white lace.

"I'm glad to see you made it safely," she said. "Did you get lost?"

Annica glanced at me. 'Don't tell her about the town,' her look said. 'It's our secret.'

"We ran into a thunderstorm," I said, "and, of course, endless roadwork. It's the same all over Michigan."

Echo rose slowly and stretched. I extended my hand for her to sniff. She pressed her soft nose to my palm.

"She's breathtaking," I said, and that was an understatement.

In fact, Echo could have served as an illustration for the collie breed standard. She was a white-factored sable with perfectly dipped ears and a winsome expression that made you want to scoop her up in your arms and hug her.

Well, not quite. She was a good weight for a female, about sixty pounds, I'd estimate, with a full coat that glistened in the late afternoon sunlight.

"What a pretty girl!" Annica said. "She reminds me of my pup, Angel."

I wanted to say, "I'll take her!" even as an image of Crane, gray eyes frosty, rose up to remind me that we already had seven collies.

Why would anyone surrender such a paragon to an animal shelter? Unless she had a hidden fault, like an aggressive temperament.

Echo tilted her head. Her tail wagged slowly, and her eyes sparkled. She lifted her paw to shake.

Aggression. That wasn't it.

Or a lack of traditional collie spirit?

A purple Kong toy lay in the doorway. She whirled around and grabbed it, offering it first to Annica, then to me.

A flaw, if it existed, was well-hidden.

"Why was she surrendered?" I asked, taking hold of the Kong and tossing it a short distance across the porch.

"I wondered that myself," Serena said. "Believe me, I couldn't pull her out of that shelter fast enough. They're so crowded; they only give a dog four days to be adopted. Echo came with an impressive pedigree. She has seven champions behind her. One is her sire."

"It had to have been a case of the owner dying with no one to take care of her," I said.

But in that case, a dog like this, an obvious show prospect, would have been worth a great deal of money to a collie fancier. Why wouldn't her owner sell her? Or return her to her breeder who must have had high hopes for her in the show ring? Echo could have been bred and produced little mirror images of herself.

Serena frowned. "I don't think her owner passed. A young girl surrendered her for someone else, a relative, I think. I wish I could keep her, but it isn't possible. I've already had to break up several fights between her and my Waffles. Would you girls like something to drink?" she added. "I have iced tea and all kinds of soft drinks."

The offer was tempting, and I was thirsty; but we had water in the car.

"We should be on our way," I said. "It's a long drive home."

"In that case, Echo is ready to go. I fed her dinner, and I'm giving you some of the brand I've been feeding her. She's a good eater."

Serena picked up a small box containing a half package of kibble and a well-chewed Nylabone bone, along with a manila file which probably contained her papers. Echo had a stuffed toy, an octopus whose legs were different colors. Serena tossed the Kong toy inside, as Echo followed the path of her possession with worried eyes.

Serena picked up a long leather leash. "You're going with the nice ladies, Echo. Be a good girl."

I expected some resistance, perhaps a natural reluctance to leave with strangers, but Echo came with us willingly enough, and we settled her in the back seat with a fleece blanket. Annica took the octopus out of the box and tucked it between Echo's front paws.

We thanked Serena on behalf of Echo for the fortuitous rescue. "Sue will let you know when she finds Echo a new home," I said, and we were off, driving south in the waning sun.

~ * ~

The journey home is always shorter than the miles covered to reach a destination. A large number of cars were also heading south on the freeway, which seemed strange to me as it was the middle of the week.

Echo was quiet. After a brief period of whining, she occupied herself by gazing out the window, first from one side, then the other.

"She's seeing it all for the first time." Annica had taken the octopus back to amuse Echo. It lay in her lap, its many legs at rest. "Think of all the wonders. Lakes and hills and even the other cars."

"As far as we know," I said. "We don't know where Echo came from."

I had glanced quickly at her pedigree. I didn't recognize any of the kennel names associated with the champions in her lineage, which wasn't surprising as I didn't follow show ring news. I *did* notice that her registered name was Golden Echo of Misty Manor. Her dam was Golden Moment. Where was Misty Manor located?

It didn't matter. Echo was about to begin a happy new life.

Presently Annica said, "This is where we reentered the freeway, and that way is the ghost town. We have to go back some day, Jennet."

I kept my eyes glued to the road, driving the speed limit, although it seemed that every other vehicle was passing me.

"I'd love to go back, but it'll have to be soon, before school starts."

"And I have a hard class this fall, Modern British Poetry. It isn't really hard, I guess, but I'm not especially interested in that subject. So I'll ask Mary Jeanne when I can have a day off."

"I can't wait to tell Crane about the town," I said.

"And I'll tell Brent. This is the sort of story he'll eat up."

I took my eye off the road for a second to smile at her. Annica's relationship with the red-haired heartthrob of Foxglove Corners was warming up nicely. I was happy for her. She had a massive crush on Brent, and Brent had a massive number of lady friends, all of them vying for his attention.

A convertible sailed past me, no doubt having grown impatient with my seventy miles an hour. The driver waved, and an English setter riding in the back seat set Echo to barking excitedly.

"We should have taken pictures of the town with our cameras," I said.

"Why didn't we?"

"It all happened so fast. I didn't think of it. Then, too, we thought we were lost."

"What if the town isn't there when we go back?" Annca asked.

"Where would it go?"

"Mmm. I don't know. Now that we're on the freeway, it seems... I don't know."

"Strange?"

"Like it didn't happen."

"But it did."

Her remark sent my thoughts back to my first glimpse of the beautiful pink Victorian on Huron Court. I had definitely seen it, had talked to the young woman who lived in it, but the next time I went that way, the house had changed, aged almost a hundred years.

I felt a familiar chill wrap around me. It happened whenever I recalled that time.

"We were together," I reminded her. "Two people wouldn't have imagined the same town or the diner and the houses."

"Who'll believe us without pictures to back up our story?"

I was surprised at her question, at the emergence of self-doubt in the usually confident young woman.

"Crane, Brent..." I said. "Anyone who knows us. And if they don't, they can drive up to Forever and look for themselves."

Four

A shred of daylight lingered in the sky as I turned off Jonquil Lane into my own driveway. The green Victorian farmhouse with its stained glass window between twin gables welcomed me home with an extravagance of brightness. It appeared that Crane had turned on every light on the first floor.

Raven, our rare bi-black collie, who lived in a Victorian doghouse lovingly built for her by Crane, provided a raucous welcome. She ran up to the Focus, barking, and jumped on the door. From inside the car, Echo set up an answering clamor. All six of the house dogs converged at the bay window to join the chorus.

"You wait here," I told Echo. "I'll be back in a minute."

I could have driven her straight to Sue's horse farm about ten minutes away, but I was anxious to see Crane first. In truth, I'd missed my home. A mission successfully completed with an adventure thrown in is always satisfying, but as I often told myself, "East, West, Home is best."

Crane opened the door for me, and Raven dashed inside. She only came in our house when it pleased her. This was one of those occasions.

I should leave for the day more often. Camille, my neighbor in the yellow Victorian across Jonquil Lane, had taken care of the dogs in my absence, and they had Crane when his shift was over, but they must have missed me, especially as I had been home with them throughout the summer.

And I also had Crane. He gave me a hearty hug and a welcome home kiss, first having to push his way through leaping collie feet and wagging tails.

Crane always looked good to me, even better after we'd been apart longer than usual. With his silver-streaked blond hair, frosty gray eyes, and rugged features, he was the handsomest and most popular deputy sheriff in Foxglove Corners. That was my opinion, of course, but so far I hadn't met anyone who disagreed with me.

"Is everything all right here?" I asked.

"It's good, but we all missed you," he said. "I saved some stew and cornbread for you."

The beef stew I'd made and frozen in containers for nights like this when I wasn't home to make dinner. All Crane had to do was defrost it and heat it in the microwave.

"Candy and Misty ate the pound cake, though," he added. "I left it too close to the edge of the counter. I found banana bread in the freezer, but it isn't thawed yet."

"They ate the whole cake?"

"You know how fast they are."

I sent a dark look in the direction of the saucy tricolor and her white apprentice. "You two had better not be sick tonight."

Well, no matter how many dark looks I gave them, the pound cake wasn't going to come back.

"I don't need dessert," I said. "I'm going to take our rescue over to Sue Appleton's. I'll just drop her off and come home. I have a fantastic story to tell you."

I paused, breaking off a piece of cornbread muffin that Crane had managed to keep away from my thieving twosome. "Come out to the car with me and see Echo. She's exquisite."

He closed the door but not quickly enough to keep Raven inside. She flew out to the car like the winged creature her name suggested. Echo barked a greeting, her pretty face wearing an endearing collie smile. The house dogs barked their indignation at being excluded.

"She doesn't look like a typical rescue," Crane said.

"She isn't. Echo comes with a mystery, but I don't think I'll ever solve it."

I opened the door, slid inside, and turned on the engine. "Keep Raven away from the car. I'll just be a few minutes."

He grabbed Raven's collar, and I drove the short distance to Squill Lane where Sue's horse farm—and little else—was located.

~ * ~

Sue was already in her night clothes, a long pink robe and slippers, when she opened the door. Icy and Bluebell bristled with excitement and all but crawled over each other to be the first to welcome the stranger collie. Because of Sue's work with the Lakeville Collie Rescue League, they were used to unknown dogs invading their space.

"Nobody wanted this beautiful dog?" Sue said. "Incredible. Come in."

"Just for a moment. I'm exhausted."

I led Echo into Sue's comfortable family room, the one we Rescue League members always gathered in, decorated with photographs of Sue's horses and the many collies who had dozed in front of the wood stove. Echo would be happy here for a while, perhaps forever, judging from the covetous gleam in Sue's eyes.

Bluebell executed a charming play bow and the three collies took off running through the house.

"How's Serena?" Sue asked.

"She seemed fine. We only stayed a few minutes."

"Was it a hard trip?"

"It was long," I said, not wanting to tell her about the ghost town. Not yet. "We got lost once but between the two of us, we managed to get back on the right road."

"On behalf of the League, I thank you, Jennet. We couldn't function without people like you."

"My friend Annica helped," I said. "I wouldn't have gone alone."

"No, that was too far. Are you sure you won't stay for a cup of coffee or tea?"

I thought of stew and cornbread and Crane sitting across the table from me. Of my pound cake bandits and of the good ones, Halley, Gemmy, Sky, Raven, and Star.

"Thanks, but I've been away from home long enough," I said. "Another time."

The dogs dashed into the family room, and I intercepted Echo long enough to give her a kiss on her head and a few farewell pats. Of course, I would be seeing her again, but our time together was over.

Although I'd only known her for hours, I was going to miss her.

"You'll be happy here, Echo," I told her.

~ * ~

We sat at the oak table in the kitchen, Crane and I, as I imagined we would. I ate beef stew and cornbread while Crane drank a cup of coffee. The dogs, who thought they should eat, too, munched on gravy bones.

"Now tell me about your fantastic adventure," Crane said.

I swallowed the last bite of stew. "Well, I got tired of dodging road work and took a detour," I said. "Only then we ran into a thunderstorm and weren't sure how to get back on the freeway."

"That's easy to do when you drive on those back roads."

As I talked, his intense interest made me realize again how extraordinary our experience had been and how, if I had been a little more patient, we would never have discovered the ghost town. Thank heavens for impatience.

"Have you ever heard of a ghost town in Michigan?" I asked.

"Sure, there are lots of them in the Upper Peninsula," he said. "Mining towns, lumber towns. One day we could take a ghost town tour."

"Forever isn't that far from Foxglove Corners."

"Where is it exactly?" he wanted to know.

Annica had taken her scratch pad with her, and the map was in the glove compartment.

"Somewhere east of the freeway," I said. "Or northeast... I'm not sure. We were on the road about two hours when we crossed the bridge."

"It sounds like a fairy tale."

"It reminds me of *Brigadoon*," I said.

"Is that a place?"

"It's an old musical about a town in Scotland that appears once every hundred years."

He got up and refilled our coffee cups. "I remember now. You have that movie in your collection. Do you mean to say there's something magical about this town?"

"Not exactly. Let's just say it has a strange ambience. Do you believe me?"

"Sure," he said, but I thought I detected a brief hesitation.

"Because Annica was with me the whole time. She saw everything I did. It's not like what happened with the pink Victorian."

"I believe you," Crane said. "Over the years you've told me stranger stories."

"We're going to go back and do some exploring. This time we'll take plenty of pictures."

"I'd like to see this ghost town, too," he said.

"Tomorrow I'm going to search for it on the Internet. Maybe I can find out why the people abandoned it."

Search for Forever. I smiled. It sounded like a sappy romance novel.

Five

The next day Brent Fowler visited us just before the dinner hour, as was his habit. He always brought wine or flowers, or treats for the collies and, sometimes, news. Today his gift was homemade beef tarts from Pluto's Gourmet Pet Shop, and he was seeking information.

The tarts having been quickly devoured by the ravenous collies, who acted as though I were starving them, Brent sat in his favorite chair, a rocker, with Misty, the white collie, sitting in his lap and Sky, the timid blue merle, lying at his feet. Among our visitors, Brent was their favorite person.

He was one of the more colorful denizens of Foxglove Corners. A handsome and wealthy bachelor—oh, happy combination!—whose dark red hair was the shade of a certain kind of maple leaf in autumn, his passions were horses, dogs, fox hunting, and any intriguing enterprise or adventure that came his way.

Like the ghost town Annica and I had discovered by accident.

"Didn't Annica tell you all about it?" I asked.

"She did, but I want to hear your version, too. She might have left something out."

"It'll be the same as hers," I said. "But if you insist. We were lost, driving on country roads, when a storm blew in out of nowhere. We had to stop along the roadside, and I'll admit I was afraid we might never find the freeway entrance. Then we came to an old wooden bridge and saw a town beyond it."

In telling the story, I felt my own excitement rising, lived again the moment in Forever when we didn't see any other vehicles or people, when we realized the town was deserted.

Forever was proving to be an elusive subject. My Internet searches had an unexpected result. There was no town by the name of Forever in Michigan. It didn't exist.

That wasn't possible. We'd been there. Driven down its Main Street.

I'd consulted a map of Michigan, pinpointing the approximate area in which we'd been lost and tried to find Forever. It wasn't on the map either.

Shades of *Brigadoon.*

"But it's there," I said, "surrounded by acres of wilderness."

Brent had clearly fallen under the ghost town's spell. Crane, who'd had time to speculate, said, "I wonder if it's one of those Christmas villages like Holiday Station. They open during the winter months and close for the summer."

"Or a set for a science-fiction movie," Brent added. "One of those end-of-the-world thrillers."

Neither explanation sounded right for Forever.

"I researched Michigan ghost towns," I said. "They're abandoned when a mine or industry like logging ends. Many of them are nothing more than ruins. I saw an old picture of a one-room schoolhouse. I can't imagine teaching English and every other subject in such a tiny room."

"Jennet and I are going to take a ghost town tour the next time we go up north," Crane said.

"We are?"

"Didn't you say you wanted to?"

I couldn't remember saying that exactly, but it would be a different kind of vacation, one we would both enjoy.

"As of now, I'm going to concentrate on Forever," I said.

"Didn't you say there's no such place?" Crane asked.

"According to the Internet. I'm going to prove it—er, them—wrong."

"And the map?"

"It's too small to warrant a place on the map."

"I'd like to explore this town myself," Brent said. "I'll ask Lucy to go with me. She's an expert on oddities."

Our good friend, Lucy Hazen, would be surprised to hear that. She was a horror story writer who specialized in fiction for young adults. In a month or so, one of her books, *Devilwish*, was going to be made into a movie filmed in Foxglove Corners. Among Lucy's talents was a flair for looking into the future and quite often seeing events before they occurred.

"Can you tell me how to find Forever?" Brent asked.

"Leave the freeway, drive around for an hour or so, and watch for an old wooden bridge. If you're lucky, you'll run into a thunderstorm."

"Very funny," Brent said.

"I'm serious. We just ran into the town. We made a few notes when we were trying to get back to the freeway. Annica has them."

"I'll find it," Brent said. "Whoever said we ran out of new worlds to conquer was wrong."

~ * ~

The next morning, I took Halley, Sky, and Star walking to Sue Appleton's horse farm. The day was summer perfection, with fleecy clouds in a deep blue sky and enough breeze to cool the sultry air.

To reach Squill Lane, we had to pass the abandoned development, a gloomy and forbidding collection of French chateau-style mansions, or what remained of them after years of neglect and exposure to the elements. The builder had gone bankrupt, leaving Foxglove Corners with a blight on its landscape and an ongoing source of danger, for often people who were up to no good sought shelter among the crumbling structures.

The ruins were a never-ending source of fascination for the collies, but my morning's walking companions were biddable. Star was my elderly rescue, Sky was still timid after having been abused, and Halley was my first collie, my heart dog.

I didn't have to worry about them responding to the call of the wild.

Sue was outside taking pictures of a gangly new colt who didn't have a name yet. Icy, Bluebell, and Echo were running around the barn. They all looked so exuberant and beautiful—both human and animals—that I snapped a few pictures of them with my phone.

Echo left her play friends to dash up to me for a private greeting. She skidded to a stop in front of me, raised her paw to shake and tilted her head. The generous sun brought out the gold in her coat. She was one of the most beautiful and beguiling collies I'd ever encountered.

"Are you going to take her to the vet and put her picture up on the website?" I asked.

"Serena took her to a vet up north," Sue said. "She's in perfect health. I've decided to keep her," she added.

Along with and Icy and Bluebell, Sue often had as many as six collies at one time. She had found good homes for her current fosters, which was fortuitous. Although I imagined Echo would have a place with Sue even if she hadn't. I was glad to know that Echo was going to stay in the neighborhood and relieved that she and Bluebell were living happily together.

Annica and I had done a good day's work and been rewarded with an intriguing new mystery. Life was good.

Six

Because our collies loved the homemade beef tarts that Brent had brought them, the next time I went grocery shopping, I made a stop at Pluto's Gourmet Pet Shop. The store was small and homey, relatively new, with a pervading aroma I wouldn't ordinarily associate with a pet store. It smelled almost like… vanilla? Something pleasant. And it was cool inside, a welcome respite from from the hot day.

Unlike most establishments of its kind, Pluto's didn't carry leashes, toys, or other dog supplies, only all-natural treats, some of them bearing a startling resemblance to human foods.

I found the tarts and added four boxes of gravy-flavored bones, and an assortment of canine cookies. Then I spied a larger treat. It looked like half a pound cake on a paper plate.

I knew two dogs who would appreciate that.

It was going to be an expensive stop.

As I walked toward the check-out counter, I noticed a poster pinned to the store's bulletin board amidst lost dog notices and advertisements for various training, grooming, and dog walking services.

It was the collie's picture in the left hand corner of the poster that caught my attention, a female, judging by her delicate features. She was a dark sable beauty with a white Lassie blaze, soulful eyes, and a silvered muzzle. Her gaze communicated elegance and dignity for she was, after all, a collie. I thought I saw a hint of sadness and loss in her eyes.

I steered my cart away from the check-out line and stood in front of the poster, reading bold black words that fairly leaped off the page.

The Foxglove Corners Collie Rescue League.

My response was immediate and emotional. *We* were the rescue league in Foxglove Corners. Was this a joke?

We were a small organization with about twenty members. Working together, we had found loving new homes for dozens of collies in perilous situations. My own Star had come to us when her owners decided they didn't have time for her.

Oddly, I felt threatened. It was as if the existence of this group were a personal affront. Who were these other people? It seemed they were trying to take something valuable away from me.

A petite silver-haired woman in a pink sundress appeared at my side, leading a rambunctious husky puppy on a leash. They were already an ill-matched pair. Before long, the husky would be leading her human.

The puppy leaped at my leg, catching the hem of my skirt in its little mouth.

"Sorry," the woman said. "Yukon. Bad dog! Down. You'll get us thrown out of the store."

Yukon didn't listen, but I didn't mind. I freed my skirt and offered my palm for the pup to sniff.

"She's gorgeous." Pointing to the poster, I added, "Did you ever hear of this group?"

"No, but it's wonderful there's a place for unwanted collies. They have rescues for every breed under the sun, don't they?"

"I guess so, but there's already one collie rescue league in Foxglove Corners. Why do we need two of them?"

She shrugged. "Who knows? You don't see collies much anymore. I haven't seen one in years."

I smiled. In her experience that might be true. We moved in different circles. All of my friends had collies: Brent, Annica, Leonora, my fellow English teacher at Marston High School, Lucy Hazen, Camille, my neighbor, and Sue, of course, who fostered them. That was at least eight collies in a small area.

"Kids today are growing up without knowing who Lassie was," she added. "They'll never know what they're missing."

I agreed with her. Foxglove Corners didn't represent the rest of the country. *Lassie Come-Home* was in desperate need of a remake.

With that, she led Yukon away. The line at the register was long, but then I wasn't in a hurry. I approached three workers before I found the manager setting up a display of treats that looked like real peaches, pears, and plums.

He was a husky young man with carrot-red hair, freckles splashed across his face, and a cheerful grin. "Good enough to eat," he said, pretending to bite into a canine pear.

I laughed at his attempt at a joke. "I've never been tempted to sample dog food. Do you know anything about the poster for the Foxglove Corners Collie Rescue League?"

"Afraid not. Some lady asked if she could put it on our board. I told her it's for all our customers except for folks looking to sell puppies. We don't allow those ads."

'Some lady' wasn't helpful, but the young manager obviously hadn't asked her any questions.

All right. I understood, but I needed to know more about the group. I returned to the board and copied the address and phone number given in small print at the bottom of the poster.

With one last look at the collie illustration, I steered my cart to the end of the line.

I was glad I'd visited Pluto's today and grateful that Brent had given me the idea. Otherwise I might not know of the existence of this group.

The competition.

~ * ~

As our president, Sue Appleton had to know about the Foxglove Corners Collie Rescue League, and I wanted to tell her in person.

At home, I handed out treats, then stored my packages in the cupboard, lest they all disappear today. That done, I walked to Sue's horse farm, for the first time without taking three collies.

Sue's reaction was identical to mine. Immediate and emotional, tempered with disbelief.

"Are you sure, Jennet?" she asked.

"I saw their poster."

"It's ridiculous." She pushed her sunglasses up into her windblown hair. "Foxglove Corners doesn't need another collie rescue group. What we need are new members in the organization we already have and more foster homes."

"We also have the animal shelter," I pointed out.

The shelter was run by the Woodville sisters, Lila and Letta, in an old white Victorian house next door to the library. For years they had been quietly saving dogs of all breeds from dire circumstances and finding new families for them.

"I have a feeling there's something not quite right about this new group," Sue said.

"The rogue collie rescue league."

"Yes, that's what we'll call them. Who's in charge of it?"

"I didn't see a name on the poster, but I copied the address and phone number."

"We have to find out more about them. Let's start with the information we have."

"I wonder if they know about us," I said.

~ * ~

Both Sue and I attempted to get in touch with the Foxglove Corners Collie Rescue League... to no avail. Nobody answered their phone, and there was no invitation to leave a message. The address, which turned out to be a fairly new house in a development called Sapphire Lake Estates, had a 'For Sale' sign in the front yard.

Anyone would think they didn't want to be found, that the numbers were fake. But that didn't make sense. What was the point in advertising then?

"Are you certain you didn't make a mistake when you copied the numbers?" Sue asked.

"I was careful, and I checked them. Maybe whoever designed the poster made the mistake."

"Let's see," Sue said. "They invite people to bring their unwanted collies to them, and they want new owners to adopt them. How can this happen if no one can contact them?"

"It can't."

"We're missing something," Sue said. "They can't be a phantom rescue league."

"This is exactly what I need. Another mystery."

"What mystery?"

I reminded myself that Sue didn't know about the ghost town.

"Oh, old ones," I said vaguely.

"What can we do about this one?" Sue asked.

There was a natural first place to look for answers to any mystery.

"Search the Internet," I said. "I'll see if they have a website."

"Depending on what you find, I think I'd better call a meeting of the League. Someone may know something. Somebody else may even have seen the poster. I don't like secrecy," she added, "and this rogue league is pure secrecy."

It was a threat, as I'd first thought, not only to us but to the collies we had sworn to help. I didn't understand the nature of it, but something told me I'd better do something to change that and do it quickly.

Seven

Brent hadn't been able to find the ghost town.

"I must have covered every inch of the Lower Peninsula twice," he said.

"You couldn't have," Crane pointed out.

"Okay, I exaggerated, but I took your advice, Jennet. I left the freeway about where you and Annica did and travelled on about a thousand country roads. I came to plenty of small towns, but they were all populated."

"Did you see any covered bridges?" I asked.

"Not the kind you described, and it didn't rain. Are you and Annica playing a trick on me?"

"We'd never do that," I said. "Forever exists. I don't care what the mapmakers or Internet gurus say."

I glanced at three empty coffee cups and the dessert plate that had held six thick slices of banana-nut bread only minutes ago. I was forgetting my hostess duties.

"I'll be right back," I said. "Talk about something else while I'm gone."

Candy trotted after me to the kitchen where I brewed another pot of coffee, sliced the other half of the loaf, and thought about *Brigadoon*. Not that I believed Forever appeared every hundred years and spent the other ninety-nine in some other place. But there was an air of mystery about the town. I'd been aware of it from the moment I'd sat in my car and seen the silent street and uninhabited houses. It was a true ghost town.

Why hadn't Brent found it? He was determined and usually competent no matter what endeavor he undertook.

The mystery deepens.

I filled a crystal plate with the rest of the loaf, thinly sliced, and poured fresh coffee, dodging Misty's paws as she pranced around my feet. I could only hope the dessert would last till the end of Brent's visit as I didn't have anything else to serve. Tonight's pie was still in the oven.

"Annica and I are going back to Forever one day soon," I said. "Would you like to come with us?"

"I'd rather find it on my own. Lucy promised to go with me. I'll have an advantage with her at my side."

I doubted that. Among Lucy's talents was an ability to foresee certain future events at times, but she wouldn't be likely to know why the inhabitants had abandoned Forever. On the other hand, if they had left their emotions behind, absorbed by the walls of the town, perhaps she *could* tell us something.

Brent turned to Crane. "Did you ever visit this mystery town, Sheriff?"

"I haven't had time to look for it," Crane said. "Someone has to keep Foxglove Corners safe."

"True enough." Brent paused to devour a slice of banana bread under Candy's watchful eye. Had she grabbed a piece for herself when I wasn't looking? Or Misty? Misty especially looked guilty.

Well, I'd never know now. Neither collie could be expected to confess.

"Let's have a competition to see who sets foot in Forever first," Brent said. "You and Annica or me and Lucy."

"That doesn't seem fair," I said. "I have to wait for Annica's day off. When are you going to try again?"

With a familiar gleam in his eye, he said, "Tomorrow."

"Don't get lost," Crane told him.

"I won't. I have my GPS."

"It didn't help you the last time," I said.

That's because Forever doesn't exist.

I ignored that pesky inner voice. Of course the town existed. Only it was well hidden, surrounded by a wilderness, beyond a wood bridge that spanned a wide stream.

"Even robot voices have an occasional day off," he said.

With an elaborate shrug, Brent reached for another piece of banana bread. At this rate, it wasn't going to last.

"I accept your challenge, Brent," I said. "May the best team win."

A search for Forever was far more enticing than trying to discover the secrets of the rogue rescue league. It promised adventure. I needed one more adventure before school started.

~ * ~

Summer vacation was winding down, the days flying by like the first falling leaves caught in the wild winds. Soon I had a wedding to look forward to.

Leonora, who taught English in the classroom next to mine at Marston High School in Oakpoint, was marrying Deputy Sheriff Jake Brown. Crane and I were in the wedding party, I as matron of honor and Crane as best man. Leonora had once avowed that she would leave teaching when she got married, but that wasn't going to happen. After a short honeymoon, she would be at home preparing for another school year.

Reality and practicality rearrange dreams.

I was happy because without her, Marston would be a lonely and sometimes hostile place with an ice-cold principal at the helm and a number of disruptive students.

Also my sister, Julia, was coming home at the end of August after an extended stay in England. I had expected her to return in July, but she had decided to tour France, Germany, Italy, and Greece before flying back to the states.

"Because I may never go abroad again," she'd written.

She was going to stay with us in Foxglove Corners until she figured out what she wanted to do next.

My end-of-summer calendar was full. If we hadn't solved the mystery of the ghost town by the time Julia arrived, she could share in the adventure.

The next day I tried again to contact the Foxglove Corners Collie Rescue League. No one answered the phone, and the house in the Sapphire Lake Estates was still for sale. I made another stop at Pluto's Gourmet Pet Shop to check that I hadn't made a mistake when I'd copied the phone number and address. I hadn't.

I recalled Sue's remark about the new group being a phantom league. No, what she'd said was that they *couldn't* be a phantom league.

I began to think they could.

The next day I saw an article in the *Banner,* a short paragraph sandwiched between announcements from the library's Summer Reading Club and dates for a photography workshop at Louisa May Alcott Middle School:

The Foxglove Corners Collie Rescue League will have a booth at the Fall Fair which will be held in Spearmint Lake. Reasonably priced collie memorabilia will be available as well as autographed copies of Heart of Lassie by local novelist Byrony Limon. All funds raised will help the Rescue League care for the town's unwanted collies and place them in forever homes.

There followed a short description of the organization and a request for donations from anyone who wanted to support the league.

I called Sue Appleton and read the article to her.

"Finally," she said. "A way to contact them."

"Did you ever hear of a local author named Byrony Limon?" I asked.

"Byrony? That doesn't sound like a real name."

"It could be a penname. She wrote a book, *Heart of Lassie.*"

"Interesting. I'm going to that Fair. I hope you'll be able to go with me."

"I will, and we should encourage our other members to go."

"We'll show them we're a force to be reckoned with," Sue said. "Remember the meeting on Friday."

I'd forgotten it. Quickly I wrote the date on the calendar.

There weren't enough days left in August for me to accomplish everything I wanted to do.

Eight

Clovers was crowded that afternoon, but Mary Jeanne had hired a new waitress, Evie, giving Marcy and Annica double breaks. Few people were ordering dinners. As the mercury soared, customers ignored the day's specials, heavy on meat and potatoes, and ordered ice cream and cold drinks.

I was no exception. Annica served me a Vernors float in an old-time soda glass. It was a simple mixture of Vernors ginger ale blended with vanilla ice cream, a perfect drink for a hot day.

"When can we go back to Forever?" she asked as she spooned sugar into her iced tea.

"You read my mind. That's what I wanted to talk to you about. I can go anytime. What's your schedule?"

"I'm free tomorrow."

"Let's go tomorrow then. In the morning, when it's still cool."

"Even the mornings are hot. This heat wave is supposed to last all week."

"Brent tried to find the ghost town and failed," I said. "At least, I assume he failed. I didn't hear otherwise. He took Lucy with him. He hoped she could use her magic powers to help him find the place."

Annica laughed. "She can't do that." Instantly she sobered. "What if we can't find it again either?"

"It isn't Fairyland," I said. "Do you think we imagined it? Because we didn't."

"It seems so strange, though. The more time passes, the more it seems like a dream."

"Two people can't have the same dream."

"This time we'll take pictures. No one will be able to say we're making up stories."

"Who thinks that?"

"My mom," she said, "and Mary Jeanne."

"They'll change their minds when we show them our ghost town photo album. I've been thinking about the dime store."

That was the building I especially wanted to explore. It might be as empty as the diner, but I hoped it was still stocked with merchandise that might reveal the date on which the inhabitants of Forever had fled to unknown places. I imagined the exodus had been hasty, occurring over a few days, which would have left people like store owners little time to strip their counters completely.

If I attempted another Internet search, this time armed with a date, would the results be different?

"Old-fashioned dime stores were before my time," I said, "but I know what they looked like from pictures and my grandmother's stories. Whittiers in Oakpoint, for instance, had a soda fountain. Grandma used to take my mom there for chocolate malted milks served with tiny wafers."

"We could do that at Clovers. I'll ask Mary Jeanne."

"I could drink one now," I said, noticing that my soda glass was empty.

"I'll pack some sandwiches before I leave tonight. Our pineapple drop cookies aren't selling. No one wants baked goods in this heat, but they'll be perfect to snack on tomorrow."

"I'll bring bottled water and fruit," I said.

"Then we're all set." Annica glanced at the clock. "I have ten more minutes." She swirled her straw through the ice left in the bottom of the glass. "It's feels wrong competing against Brent. I like to think of us as a team."

"It's all in fun," I said.

Annica had gone from having a crush on Brent to an occasional date to a fledgling relationship with him. They had bonded over planting wildflowers where the pink Victorian had once stood. Which reminded me of the mysterious violet that grew amidst the chosen varieties.

"How is the violet doing?" I asked.

"It's as tall and beautiful as ever. It hasn't lost a bit of its color or freshness. I drove out to see it the day after we came back from Forever and took another picture. Somehow I think it's connected to Violet Randall. She doesn't want it to die."

Sometimes I thought so, too.

"It's not going to live in the snow," I pointed out.

"Are you sure?"

"Reasonably."

But I wasn't. "We'll have to see if it comes back next spring."

"I thought of a way to preserve it," she said. "When the other flowers start to die, I'll cut it and make a potpourri."

"You'll need more than one flower for potpourri."

"I'll add rose petals. My mom has a recipe."

"It won't be alive then. Not really."

"I haven't made up my mind," Annica said. "I'll have to talk it over with Brent."

Brent didn't share Annica's obsession with Violet Randall's flower, although he believed wholeheartedly in Violet. He'd suggested simply picking it.

"Let's concentrate on Forever," I said. "One mystery at a time."

~ * ~

As predicted, the heat returned the next morning, bringing with it a mist that hung heavily over the freeway. Although traffic was light, I felt nervous with speeding drivers passing me and diminished visibility. Oh, to be driving on a country road, even though it would still be difficult to see until the mist burned off. Unfortunately neither Annica nor I remembered where we'd exited the last time. And it mattered.

We had been on the road an hour and a half when Annica said, "Let's get off the freeway as soon as we can. We know the general direction. Maybe with luck we'll run into Forever again."

"All right, but I don't think we can count on luck."

"Well, we sure can't count on the map."

Exits were few and far between, but at last we came to one— Exit, Lorne Lake. The mist followed us onto a road lined with conifers, their branches wreathed in shreds of white gauze. I turned the air off and opened the windows, letting the sweet smells of woods in summer drift in.

"It's pretty around here," Annica said.

She held the unfolded map on her lap even though it hadn't helped us.

"That must be Lorne Lake," she said.

I looked to the right where a glimpse of still blue water shone through the mist. It didn't appear to be a large lake, but perhaps Annica was mistaken. A sign pointed the way to Lorne Lake—Five Miles.

Lorne Lake turned out to be the name of a cluster of rustic cottages built around a larger body of water. A few boats were out on the water and children played on the beach as a reddish dog dashed in and out of the lake. It was heartening to see a sign of life in what I had been thinking of as a never-ending wilderness.

"*This* is Lorne Lake," I said. "I don't remember it. I hope we're going the right way. These country roads seemed to go on forever."

Annica held the map up to the light. "I don't see it. We need a more detailed map."

Leaving the lake and cottages behind, I followed the curves in the road, hoping to see a familiar sight, although, in truth, the scenery didn't vary much from mile to mile. Woods, ponds, lakes, more woods, and flowers with vibrant colors blooming along the roadway.

"Shouldn't we be seeing some cars?" Annica asked.

"You'd think so."

"Do you think that's significant?"

"No. I hardly ever see traffic on Jonquil Lane, and this area isn't as developed as Foxglove Corners."

Which was an understatement.

Eventually I turned on a narrow road lined with towering evergreens whose shadows blended into one another across its winding expanse. It reminded me of the seemingly endless one we'd traveled when we were caught in the storm.

If so, we'd soon come to a crossroad.

"I wonder if it's this hot on Mackinac Island," Annica said.

I glanced at her as she brushed strands of red-gold hair that had come loose from her hairband... or been left loose deliberately to lie across her cheeks. Her earrings, long green tassels, complimented her hair color but didn't jingle like her favorite silver bells.

"Why?" I asked.

"I'm thinking about taking a mini-vacation there."

"Alone?"

"Uh, no. Brent mentioned something about our going together before my new semester starts."

"That'll be fun."

I hoped she would elaborate, but she embarked on an intense perusal of the map. Why had she brought it up? I wondered. Why now? On the subject of Brent, Annica was usually reticent. Well, when she was ready to talk about him, she would.

Finally forty-five minutes of driving brought us to an area that seemed vaguely familiar, and beyond the next curve in the road, a wood bridge—*the* bridge?—took shape in the mist.

"We found it!" Annica cried. "Any minute now we'll see the ghost town."

And there was the Forever Diner beckoning to us, its pale colors a glowing beacon.

"Yes," I said. "And without proper directions, just driving blind. It's luck all right."

"Or magic," Annica said.

Nine

An unearthly silence hovered over the abandoned buildings that lined the main street of Forever. I had expected to hear birds chirruping or see squirrels scampering up a tree, but it was as if even forest creatures avoided the borders of this strange town.

The quiet had a life of its own. A heartbeat. I could almost feel it beneath my feet.

I shivered and thought of *The Martian Chronicles*, a novel I'd soon be teaching in my American Literature class. In one of the stories, Ray Bradbury's character realizes that he is the last man left alive in a silent Martian town. It didn't really apply to the situation, because I had a companion, but the ambience was the same.

Grocery stores, candy stores, department stores, all at your disposal with no one to prevent you from helping yourself... No one to talk to...

Eventually he had found a female companion, but she wasn't the kind of person you'd like to be paired with in any circumstance.

Annica looked around, lowered her voice. "Was it like this before?"

"Quiet, you mean?"

"Yes, quiet and creepy."

I parked the car and we stepped out onto the sidewalk in front of the diner.

"Nothing appears to have changed," I said. "When we first saw the town, we didn't know it had been abandoned. Remember, we were planning on getting out of the rain and having something to drink."

That was what I said, but something *was* different in Forever. Something intangible, neither seen nor heard but nevertheless *present*. Was it threatening? I didn't know. I *did* know there was no point in sharing my apprehension with Annica. It was too vague, too undefined.

"I wish I'd brought Misty," I added, thinking that my psychic white collie would sense whatever it was I felt.

And protect us?

What an odd notion! How could we possibly be in any danger in a ghost town?

"We'll bring her along the next time," Annica said.

She brought her phone out of her jeans pocket and, aiming it at Main Street, took pictures from different angles. "We're here to explore. Where shall we start?"

"We've already been inside the diner. How about looking in the dime store? Then we can let ourselves into a few of the houses, if they're unlocked."

"That seems intrusive."

"It is, I guess, but there's no one to know or care."

"Why are we keeping our voices low?" she asked. "No one is going to hear us."

"I wonder."

"What does that mean?"

I shouldn't have spoken. "The ghosts," I said. "You know. Why else do they call them ghost towns?

"You are too funny, Jennet. Let's leave the car here and walk."

~ * ~

A strong aroma greeted us as we entered Claymore's Dime Store. It wasn't unpleasant; it was somewhat familiar. Popcorn?

How long do scents last in an empty building? I could almost see golden-white kernels popping in their machine and cardboard cartons waiting to be filled to the top. As if the ghosts had to have their favorite snacks.

"It smells like strawberry bubblegum," Annica said.

"It makes me want popcorn. And look! No one cleared the counters in here. It's like the clerks just stepped outside for lunch."

At the diner.

The display closest to the door consisted of cosmetics: compacts, lipsticks, and fingernail polish ranging from pastel pink to dark red, and eyeshadow in all shades. Beyond, imitation jewelry sparkled in the dim light that stole in from the street. Curtains and rods decorated a back wall, along with mirrors and uninspired prints of landscapes.

The dime store had only two aisles with no room for the lunch counter or soda fountain of my imagining. So much for the chocolate malted.

Annica picked up a compact. "Ponds, Ivory Angel pressed powder. This isn't a twenty-first century product." Replacing the compact with a tube of lipstick, she said, "I've never seen this brand. Here's a pretty shade of red."

I glanced at the array of perfume. "Wood Violet toilet water. Ann Haviland. I'd say this was vintage, too."

I opened the bottle and held it up to my nose, preparing to recoil from a rancid odor. To my surprise, the fragrance was still light and fresh. After how many years? There was no way of telling. Even if there were, I had no idea what the life span of perfume was.

"Do you see any comics or magazines?" I asked. "We might be able to pinpoint the last day the store was open for business."

She took a whirlwind tour down the second aisle. "Just these tiny books."

She handed me a children's adventure story. It was thick but the pages had large print and it was the size of a compact disk.

"Let's move on," she said. "There's a lot more to see in this town. I wonder if anyone would mind if I helped myself to a lipstick? I could leave money. A dollar, maybe?"

"For the ghost? I'd just take it and keep the dollar. But are you going to wear it?"

"Sure. Why not?"

I didn't have an answer for her. It wasn't something I'd do.

She slipped the lipstick in her purse, and we stepped outside. I took a breath of fresh air. We hadn't been in the five and dime long, about ten minutes, but the temperature seemed to have climbed a few degrees, and a wind had suddenly sprung up. The dead, dried leaves of past autumns went flying down the street, their rustling the only disturbance in a silent world.

The silence made me aware of little sounds I'd never have noticed on an ordinary day. Our footfalls and breathing, a sigh (the wind?), and the echoes that threw our voices back at us.

We made our way slowly down Main Street, pausing to take pictures and peering into each store. Some were as empty as the diner with certain bulky items left behind. Others were fully stocked.

"It's funny," Annica said. "Did the people all leave at once? Did some have trucks to haul away their possessions while others didn't? I wish we knew. More important, why didn't they come back for their stuff?"

"I have no idea."

All I knew was that we were alone in Forever. However, without evidence to the contrary, I felt as if our progress were being observed by an unseen watcher.

Leave it to you, Jennet.

Pure imagination, given a fertile field, that field being the haunting little town of Forever, was all I needed to create an impossible scenario. An entity without footsteps or breathing? How was that possible?

Only if said entity is a ghost.

Annica gasped as she inadvertently kicked an object lying at the side of the street.

Object? It was an apple, as red and glossy and perfectly formed as if it had just dropped from a non-existent tree.

She bent to pick it up.

"Don't touch it!"

"Why not? It can't be poisonous."

"You don't know that, and you don't know how long it's been here."

"Good point, but I wasn't going to eat it. I wonder how it got here."

"That's easy. An animal must have decided it didn't want an apple after all and dropped it."

She turned the apple over with her shoe.

The huge bite lay exposed to the light. I was no expert, but I knew the apple had been sampled and summarily discarded by a human.

And this hadn't happened several years in the past.

Ten

"What kind of animal?" Annica asked, studying the apple closely. "A deer? Or a coyote?"

"Unless I miss my guess, that bite was made by a human mouth," I said.

She paused to absorb that. "But we're the only humans in Forever."

Were we?

I didn't want to alarm Annica by talking about unseen watchers. Besides, another explanation occurred to me.

"Who's to say we're the only people who know about this town? It's certainly out of the way, but it isn't hidden."

"But then, we'd have read about it in the paper, wouldn't we?"

"You'd think so. It's obviously been here for a long time. It's possible it's an old story, and we missed it."

"Maybe Brent and Lucy found it after all. Brent always travels with fruit. He especially loves apples."

I doubted that, simply because neither one would have littered the countryside, let alone a unique ghost town, with a discarded apple.

I pointed that out and added, "It could be anybody. Annica, stand in front of the hardware store, and I'll take your picture. Then you can take one of me on the other side of the street."

She brightened, the possibility of previous visitors to Forever apparently slipping out of her mind. "I almost forgot. You and I have to be in the pictures if we're going to prove our ghost town is real."

The pictures taken, we turned our attention to the houses, walking slowly down a shaded street, considering.

"Which ones should we explore?" Annica asked.

"Any one."

I stopped in front of a yellow bungalow shaded by pine trees whose lower branches were dead. Ungainly weeds sprouted from cracks in the walkway, and the lawn had more bare patches than grass. A crawling vine almost covered a fallen 'For Sale' sign.

"How about this one?

"Do we break in?"

"We may not have to. Wait a minute."

I turned the knob and gave the door a shove. It swung open, revealing an uncarpeted expanse of wood floor—a long sparsely furnished living room with a kitchen on the right, facing the street. A small closet with an open door was crammed with clothing, mostly jackets for both warm and cold weather.

The air was stuffy, trapped within the walls, and the pines blocked much of the sunlight. I turned the switch of a floor lamp, not expecting a burst of light. Nothing happened. The lamp was dead or, more likely, the town had no electrical power.

No gas, no water. No life.

Annica looked around, a frown forming on her face. "They didn't have a television, and I don't see any photographs or personal possessions like figurines. It doesn't look like anybody ever lived here."

I agreed with her assessment. Still… the uneasy feeling that we weren't alone in the town returned. It seemed to me that the spirits of a once-happy family had stayed behind when the bodies left.

At that moment, I remembered one of Ray Bradbury's Martian chronicles. His futuristic house lived on, untenanted, its various mechanisms continuing to perform their functions, while the family escaped to Mars.

My notions were growing wilder with every passing minute.

"The people who lived here may have taken their family pictures with them," I said, "and, depending on the season, only minimum clothing."

"Only the necessities. Leave the rest."

I could almost hear the echo of harried voices, both inside and outside the house.

"I'd guess it happened in the summer," Annica said.

She walked toward the back of the house into a small hallway. "There are two bedrooms and a bathroom here. The beds are stripped, and I don't see anything in the bathroom, not even a bar of soap."

In the kitchen the refrigerator was empty except for a few cans. Beets, stewed tomatoes, sliced pears, and peach halves. Why hadn't they taken them?

"We really are intruding," Annica said.

"And we're not learning anything new. The people who lived in Forever abandoned their town, taking only what they could carry in cars. Some people left more behind than others, but it doesn't appear that anyone stayed behind. Whatever drove them out must have been catastrophic. I don't think we need to go through other houses today. It'll be the same in every one. But we should take more pictures before we leave."

That was what we did. There were perhaps twenty-five or thirty houses in the ghost town and one vehicle, the rusty blue Volkswagen with no tires that wasn't going anywhere. As we walked back to the car with dozens of pictures on each camera roll, I said, "This was enlightening but unfinished. I simply have to know more about this town."

"Then we'll come back?" Annica asked.

"Yes, and I'm going to continue my research. I can't remember when I've been so curious about anything."

And apprehensive as well. I'd learned that having unsettling feelings was part of my make-up and usually assigned them to imagination running wild. However, there was something secretive about the town of Forever, something that perhaps needed to be known.

Then there was the apple.

~ * ~

On the way out of town, Annica pulled the map and a sketch pad out of her purse and began writing.

"What are you doing?" I asked.

"Jotting down directions to Forever—in reverse. No more flying blind."

"You realize I'm not sure where I'm going."

"That's okay. I have confidence that you'll find the freeway eventually."

I intended to find it eventually. Emphasis on eventually. It existed somewhere beyond endless country roads, beyond stretches of forest and glimpses of water. I hadn't noticed any landmarks on the way to the town and saw none as we motored our way back to civilization as we knew it. Everything was the same. Everything green.

"I give up," Annica said after a while. "I can't see any names. Don't they name roads out here?"

It was a rhetorical question, but I answered it anyway. "The trees may cover the signs. They're easy to miss with all the leaves. Or I may be going too fast."

"Yeah, you are. Slow down. You might hit a deer."

That was what was missing. The Deer Crossing signs I was used to seeing in Foxglove Corners.

As for speeding, all I needed was to attract the attention of a state trooper. But that would be good. I could ask him questions.

As we left Forever behind, the past hours took on the colors of illusion. It seemed as if we had left the realm of make-believe far behind and were even now entering the real world. Of collies and a husband to feed, a rogue rescue league to investigate, and a bride-to-be who might need the help of her matron of honor.

But my thinking was wrong. The ghost town was as real as the water shimmering in the sunlight as I drove past an unknown lake. Annica and I had pictures on our phones to prove its existence.

Pictures tell the truth.

But…

I remembered a time when they hadn't reflected present reality. Once I had taken a picture of a pink Victorian house in all its glory. The camera had recorded the same house in a dilapidated state. An instance when the camera told the truth.

A sudden panic tagged at me. I had to know.

"Annica, check your camera roll."

"Why?"

"To see if the pictures are still there."

"Why wouldn't they be? Oh, all right."

She pressed a few buttons on her phone. "They're good pictures, Jennet. Especially the one of you in front of the hardware store. You should wear maxi skirts all the time."

"I do. Pretty much."

"They make you look old-fashioned," she added. "Like a pioneer lady in an old-time western town."

"Then they're all there?"

"Every one."

All right. Forever was nothing like the pink Victorian. The camera had recorded what was there, what we saw. Its particular power remained to be discovered, and discover it we would. Only not today.

Eleven

Later that afternoon, I took a strawberry pie across the lane to thank Camille for taking care of the collies in my absence. Camille, the master baker of Foxglove Corners and well-known author of cookbooks, was delighted, as were her dogs, Twister and Holly, who had seen or smelled the treat from their porch.

"I haven't baked a strawberry pie in ages," she said. "I've been making preserves with berries instead. Will you have a piece with me?"

Annica and I had stopped for lunch on the way home, and I'd had a slice of ice cream cake roll with hot fudge sauce for dessert.

"I couldn't eat another bite, but a cup of tea would be nice."

Twister and Holly followed us into the blue and white country kitchen hot on the trail of the pie. Camille set it on top of a high cupboard.

"Tea it is," she said.

While the water boiled, I showed her the pictures of Forever.

"Some people thought we were making up stories," I said. "These should prove them wrong."

"These are amazing," she said. "Fascinating." She handed the phone back to me. "You should contact that reporter friend of yours at the *Banner*. This is truly newsworthy."

She meant Jill Lodge, the *Banner* owner's cousin, whom I hadn't seen in years. It was a good idea, but I knew I wouldn't do it.

"I want Forever to be our secret for a little while longer," I said.

"Who else knows about it?" she asked.

"Crane, of course. Brent, Lucy, Annica's mom, and Mary Jeanne at Clovers. There may be others."

I told her about the apple.

"Were there any apple trees around?" she asked.

I tried to remember, but I'd been concentrating on the houses rather than the surroundings and retained only an impression of all-encompassing neglect. "There might have been. I didn't notice."

"What kind of apple was it?"

"Red Delicious, but not one of those little schoolboy kind."

"Was it rotten?"

"Well, brownish, where it was bitten. I can't guess how long it had been exposed to air."

"I wonder why it was tossed away after one bite," she said.

"Some red delicious apples taste rather bland in spite of the name."

"My guess is a person threw it out the window of a passing car and an animal carried it to Forever and left it there."

It was comforting to sit at Camille's table and speculate about a piece of fruit that might become a clue to solving the ghost town mystery, and good to think that no faceless, apple-eating entity roamed the streets of Forever.

"And the scrounging animal decided it didn't like the taste of apple," I said.

Camille gave me a triumphant. "There! We've solved the mystery."

Except I hadn't mentioned the feelings that had assailed me. The sense of not being alone in a place that was undeniably empty. The burn of eyes boring into the two mortals who dared to desecrate the streets of the town. The hint of a presence moving quietly in the silence.

I had to know more before I spoke of them.

"I wish Brent and Lucy had found Forever," I said. "If there's anything unnatural about it, I'm pretty sure Lucy would be able to detect it."

~ * ~

That evening Brent scrolled through my pictures. He had already seen the ones Annica had taken.

"They look real enough," he said.

"They *are* real."

"I can't understand why I didn't find Forever unless it's hiding from me. I didn't even see the bridge."

"How could a town hide?" Crane asked.

"Oh, it's there," I said. "In real life, if not on the map."

"Lucy and I drove around for a couple of hours looking for it. Then we got back on the freeway and drove north a ways. We had dinner in a restaurant on the lake. Are you sure this so-called ghost town isn't a movie set?"

"It's a whole town," I said. "It couldn't possibly be a movie set."

Or could it? Was it possible our mystery town was a set constructed for a science-fiction movie?

Everyone in a town disappears. Why? Where did they go?

Crane had mentioned the possibility when I'd first told him about our discovery.

I considered and promptly rejected the idea. I doubted that anyone would go to the expense of constructing an entire town with stores and houses to shoot scenes for a film.

"The next time we go, you and Lucy can come along with us," I said.

"That's not the same as finding it myself. It should be a piece of cake."

Brent was eating a slice of orange chiffon cake that the collies had their eyes on. To make his point, he speared a generous chunk with a fork and waved it in the air—under Misty's nose. Predictably it disappeared. He stared at the empty fork.

Crane laughed. "You asked for it, Fowler. Next time I'm free, I'll go with you. I'd like to see this ghost town myself."

I pounced on the idea. "Why don't we all go? We'll choose a time when Annica and Crane are off. We can make an excursion of it, pack a lunch, take more pictures. And we'll take Misty with us."

"Yes!" Brent said, apparently forgetting his desire to find the town on his own. "Let's do it soon."

I glanced at the calendar. September was drawing inexorably closer. September... School... Free time left behind in a memory of summer days.

"Just as soon as we can coordinate schedules," I said.

~ * ~

While the excitement of exploring a ghost town was still fresh, I kept the matter of the rogue collie rescue group in the back of my mind. When the day of Sue Appleton's emergency meeting of the Rescue League arrived, it leaped to the forefront. Leonora set aside her reception planning for a few hours and picked me up so we could drive the short distance together.

Sue's horse farm, with its picturesque ranch house, was located on Squill Lane, where Jonquil Lane ended. To the left, at the end of acres of woods and farmland, stood a yellow Victorian cottage more often than not untenanted. The cottage backed up to a cornfield presided over by a frightfully realistic scarecrow. To the right were more farmland, woods, and finally Sue's home which sheltered her collies and rescues, along with her horses.

Judging from the six cars parked around the house, only a portion of the membership would be attending the meeting, and that was regrettable.

"We have to learn everything we can about this new rescue group," I said.

"And stop them," Leonora added.

If that were possible.

"I hope Sue impressed the importance of this meeting on everyone," I said.

"I can understand why people would rather sit this one out. It's such a beautiful evening."

I couldn't disagree with her, but if we wanted to belong to the group, we had to support it, even when it was inconvenient.

With wagging tails, Sue's rescues, Icy and Bluebell, met us at the front door that had been left ajar. Yelping with joy, a third member of the welcome party pushed her way between Icy and Bluebell. It was our rescue collie from up north, our golden girl, Echo, looking as if she had been a part of Sue's pack from puppyhood.

Yes, Sue was going to keep her. I didn't doubt it.

I gave Echo a long caress on the top of her head. Nothing is happier than a foster failure.

We made our way through the house to the spacious family room, to the light and hum of conversation.

"Welcome, Leonora, Jennet." Sue set a bowl of mixed nuts on a side table. "We're just about to get started." She sat in her favorite chair and looked over the small gathering. Her expression was neutral, although the low turnout must be a disappointment.

"Where is everybody?" Leonora asked.

Sue shrugged. "Various places. I fielded a lot of phone calls today. Help yourself to the refreshments, girls."

Besides the nuts, there were chocolate chip cookies, tea, and coffee set out on a low coffee table. If my chowhound, Candy, had been one of the canines in the room, this arrangement would never work.

I helped myself to a cookie and took a seat near Emma Brock, while Leonora poured herself a cup of coffee.

"You've all heard of the Foxglove Corners Collie Rescue by now," Sue said.

Nobody contradicted her.

Emma Brock sat forward in her chair, lamplight shining on the silver streaks in her hair. "Did you learn anything about them?"

"Nothing at all. It's like they don't exist, but they do. They're out there. That's what I want to discuss tonight. We can't find a way to contact the new rescue, which leads me to believe something other than collie rescue is going on."

Sue's words inspired a murmuring in the gathering. Something else? Something bad?

A vague threat is more fearsome than one you can see.

Emma said, "I want to know why they—whoever these people are—didn't contact one of us instead of setting up their own organization. We could use the help, and we need more foster homes. If they merged with us, we'd double our power to help homeless collies."

"How many collies in Foxglove Corners need rescuing?" Diane asked. "For that matter, how many collies are there in Foxglove Corners anyway?"

"More than you'd think, Diane," Sue said. "Too often city people drive their dogs out to the country and abandon them. They figure some farmer will take them in."

"Surely there can't be enough collies for two groups."

"No," she said. "This new group is going to be at the Fall Fair. I hope everyone can attend. We'll bombard them with questions and find out what the heck is going on."

Vanna, one of our newer members said, "I may have some news. I asked around and came up with a name: Ann Clarke. No 'e' in Ann but one in Clarke. She's supposed to be the group founder. I can't reveal my source. She's afraid of repercussions."

No one said a word, but all of a sudden, electricity seemed to crackle through the air.

Repercussions? What kind of organization was this?

Twelve

"Repercussions?" Leonora said. "What kind?"

"She wasn't specific, but that was the impression she gave me."

"Are they a rescue group or a secret society?" Vanna demanded.

"I call them the rogue rescue group," I said. "The name seems to fit."

"I hope we're overreacting, but that's better than letting these people move into our town and operate in the shadows."

Sue's words reminded me of Lucy Hazen's Gothic rhetoric. She had me picturing secret meeting places, hooded faces, and candles burning. Which was way beyond melodramatic. Whatever was going on, we needed to know their mission.

"If we can find this woman, Ann Clarke, we may have all our answers," Emma said.

By then, influenced by Sue's attitude, the League members had had time to react to the new threat. I heard outrage in their murmurings and even anger.

Diane said, "How dare they copy us? Why don't they concentrate on another town in Michigan?"

"I wondered about that, too." Sue set her coffee mug on the table with a bang. "Their choice of Foxglove Corners makes everything seem personal."

"How about Maple Creek?" Emma asked. "They don't even have an animal shelter, let alone a rescue group."

"Oh," Diane said. "That reminds me. I saw the cutest collie pup for sale at the Pet-Go- Round last week. You know he'll likely end up being surrendered by a family who wants cuteness and doesn't know how much work a puppy can be. He was seventy-five dollars."

"No!" Sue couldn't mask the horror in her voice. "They're not supposed to sell animals at the Pet-Go-Round, just food and supplies."

"I almost bought him," Diane said. "He looked pathetic, and he seemed so friendly. He's a sable, maybe three or four months old. He knows how to shake hands," she added. Her voice broke, then took on a decisive note. "You know, I just decided. I'm going back and see if he's still there."

"You're asking for heartbreak, Diane," Sue said. "You're holding the door open and inviting it in. You won't know anything about his breeding or background. He may get sick or be sick already."

"But what about the puppy? His life is at stake. There's a sign on the cage. His name is Chief."

With seven collies at home, I was glad I hadn't seen the pet shop puppy.

"You do what you have to, Diane," Sue said. "Just so you're aware of problems down the line. If you do buy him, take him to the vet right away. And who knows? There may not be anything wrong with him. Now Jennet…"

All eyes turned to me. I knew what was coming and couldn't dodge it.

"You're so good at ferreting out information," Sue said. "Do you suppose you could use your contacts to find Ann Clarke?"

"Contacts? I don't have any contacts."

"You must have something. How else could you solve so many mysteries?"

"Luck," I said.

"You're the best one for the job," Emma said, obviously hoping flattery would sway me.

"Will you do it?" Sue asked. "Ultimately it's for the collies."

How could I possibly refuse even though exploring the ghost town headed my list of things to do before the start of school? Besides, discovering the elusive Ann Clarke seemed like a hopeless enterprise to me. Still… For the collies.

"I'll try. No promises."

"Thank you, Jennet," she said. "I know you won't fail us."

~ * ~

Leonora and I stayed at Sue's after the others had left. Sue wanted to know all about the wedding.

Echo lay with Bluebell and Icy in front of the wood burning stove looking as much at home as if the stove had been installed for their benefit, as if Sue had built a roaring (and unnecessary) fire for them.

The winsome pair had been bred by Rosalyn Everett for health and intelligence rather than beauty, which wasn't to say they weren't stunning collies. But Echo had a certain sparkle along with beauty. She could have competed with any outstanding collie and come home with a first prize ribbon.

She stared back at me, and her tail thumped on the hardwood floor. Could she possibly read my thoughts?

"You're not worried that someone made a mistake then?" I asked Sue.

Her eyes narrowed. "What kind of mistake?"

"That Echo was wrongly surrendered without the owner's permission. Didn't something like that happen before?"

Echo rose and padded over to me, ears flattened, eyes shining with the joy only a collie wanting to play can convey.

I found a small stuffed hen on the floor, squeezed it, and threw it to the middle of the room. Bluebell lounged for it, while Icy looked on in amusement as the two girls engaged in an impromptu game of tug-of-war.

Sue watched the collies' antics with a fond smile.

"I'll admit I've thought about that," she said. "It's one reason I'm not offering Echo for adoption."

"And the other?"

"It's simple. I already love her. Bluebell and Icy love her. Anyone would think she'd been on the farm all her life."

"I sure hope nobody is missing her," Leonora said softly.

An uncharacteristic hardness sharpened Sue's voice. "If they are, they'll never find her here."

~ * ~

I asked Leonora to come in for a while to have a cup of tea and finish my now famous orange chiffon cake. Crane greeted her and disappeared into his office on sheriff's business.

"I've been away from my dogs too long," Leonora said. "But ten more minutes or so won't make a difference."

I'd thought we should offer to take care of Leonora's two collies during her honeymoon. When I mentioned it to Crane, he said, "Nine dogs! We might as well be a kennel."

"Leonora's neighbor is willing to keep them, but I thought they'd be more at home with our gang."

"She has a pet sitter. Good. Just so we're on the same page, Jennet, seven collies is enough. Right?"

"More than enough," I'd said. "Don't worry."

After his reaction, I abandoned the idea.

I remembered that conversation as I brought the cake down from the cupboard. What would I do the next time the Rescue League had no foster home for a collie in need? And that would happen.

Well, I'd cross that bridge when I came to it.

"Are we all ready for the wedding?" I asked. "Is there anything else you need me to do for you?"

"I can't think of another thing."

"Then maybe you'll have time to come with us on our next trip to the ghost town," I said.

For a moment it seemed as if she might accept my invitation. Then the moment passed.

"Not this time," she said. "I don't want to take a chance on anything happening before the wedding."

"What could happen?" I asked.

"Anything. I might trip and sprain my ankle. There might be some germs floating around in the air. Or... Well, you don't know what's really going on in that town."

When I'd told her about the apple, we had speculated about the many ways in which it could have ended up on the main street of Forever. Leonora thought it was a sinister piece of fruit and alluded to the wicked queen's poisoned apple in *Snow White*.

Ridiculous. Neither Annica nor I had ever considered eating the apple. Certainly we didn't have a secret enemy who would leave a poisoned apple in the street for us to find on the off chance we would return to Forever.

"I've missed sharing adventures with you in the past," Leonora said. "We had some great times. After I'm safely married, I'll join you on the next one. Unless Jake disapproves, of course."

Clearly I would have to give Leonora the benefit of my experience with Crane. It was, after all, part of my duties as her matron of honor.

I refilled out teacups and cut the last piece of cake in two... and thought of something else.

Leonora was concerned, but not about a wrinkle in her carefully wrought wedding plans. She seemed to be afraid that Forever held danger for us. And not the danger of tripping on a rise in the sidewalk, or breathing germ-filled air.

I could only hope her fears were groundless.

Thirteen

Our multi-person expedition to Forever slowly fell apart. Annica was free the next day, but Crane received an unexpected assignment that would take him out of town for two days. Meanwhile, Brent expected to welcome a new horse to his stable and was eager to spend time with him.

"I'll go when Andromeda is settled in," he'd said.

At Dark Gables, Lucy was immersed in her latest novel but said she could join us any day. It looked as if we would be a group of women.

Annica didn't want to wait for everyone's schedule to coordinate.

"Before we know it, you'll be in school," she said. "I've been thinking about that apple. If we look, really, really look, we may find something else on another street that shouldn't be there."

"It's possible."

I'd had the same thought. A careless individual might discard an object even more telling than an unwanted snack.

"The town is small enough for us to walk through it," she said.

"And this time we can go through some of the other houses. I shouldn't have rushed us away, but I was anxious about finding the way back home."

"You can bring Misty," Annica added. "We'll be the scouting party for the next expedition with the men."

So it was settled. Annica's mention of school set off alarm bells. In September I'd have to rise two hours earlier in the morning, wear dresses instead of denim skirts, and drive an hour to teach English to kids whose minds were still on summer vacation.

The next morning I woke from vague dreams of school classrooms and fixed Crane an old-fashioned country breakfast before he departed on his mission.

"If you and Annica are going to the ghost town again, be careful," he said as he speared a hunk of blueberry pancake with his fork.

He had been thinking of the apple, that mysterious piece of fruit that set everyone to wild speculation. To him, it suggested the presence of another person, a man. Translation: danger.

"You don't know what you'll run into," he said. "If something happened, no one would know where to find you."

At times Crane was overly cautious. I had to concentrate hard to keep his concerns from chipping away at my confidence.

Nothing was going to happen. Hadn't I just said something like that to Leonora?

"We'll be very careful," I said. "Lucy is coming with us, and we're taking Misty."

"I wish I could go, too."

"So do I, but we'll go again soon, all together, like we planned."

"You have a nice sunny day for your expedition," Crane said.

His plate was almost empty. Soon he would be gone. The collies were unusually clingy this morning. They sat close together in a semi-circle around Crane, and I didn't think it was only in the hope of leftover pancakes.

Dogs know when a change is imminent. They can sense our emotions. They heard the reserve in Crane's voice and, I believed, could read my mind. I worried about Crane, too. I didn't know what his current project entailed, but he assured me that he'd be safe. I imagined it was more dangerous making random stops on the roads of Foxglove Corners.

All too soon he left with a goodbye kiss and a promise to call me this evening.

Look on the bright side, I told myself. For the next two days, I wouldn't have to cook dinner. I could make do with a salad or sandwich, and I'd have an adventure of my own.

Still I'd rather have Crane sitting across from me in the dining room with the light from the taper candles bringing out the silver streaks in his light hair and the glints of frost in his eyes.

Well, being alone would be my reality for a few days. It wasn't as if he were a soldier, going off to war.

I cleaned the kitchen, called Camille to ask her to look in on the dogs, and bid them a low-key farewell. Finally I set out with phone, (useless) map, bottled water, and a bag of fruit to pick up Annica and Lucy.

Let the day begin.

~ * ~

I left the freeway and turned on a rutted country road whose top branches met each other overhead, creating the illusion of a green tunnel. The sun seemed to recede behind a ceiling of rustling leaves. We'd left the air off and opened the windows. All the wondrous scents of nature wafted in, and all the sounds. On the other side of the tunnel, the world was bright and fresh, the woods washed clean with a recent rain shower.

"Brent thinks you have a special map that takes you straight through to the ghost town," Lucy said. "That's the reason you always find it and he doesn't."

Annica laughed, and Misty whirled around in the back seat to see what she had missed. "In his dreams. Jennet is the better navigator."

"There's no written route," I said. "I just keep driving, and eventually we come to the bridge."

"All these roads look alike to me," Annica confessed. "I've searched for a landmark but have never seen one. Not even a road sign."

"We're in the deep, deep woods," Lucy said. "There's a magical quality in the air. Dark magic," she added.

Annica sniffed. "I smell pine."

What would Lucy think of Forever? I could hardly wait for her impressions, could hardly believe that I counted this amazing woman among my close friends.

Of course, this might be the day I drove and drove and didn't run into the ghost town. How long a life span did luck have?

Annica didn't share my doubts. "We're getting close. I wonder if the apple is still there."

"It must be, unless an animal carried it away. Crane thinks someone else was in the town. He warned me to be careful. So be warned."

"That's what Brent thinks, too," Lucy said.

"Then he should have come along to protect us," Annica pointed out.

"We don't need a man for protection," Lucy said. "I'm confident we can deal with any problem that may arise. If not, we have a guard dog."

"Woman power!" Annica added. "And canine power!"

I let them ramble on and watched the road. That patch of spindly pink wildflowers… I remembered passing it and wishing I'd brought a shovel. It was a landmark of sorts, likely to still be in the same place for a few weeks.

The point was that we were on the right track. Forever would be around the next curve in the road. Or the next.

And there was the bridge over the shining water, and beyond the bridge, the town.

"Where did all the sunlight go?" Lucy asked.

I glanced at her. Misty began to whine.

The sun was where it should be, where it had been all morning, high in the sky. It had turned the water under the bridge to silver and bathed the town in golden light.

"Suddenly it's gotten so dark," she said. "I hope we're not heading into a storm."

"Jennet?" That was Annica. "Do you think Misty needs to go out?"

"No, I think…" I paused, striving for diplomacy. "I don't think it's that dark, Lucy. Just the opposite."

"Oh." Lucy rubbed her right eye. "Oh, you're right, Jennet. For a moment the sky seemed overcast."

Not knowing what else to say, I said nothing. Annica was murmuring something intended to soothe Misty, who was still whining.

Lucy often saw that which was hidden to ordinary people. Annica and I saw the sun shining on a forgotten town built in the wilderness. Lucy saw darkness.

In the end, whose view would prove true?

Fourteen

The apple was still there. It looked a little duller, as if rain had washed away most of its rosy color. Misty sniffed at it warily, then looked abruptly to her right, her eyes fixed on something in the distance that I couldn't see. I took a firmer grip on her leash.

"I'm surprised a bird hasn't eaten it," Lucy said.

Annica touched her arm lightly. "Look around, Lucy. Do you see or hear any birds?"

"Now that you mention it, I don't."

And thank heavens for that. I was fond of birds flying through the air and enjoyed listening to their cheery singing, but in this mysterious town, I couldn't help but remember Alfred Hitchcock's classic horror movie, *The Birds*. A black vulture wouldn't improve the ambience, and we didn't need to be besieged by a flock of rampaging feathered creatures.

I had left the Focus in front of the dime store, and we strolled to the end of Main Street, surveying the silent houses. Lucy marveled at the sight of the empty buildings and snapped pictures constantly with her phone.

"I can hardly believe this is all real, and that I'm here, experiencing it," she said.

"We thought we'd split up and let ourselves into as many houses as we have time for," Annica said.

"We don't have to hurry," I reminded her. "We have all the time in the world."

Until darkness, that is, which would give us most of the day. Oh, wait. Not quite that long. I didn't want to navigate unfamiliar country roads without full sunlight.

"Is it wise to split up? Lucy asked.

"We can cover more ground that way," Annica said. "But if you'd rather team up with me…" She let the sentence trail off.

"No, it'll be all right. I see your point. Tell me, are we going to break in? Because I never did that."

"Some people may have left their doors unlocked," Annica said. "I guess nobody worried about looters, not if they all left."

"Our purpose is to observe," I added. "Look for anything like a newspaper or magazine with a date. Look for something that doesn't belong, like the apple. Oh, and is there any sign that someone stayed behind?"

"Why would anyone stay behind if the whole town was clearing out?" Lucy asked.

"We won't know that until we figure out why the townspeople abandoned Forever. Let's give ourselves about an hour," I added. "Then we can meet at the dime store and compare notes."

I'd noticed that Annica was wearing a new shade of red lipstick. Her five and dime purchase, I imagined. She'd have an opportunity to make another one. Maybe I'd help myself to a bottle of Ann Haviland's toilet water.

"I'm off to find the house with the disabled Volkswagen in the driveway," I said.

Lucy snapped a picture of a small cottage whose paint was faded and peeling. "This is mine. It looks so forlorn."

Annica gestured to a street lined with maple trees. "I'll take this one and pick the first house that appeals to me."

"Come, Misty." I gave her leash a tug.

My psychic collie was eager to move on. Having her with me gave me a slight advantage. If Crane's specter of danger lurked around a bush or the side of a house, she would warn me.

Not that that would happen.

I felt that, at least today, we were alone in Forever. No wary eyes followed our progress and no foreboding tugged at me. This was an adventure, pure and simple: *The Foxglove Corners Girls in the Ghost Town.*

~ * ~

A scream fractured the deep silence that enveloped me. I froze in the middle of the porch, and Misty tried to break my hold on her lead.

That was a woman's scream. Annica? Lucy?

Misty cast me a look over her shoulder that all but cried, *Hurry!*

Stumbling over the uneven sidewalk, I let her lead me back down the street, retracing our path. We found Annica racing toward us. She carried a long branch in her hand, letting it drag on the ground. With an excited yelp, Misty lunged for it.

"Snake!" she cried. "I almost stepped on a monster snake!"

"Oh, my God! Did it bite you?"

"I… No, I don't think so. Almost."

She bent down to examine her ankle. It was trim and tanned, free of puncture wounds or redness.

"Where did this happen?" I asked.

"Back there." She pointed toward the house she'd chosen. "It was hiding in the grass. I thought it was a fallen tree."

I hadn't expected danger to take the form of a reptile.

"It wasn't one of those little snakes either," she said, "although they're bad enough. This one had a long, thick body like an alligator. I didn't think we had such large snakes in Michigan."

Misty wrested the stick from Annica and tried to break it in half. Annica didn't seem to notice.

"I was just scared, but I'm okay now," she said.

I didn't think she was. She was trembling and pale and kept looking at the ground.

"Let's stay together," I said, remembering Lucy's initial misgivings about splitting up.

Lucy?

Where was Lucy? She must have heard Annica's scream.

Don't frighten Annica anymore.

"Let's find Lucy," I said.

~ * ~

As we hurried down one street, then another, I called Lucy's name and listened. Echoes bounced by. Misty whimpered, her branch forgotten.

"Why doesn't she answer?" Annica's voice was an octave higher than normal.

"You know Lucy," I said. "She gets distracted. She's probably thinking about a new book set in a ghost town."

That's right. Don't jump to conclusions. Just because Crane's warning is playing in your head and that eerie sense of a watching presence is back.

"Lucy!" Annica's voice shook. "Be careful where you walk, Jennet. There may be more snakes."

I wished she hadn't said that. At the same time I was grateful for the reminder. We might be in a jungle for the height of the grasses and weeds.

Didn't snakes tend to blend into their environment as a way of hiding from predators?

A snake as large as a fallen tree.

"What color was the snake?" I asked.

"Brownish... Greenish. Ugly."

"Like the grass."

"Something happened to Lucy," Annica said. "Something took her."

"What nonsense!" If only I'd been able to inject a little force into my voice.

"Maybe she met up with a snake, too. We have to find her."

"We will. Misty," I said, "find Lucy."

I balked at taking her off her leash. Where there was one snake, there might be more. I'd read somewhere that dogs consider snakes a natural enemy. Nonetheless, I didn't want Misty to encounter one.

So I'd hold on fast to the leash and try not to fall.

She took off like a white rocket streaking above the ground, ran as if she knew exactly where Lucy was, trusting me to follow as I was on the other end of the leash. If only I could have let her run free.

We turned a corner and Misty dragged me to a forbidding brown house at the end of the street. It towered over its neighbors and appeared to be in better shape, perhaps built at a later time than the others. Misty came to a halt, barking. She barked, a frantic note creeping into her voice, and strained to break free of her restraint.

The door was ajar.

"She's in there," Annica said. "Lucy!"

As I tried to fill my lungs with air, Lucy came out on the porch, her black skirt blowing in a sudden wind.

Thank God! For a minute, I thought... No matter what I thought.

"What's wrong?" Lucy asked. "Did you find something interesting?"

Ignoring her question, I said, "Lucy, didn't you hear us calling you?"

"Didn't you hear me screaming?" Annica demanded.

Lucy leaned back against the door, patting her knee to summon Misty. "I heard lots of things. It was so noisy."

"What was noisy?"

"Come in, and I'll tell you. I want to know if you hear it, too."

Hear what? The wind? Misty panting? The clinking of Lucy's zodiac charms as she moved her hand along Misty's rib cage?

She ushered us inside to a living room as dark and gloomy as the house.

"Voices," Lucy said. "I didn't find anything noteworthy in that cottage, so I checked out another house, then I saw this one so much larger than the others. As soon as I stepped inside, I heard people talking."

"Is someone here?" Annica asked.

"I don't think so. Their voices were coming from another... How shall I describe it? Another plane? I couldn't make out what they were saying, but they sounded fearful. Frantic. I sat down and listened, trying to put their words together to make a conversation, but I couldn't. All I could tell was that it seemed to be three people speaking. So I'm sorry, but I didn't hear anything outside the house. Why did you scream, Annica?"

"I met up with a snake," she said.

Lucy shuddered. "How ghastly! It doesn't surprise me, though. Jennet, you should have brought your gun."

"I didn't think I'd need it."

Lucy pointed to a chair with worn dark upholstery. "Here's where I sat. Do you girls hear anything now?"

Annica shook her head slowly. "Nothing that can't be accounted for," I said.

"Well, now, I don't either, and I didn't find anything unusual."

It didn't matter. What did matter was that Lucy had heard voices from the past or the future, and they hadn't originated in the house, in the here-and-now. There had been a time when she was certain she was losing her powers and, in some strange manner, transferring to me the ability to hear sounds from another world.

The situation had righted itself, leaving us with another aspect to the mystery of the ghost town.

"I had a narrow escape, and I'm still shaking," Annica was saying. "Let's get out of this neighborhood and go back to Main Street. I hardly think a snake would go there."

"You can't tell," I said. "We'll keep our eyes open. Remember, forewarned is forearmed."

Fifteen

The wind pushed us along, gathering more strength with each gust. It blew my hair across my face and sent debris from the nearby woods flying down Main Street. Walking was an effort, but we were determined to leave the eerie neighborhood behind.

"I'm the snake watcher," Annica announced. Her natural good humor had tempered her fright.

She had retrieved half of her branch, and Misty carried the other half proudly in her mouth. They were ready for any eventuality.

We didn't see a single errant reptile, but the apple still lay in the street, taunting us with its mysterious origin. You'd think it would blow away with the wind. One day, I thought, we'd find it missing.

"I guess we didn't accomplish anything today," Annica added.

"I wouldn't say that."

I'd had time to walk quickly through two houses before the snake incident. Both had faded 'For Sale' signs on the front lawn. As I had anticipated, the townspeople had left their bulky furniture behind while taking personal possessions, some of their clothing, and food.

To go where? That was another aspect of the mystery. Did they go their separate ways or flock to the same place?

"I suspected that a catastrophic event caused the mass exodus," I said. "Lucy's description of the voices as fearful and frantic reinforces that idea."

"Fear," Lucy mused. "What on earth could have been so terrifying that it made the people of Forever abandon their homes and everything they cherished?"

"Maybe it wasn't something on earth," Annica said. "How about an alien invasion?"

"Mmm." Lucy was always open to the extraordinary. "It could be, but I don't recall reading about flying saucers in Michigan."

"That doesn't mean there weren't any," Annica said. "The alien invaders could have come to earth some other way."

"Other than from the sky?" Lucy asked.

"From the sea?" Annica said.

"There's the dime store," I said, bringing this wild speculation to an end. "Everything inside is just as it must have been before."

Annica brandished her branch. "I hope there won't be any snakes in there."

"Just spiders." I pushed open the door. "Didn't you notice all the cobwebs?"

A delicious aroma wafted out into the air. Popcorn. Warm. Salty. I could almost taste it, practically feel the kernels in my hand. Misty licked her chops, and Lucy frowned.

"That's odd," Lucy said. "It smells fresh, but how can that be?"

"It can't. Maybe with the store closed for so long, smells were trapped inside."

"My lipstick still has a light fragrance," Annica pointed out.

"That's different."

Lucy walked down the aisle, gazing in wonder at the store's many offerings. "This is amazing. It's like stepping back in time, but that's not what's going on here." She picked up a blue apron with gingham checks. "One dollar and ninety-nine cents. Imagine! My grandma used to make aprons just like this from leftover material."

"I wonder why the owner didn't take his stock when he left," Annica said.

I didn't find that mysterious. "Obviously there was way too

much to load. And what would he do with aprons, make-up, curtains, and toys?

I wandered over to the perfume display, lured by six bottles of Ann Haviland toilet water. Wood Violet! I slipped one in my straw purse and promptly felt guilty, even though, in these strange circumstances, that made no sense. To assuage my conscience, I left a ten dollar bill in the space where the bottle had lain and strolled toward the back of the store.

I'd done an Internet search for that Wood Violet toilet water once and found it on sale at eBay for thirty-two dollars. Then I discovered that was the price for the empty bottle.

A half door at the back of the store led to a dark cluttered room filled with boxes. Perhaps the contents could tell me something. A brown cardigan sweater and an umbrella hanging from a peg. A pair of boots lying on their sides. An overturned chair. That spoke of haste and flight. What else? A desk holding one of those small battery-operated clocks that had stopped at three-thirty on some past day and nothing else.

Finally a clue! On the wall behind the desk hung an old calendar whose picture for September was a pair of handsome English setters posed in a red and gold autumn landscape.

At last I had a date. September, 1998.

~ * ~

"What are we going to do with the date?" Annica asked as we walked back to the car, struggling to remain upright in the wind. Misty, white fur blowing, seemed reluctant to leave Forever. She was the only one.

"It's a starting point," I said. "What happened in southeastern Michigan in September of 1998?"

I could hardly wait to get home and turn on my computer.

"Your catastrophic event," Lucy murmured.

"The alien invasion," Annica said.

"It may not be easy. Suppose there's no record of any unusual happening?"

"Then we're back to Square One. The ghost town keeps its secrets."

"Is it getting darker or am I imagining it?" Lucy asked.

I looked around, glanced at the sky. The sun was still visible, burning down on the town, and the clouds were puffy. I saw blue and white... and shadows. "No, but it's getting windier."

"I can feel the darkness," Lucy said. "It's the town, and I hear something."

"Voices?" Annica asked. "What are they saying?"

"It's more like a hum."

I shivered. Lucy saw a different kind of darkness, one that wrapped itself around the town, and, in a sense, isolated it from the rest of the world.

Why had the town allowed us to breach its defenses?

As we neared the Focus, an apple flew past us, like a red bird flying close to the earth. Misty launched herself at it. I gave the leash a tug, and she gave me a whine of protest.

The apple?

I kicked it and breathed a sigh of relief when I saw the chunk bitten off.

It was *the* apple.

"Let's get out of here," Annica said.

~ * ~

"Now to find the way home," Lucy said. "Do you think you can do it, Jennet?"

"Well, I hope so."

We had left Forever well before sunset. At this point I was a bit hesitant, but I'd grown used to driving without a specific route. When I passed the pink flowers, I knew I was heading in the right direction.

After a moment, Lucy said, "I brought a souvenir out of Forever."

"What is it?" I asked.

"The blue apron. It's in my purse. I don't wear aprons. I don't even cook that much. But when I touched it, I felt a moment of panic that wasn't mine."

"I took a bottle of toilet water," I said. "It didn't communicate anything to me. I just liked the scent."

Annica drew a tube of lipstick out of her purse. "I'm wearing Riding Hood Red from the dime store." She proceeded to apply another layer.

We each had something from the ghost town, along with three sets of photographs on our phones. Lipstick, toilet water, and an apron. If they had anything in common, I couldn't see it.

A woman with dark red lips wearing an apron and smelling of toilet water? Perhaps there was nothing significant to find.

"There'll be a day of reckoning," Lucy said.

I could have asked her to explain that cryptic remark, but I didn't really want to know what she meant.

Sixteen

On the way home, a familiar feeling assailed me. It told me that Forever existed only in my imagination. The real world was the southbound freeway with cars speeding past me and sunshine so bright it hurt my eyes.

"Does anyone else feel like we just left an enchanted place?" I asked.

"A place of dark enchantment," Lucy said. "But it's real enough."

Annica nodded. "I can't understand why no one else has found it."

"We don't know that," Lucy pointed out. "It isn't on the map, but it's there. It may be the locals' best-kept secret."

"What locals?" I asked.

"The nearest town, whatever it is." Annica unfolded the map. "Let me see. That would be Candorville to the east."

"If even one person had visited Forever, everyone would know about it," I said. "Reporters and photographers would flock to the site. Archaeologists, too. All the papers would run feature stories. Some developer would step in and try to turn it into a resort."

"Before that happened, the F.B.I. would investigate," Lucy added.

I hadn't thought of that.

"If Annica's flying saucer theory is true," she added.

"Maybe we ought to tell someone," I said. "Or should we wait?"

My companions were silent. I imagined they were considering the loss of our private ghost town and other possible ramifications.

Finally Lucy spoke. "Let's wait. A week or so won't make any difference."

We agreed to keep Forever a secret for now. Enough people already knew about it.

"I've been wondering about something, Lucy," I said. "I don't understand how an inanimate object can transfer feelings to you, or even have them, but I accept it. Still, an apron in a dime store that no one had purchased... How can that absorb fear?"

"I don't understand it either," Lucy said. "Except that every stick and stone, every item left in Forever, holds a memory of what happened there. I'm fortunate enough to be able to feel the fear. I only wish I could pick up details."

"Well, we have one detail. The date."

I read the freeway sign as we passed the next exit. *Foxglove Corners—Twenty Miles*. We were almost home. Back to reality with our souvenirs from the Twilight Zone, with more questions and no answers.

We would have to visit Forever again, the next time with Crane and Brent.

~ * ~

Reality was a houseful of wild collies and no husband coming through the door. It was being suddenly exhausted and wishing I could go straight to bed. It was Camille's note telling me to look in the refrigerator. She had brought over a homemade chicken pie for my dinner.

And reality was taking care of my collies, fixing their meals, and watching over them while they worked off stored-up energy in the yard. I never let them out alone because of the coyotes, our unfriendly neighbors who lived in the woods. Only Raven was a match for the wild canines.

I was home in plenty of time to take Crane's phone call. He wanted to know about our trip to Forever. I wanted to know what he was doing. He fell back on his favorite 'sheriff's business' excuse.

"Do the dogs miss me?" he asked.

"Of course. So do I."

"I'll be home late tomorrow," he said. "We'll make up for lost time."

"How's the weather?" That was always a safe subject.

"Nice and cool. The leaves are just starting to turn."

He was up north then. Somewhere. Darn sheriff's business anyway. I'll bet Veronica the Viper knew where Crane was and what he was doing. Veronica was the female deputy sheriff in the department who made no secret of her romantic interest in Crane.

"Did anything exciting happen in Forever?" he asked.

"Annica almost stepped on a snake, and I saw an old calendar from September, 1998. I figure that's the month and year the people abandoned the town. Lucy picked up her usual vibes. Otherwise it was an uneventful day."

A bottle of toilet water and an apron. The apple still in the street. Crane didn't need to know about them. As for the darkness that Lucy had seen on the other side of the bridge? That was part of her vibe collection.

"Well, be careful," I said.

"You, too, if you decide to go back to Forever. It may be crawling with snakes."

"If anything could keep me away, that would be it."

"What are you going to do tomorrow?" he asked.

"Something around the house. Something quiet."

On the computer, I thought. I had to go back in time almost two decades and jot down major happenings in my corner of the world—and while I was at it, find a catastrophe.

~ * ~

Before settling down to research, I cleaned the guest room. Julia would be here soon, and I wanted everything to be warm and welcoming for her. All I needed was a bouquet for the night table and an assortment of American magazines which I'd buy at a later date.

After exploring a secret ghost town, I found life in Foxglove Corners bland. Without Crane, the house lost its luster. I took my three most docile collies for a walk on Jonquil Lane, and, on returning, was overcome with guilt when Candy gave me a long, reproachful look.

Because she had proven too strong for me to control when she wanted to choose her own route, Crane had decreed that henceforth he would be responsible for her exercise. But Crane wasn't here, and Candy needed a walk. She must have read my mind. One pitiful whine convinced me to take a chance.

"Come, Candy," I said, attaching her lead to her collar. "We'll go. And you'd better behave yourself."

As it turned out, Candy was as good as the proverbial gold, and when I returned, while she dozed, I started my research, searching for memorable happenings in Foxglove Corners in 1998.

What I needed was one of those reprints of newspapers' front pages published on a particular date—the date of your birth. Without that resource, I was once again flying blind.

In 1998 people were already beginning to worry about electronics going wild at the turn of the millennium. I found an article listing necessities to store in case the grocery shelves were depleted. In March a strong wind storm wiped out power to a sizable portion of Lakeville. A private plane crashed in a lake near Maple Creek, killing the pilot and his passenger.

Other happenings were run-of-the-mill, in my estimation. Nothing accounted for the mass exodus of people living in a secluded town in southeastern Michigan. Whatever had occurred was either unknown or had been covered up.

Covered up, I decided. But why? And what would happen to a person who inadvertently snatched away the cover? Unknown would be a safer option.

In any event, I'd have to think of another way to solve the mystery of Forever. It would involve another trip to the ghost town, which we'd already planned.

While I was at the computer, I typed Ann Clarke's name into the search engine. I found several Clarks and Clarkes but no Ann. Under 'collie rescue' I found a few groups with which I was already familiar but no Foxglove Corners Collie Rescue League. Well, obviously, this wasn't my day for revelations.

I left the computer room feeling frustrated. I'd thought one could find information about anything on the Internet: the name and whereabouts of an old boyfriend, the background and picture of a mysterious flower, like the violet in Brent's wildflower field, the title of a half-remembered song from long ago.

You still can, logic whispered to me. *But you have to look in the right place.*

Seventeen

Candy dashed through the house barking as if her tail were on fire. She threw herself against the side door and began to whine frantically. This dramatic display heralded the appearance of Crane, who moments later walked into seventy-two pounds of collie fur and muscle.

"Whoa, Candy!" he said.

The rest of the dogs came running from every corner of the first floor to greet him. While this was happening, Raven, our outside girl, slipped into the kitchen ahead of Crane. The master returns!

"I think they missed you," I said.

He waded through his welcome committee to give me a kiss. "How about you, honey?"

"Do you have to ask?"

"Guess not."

"Did you have dinner?" I asked.

"A quick burger on the road."

"I baked an apple pie this afternoon," I said. "It's cool enough to eat. "I'll make us some coffee to go with it."

Crane locked his gun in its cabinet. The collies went back to their respective corners except for Candy, who stood so close to him she risked getting her foot stepped on.

"Can you tell me about your trip now?" I asked.

"All that matters is that it was successful."

I had to be satisfied with that vague answer. I couldn't imagine what business the sheriff had that needed to be wrapped in a cloak of secrecy. It wasn't as if he had discovered a ghost town.

Well, Crane was home again, looking infinitely desirable, and I didn't expect any company to interrupt our quiet evening together.

He played with Candy and Misty until the coffee was ready. Outside the coyotes began their ghostly howling. I lit the tapers in the heirloom candlesticks that had been the property of Crane's Civil War era ancestress, Rebecca Ferguson, and served the pie and coffee in the dining room.

Unbidden, a thought dropped into my mind. I was home with my husband and our canine family, safe and sheltered from whatever lurked in the darkness that surrounded us.

How would I feel if a major catastrophe—a wild fire, a killer flood, an alien invasion—forced us to leave everything we loved and seek safety in another place?

That couldn't happen to us.

But it had happened to the inhabitants of the ghost town. Probably they, too, thought they were safe in their homes.

Misty's purple Kong toy landed in my lap. She'd tossed it there, in a blatant attempt to lure me into a game.

"Not till we're through eating," I told her sternly.

She sat and watched us, hoping for a handout even though she'd never tasted my apple pie.

Almost everyone has a dog or a cat. Did the people of Forever take their pets with them when they abandoned their homes? Or did they leave them behind?

I'd read a story once in which an Irish family who was fleeing from the potato famine didn't take their faithful dog with them, leaving it behind to starve. I think it was a collie. At that point I set the book aside forever.

Imagining myself forced out of the house on Jonquil Lane with Crane and my seven collies, I balked at carrying this scenario to its conclusion. The outcome was sadness guaranteed.

In any event, it was extremely unlikely that would happen to us.

~ * ~

The next day's mail included a postcard with views of the Isle of Capri. It could only be from Julia. Turning it over eagerly, I read her brief message: *Decided to finish the summer with an extended tour of Italy. See you sometime in September.*

Well, darn. I didn't realize how much I'd counted on seeing my sister this month. I understood the reasoning behind her change of plans, though. She'd stated it herself. Who knew when she'd be able to go back to Europe?

In truth, I envied her. I'd love to travel to foreign countries again. But only if Crane could go with me, which was impossible at present.

I told myself that my summer held plenty of excitement and I should be satisfied with what I had. That realization took the edge off my disappointment.

Later, Sue Appleton called to remind me of the Fall Fair.

My mind gave me a blank screen. Then I remembered. The rogue collie rescue league and Ann Clarke, its supposed founder. In the excitement of exploring the ghost town, I had almost forgotten her.

"Sure," I said. "If you still want to go."

"We have to, Jennet. You, me, and Emma. I heard through the grapevine that one of the members rescued a collie abandoned at the Maplewood Mall. The group is doing our work."

"As long as someone saved the collie," I said.

"But what happened next? Did they take him to a vet, then place him in a foster home the way we would?"

"What else would they do?"

"That's the trouble. Who knows? Maybe they're a front for a dognapping gang. Why else would there be this air of secrecy about them?"

I thought Sue's fear was over the top, but it wouldn't hurt to investigate. From the first I'd thought something was off about the group.

"I wonder if they chose their name deliberately, hoping people would think the two groups were the same," Sue said.

"They might have, but I don't see what that would accomplish."

"Other than to confuse people, neither do I. Well, the fair opens at nine," Sue said. "We should be there at least by ten."

I remembered the author, Byrony Limon, who had written a book about a collie, planned to autograph copies at the event.

Yes, we had to attend the fair. With luck, we would meet the mysterious Ann Clarke there.

~ * ~

The day was made for fair going, warm with a mild breeze and bright golden sunshine. The primary attraction was a merry-go-round filled with seven colorful jungle animals.

"If I were a kid again, I'd ride that tiger," Sue said.

I gazed at the prancing creatures. "I like the zebra."

"I'd choose the elephant," Emma said as she reinforced the knot on her yellow scarf. "I always wanted to ride one."

We wandered through a wonderland of music, balloons, crafts, screaming children who dashed in front of us, and noise. In other words, happy chaos.

The tempting smell of hot dogs wafted through the air. Close at hand I spied a stand selling coffee and doughnuts which were more appealing fare at this early hour. Thus fortified, we followed the sound of barking to a booth on the far side of the fair manned by a long-haired girl in a floral patterned dress with a pretty tail-wagging sheltie at her side.

The sign told me we'd come to the right place: the Foxglove Corners Collie Rescue League. The girl's name tag identified her as Geneva.

The sheltie flattened her ears and lifted a paw to shake. I obliged.

"Is that a collie?" Emma asked.

Geneva's warm smile seemed designed to attract passersby to her cause. "Yes, she's a small one. Her name is Lindy."

I doubted that Lindy was a purebred rough collie, but Geneva appeared to think she was. I wasn't about to challenge her.

"We're looking for Ann Clarke," I said. "I read in the paper that she'd be here today."

She had a quick answer. "You'll have to make do with me. Ms. Clarke had an emergency. How can I help you?"

"We're interested in collie rescue," I said. "Do you have any literature about your group?"

"Also a form for new members?" Sue added. "We want four, one for each of us and another for a friend who couldn't come today."

"Just a second."

Geneva scooped up four packets of papers, done on a computer, and forms consisting of several pages. This was all well and good, but it wasn't the outcome I'd hoped for.

"Then Ms. Clarke won't be here later?" I asked.

"I don't expect her."

Emma slipped her packet into her large yellow tote, while Sue flipped through the pages. "How long has your group been in the rescue business?" Sue asked.

"Since May. We're relatively new and small, but so far we've had remarkable success saving collies and rehoming them."

I tried to keep the confrontational tone out of my voice. "Did you know that Foxglove Corners already has a collie rescue organization? It's the Lakeville Collie Rescue League."

Geneva narrowed her eyes. "I've heard of them, yes."

"Why didn't you just join the existing group instead of starting a new one?"

"That's right," Sue said. "Lakeville and Foxglove Corners are small towns. Two collie rescues are excessive."

Geneva's smiled vanished, and her voice acquired a sharp edge. "I'll tell you why. That other group is corrupt. It's all about politics. We put the collies who need help first. Also, we don't turn away older dogs, and we don't care about pedigrees. If they look like a collie, they're welcome."

This accounted for the sheltie. No one could say that shelties didn't resemble collies.

"You're starting to sound like a reporter," Geneva snapped.

Lindy gave a little yelp as an enormous black dog strolled by, his leash held by a little girl.

"Lindy!"

At the implicit command in Geneva's voice, Lindy melted into the ground.

"We're not reporters," Sue said. "Just curious. My friends and I have collies. We want to help dogs who lose their homes."

"It's horrible, but some heartless people abandon their pets in the country," Emma added. "They figure that with all the farms, someone will take them in. Sometimes it happens, but not always."

"Hence the need for the Foxglove Corners Collie Rescue League." Geneva looked over our heads into the crowd. "The famous Michigan author, Byrony Limon, is one of our members. She's here today signing copies of her book."

With that, Geneva began to fuss over Lindy.

"We'll look for her," Sue said.

"What do you make of that?" Emma asked as soon as we were well out of earshot.

"Not much. I'm more suspicious than ever. I wonder where she got that ridiculous information she spouted."

"And how convenient that the mysterious Ann Clarke had an emergency," Emma said. "You notice Geneva didn't say anything about her."

I thought of my many Internet searches, of zero results. "Maybe there is no Ann Clarke."

"Then what's going on here?" Sue asked.

"I haven't a clue. What do we do now?"

"We fill out the forms using fake names and send them in." Maybe they'll send somebody to interview us and we'll have another chance to ask questions."

In my estimation, that was a good second step. They couldn't very well ignore us.

Eighteen

Byrony Limon had set up her table near the hot dog stand, which was an ideal location. She sat between two high stacks of books, her ash brown hair blowing in the wind which had suddenly sprung to life. Her cobalt shirt bore a laudable inscription: *Protection for the Collies.*

A sable and white collie with a blaze graced the cover of her book, *Heart of Lassie*. To encourage sales, a sign taped to the table promised that all proceeds would be donated to the Foxglove Corners Collie Rescue League. She was charging eleven dollars for a handsome trade paperback published by… I opened the book. The Winged Dog Publishing Company.

An unfamiliar name.

Emma looked over my shoulder. "Whoever heard of a winged dog? A winged horse, yes. That's Pegasus. But a dog?"

Byrony glanced at the book in my hand. "It's a charming story, if I say so myself. A bit of a tear jerker, but so is life." She brushed a strand of hair off her face.

I reached for my wallet. "I'll take it."

"I'll have one, too," Sue said. "As long as the money will be used to help a collie."

Emma hesitated, then opened her tote. "I'll buy one for my granddaughter."

I tucked the book into my shoulder bag. "You must belong to the rescue league, Ms. Limon. My friends and I are thinking about joining."

"You won't be sorry," she said. "We're a dedicated group, and all of us are young and energetic. Those are qualities you need if you're going to be a real help to the dogs."

"We qualify." Sue's surreptitious smile clearly said, 'Young? Energetic? If you say so.'

"I'll see you at the next meeting then." Byrony shifted her attention to a woman and little girl in matching green sundresses. They had come up behind us, and the child pushed rudely ahead of me.

"Mom, look! A book about a collie!" she said.

Our second encounter with a member of the rogue had come to an abrupt end.

We walked back to the merry-go-round, drawn by its cheery tune.

"A tear jerker, huh?" Sue said. "I don't know if I want to read it."

I stopped for a moment mesmerized the sight of the rainbow-colored animals as they circled around and around. Beside me, I heard the rattle of pages and an angry exclamation.

Sue came to a standstill. "Well, of all the nerve! I don't believe this."

"What?"

"This is *our* form. Word for word. I should know. I created it."

One more odd fact associated with the rogue group.

"I wonder what else they stole," I said.

Sue jammed the form into her purse. "Some of our members? Oh, no, they couldn't have. Our people are loyal. Many of them have been with us from the beginning."

"That settles it," I said. "One of us is going to have to infiltrate the group."

"Which one?" Emma asked.

I thought of the fourth form. How fortuitous of Sue to have requested it.

"Brent Fowler could join them and spy on their activities."

"But he must be a busy man," Sue pointed out. "Would he do it?"

"He'd love to. When I first met Brent, he was pretending to be an animal activist to get to know Caroline Meilland better."

"Pretending?" Sue asked.

"Yes, and all the time he was a fox hunter," I said.

Brent would be able to charm the secrets out of the rogue league members. They'd never know what hit them.

~ * ~

"You want me to do what?"

Brent looked up from the platter of sliced roast beef I had handed to him.

"Join the rogue collie rescue group," I said. "It won't be a stretch. You love dogs, and you have a rescue collie."

"That's true, but I'm a busy man. I don't have time to join organizations."

"I told you he wouldn't go for it," Crane said. A telltale sparkle appeared in his frosty gray eyes. We both knew Brent couldn't resist a challenge.

"If I join any collie group, it'll be Sue Appleton's," he added.

"That won't help. We think there's something suspicious about the Foxglove Corners Collie League, and we need a person we can trust to spy on them. Someone charismatic and clever."

Brent speared a thick slice of beef and doused it in gravy. "Spying! That's something I can do. Tell me more."

"Their founder, Ann Clarke, can't be found. One of their members accused our league of being corrupt. She claimed that we only want to save only purebreds and reject older dogs."

"That's not true. Look at your Star."

Star heard her name and tilted her head, fixing Brent with a soulful look from her station in the living room. Star's family, the one she'd had since puppyhood, had surrendered her to rescue in her twilight years, claiming nobody had time for her. Because no foster homes were available at the time, she became our seventh collie.

"Of course it isn't true," I said. "Sue suggested they may be selling dogs for nefarious purposes. I wouldn't go that far, but we need to know exactly what they're doing."

"What if it turns out to be a legitimate rescue group?" Crane asked.

"Then we'll refute their baseless accusations and find out where the stories came from."

"I'll do it," Brent announced.

"Great! I knew I could count on you."

I had the spare application on my desk. I would serve it to him with dessert.

"Now I want to hear all about the ghost town," Brent said. "I wish I could have gone with you, but I had to get Andromeda settled. He's on the high spirited side. Then my Tempest had her first foal."

"Didn't Annica tell you?" I asked.

"I haven't seen her. I've been pretty much tied up at the barn."

"There isn't much to tell. Annica almost got bitten by a monster snake, and Lucy sees a darkness beyond the bridge that we don't."

"That doesn't sound good," Crane said.

Trust Crane to zero in on the one truly troubling aspect of our trip.

"Lucy is responding to the emotions of the people who had to leave Forever, probably with little or no warning. Like at Pompeii."

"Didn't most of those people die when that mountain erupted?" Brent asked.

"Most of them. I thought a few escaped."

"It's not at all like Pompeii," Crane said.

"Are you going back to the town?" Brent asked. "Because if you are, I'm coming with you. How about you, Sheriff?"

"It depends on the date. I hope I'll be able to make it."

"We all want to return, even Lucy," I said. "Especially Lucy. There are many more houses we could check out and maybe some clue we haven't found yet. The next time, I'll bring my gun in case we stumble across a snake."

So I said, even though I couldn't see myself shooting a mammoth snake like the one Annica described.

"It sounds dangerous to me," Crane said.

"Aside from the snakes…"

"And the apple," he pointed out. "And whatever drove the townspeople out of Forever in the first place. Who knows if it's still a threat?"

I hadn't thought of that. I pulled the images of Forever from my memory. A silent town with deserted stores and houses. A fully stocked dime store with no customers. Lawns and yards that had been largely reclaimed by nature. Relics of a past that had been left behind.

Added to these was the darkness Lucy had seen and sensed. The dark beyond the bridge.

"I can't imagine what kind of threat Forever could still pose to people like us who are just passing through," I said.

"You're not just passing through," Crane pointed out.

He was right. We were snooping. Helping ourselves to inexpensive items from the dime store, but still, we had taken them out of the town. We had entered people's homes and noted the contents of their refrigerators. How much more intrusive could we get?

At times I'd had the unsettling sense that someone was watching us, outraged at our intrusion, planning revenge.

Don't get carried away, I told myself. *These aliens exist in Annica's mind.*

We all wanted to know what had happened to the people of Forever. That was a positive goal.

"Don't go without me," Brent said. "And you don't have to bring your gun. I can take care of any snake, even if it is a monster."

For the first time, I thought of Brent in terms of protection. Who knew? We might need it.

Nineteen

On the morning of our third trip to Forever, I dressed for a hot day in jeans and a sleeveless green blouse, after which I dabbed the toilet water I'd brought out of the ghost town on my wrists.

Apparently Misty didn't like the fragrance of wood violets. She immediately began to bark. You'd think that by this normal act I had transformed myself into another being, a fearsome one.

What possessed the creature?

I rarely wore perfume, never in school, and only when Crane and I went out for the evening, so she wasn't used to it. But this reaction was over the top, and it continued as I hurried downstairs to fix breakfast. An agitated white collie yapping all the way to the kitchen, she grated on my nerves. Well, I couldn't very well wipe the fragrance away. Nor should I have to.

"Stop that infernal racket," I told her.

Crane joined me a few minutes later. "What's gotten into Misty?"

"She doesn't like the way I smell."

"Be quiet, Misty," Crane said. "You'll wake the dead."

He pulled me into a close embrace. "You smell just fine to me. Like flowers."

"It's the scent of wood violets," I said. "I bought a bottle of toilet water at the dime store in Forever."

"How did you manage that?" he asked.

I remembered that I hadn't mentioned my unusual purchase to him. "I just took it and left money on the counter."

"Who is supposed to collect it?"

"You never know. Someday the owner may return."

That wasn't likely, though, and we both knew it.

"Perfume from a dead town," Crane said. "Maybe that's why Misty has gone bananas."

In a way, her behavior was amusing. Instead of weaving in and out, trying to trip me while I mixed pancake batter, she retreated to the dining room where she lay with her front paws crossed and regarded me balefully. If only dogs could talk. Fortunately none of the other collies noticed anything different about me or, if they did, it didn't bother them.

"I'm glad you're taking Fowler along today," Crane said. "Just in case there's trouble."

"With snakes, you mean?"

"Any kind of trouble."

"I'm not anticipating any," I said, knowing that often trouble makes its appearance when one is oblivious.

I dropped the batter for the first pancakes into the frying pan and took my eye off the stove long enough to pour orange juice. A stack of pancakes was a heavy breakfast on a hot summer morning, but both of us were going to have a long day.

When everything was ready and we sat down to eat, Misty maintained her curious vigil in the dining room well behind her sisters who had gathered around us, hoping for handouts. I was glad she wasn't going to be part of our expedition.

~ * ~

We had decided to drive to Forever in separate cars. Annica and I would lead, and Brent and Lucy would follow in Brent's vintage white Plymouth with its fantastic green fins. Taking an old time automobile to a ghost town seemed fitting. If the watcher existed, and, if he or it were paying attention to the comings and goings in Forever, he would be confused.

I had promised to drive slowly and not lose Brent in the convoluted route to the ghost town. There would have been hard to do in regular traffic, but once we left the freeway, I didn't imagine we'd have any company on the country roads.

The freeway exit loomed ahead, wreathed in a soft, entrancing haze. I saw the Plymouth in the rear-view mirror, turned on my signal, and entered the alluring green world that was by now familiar to me.

Brent turned with me, keeping three car lengths behind. So far, so good.

"I hope this isn't the one time we get lost," Annica said.

"We won't. I have my reputation to uphold."

"It's so beautiful out here, so green and peaceful. It's really like we're on another planet."

"I *do* feel like an explorer every time we come this way," I admitted. "And when we leave, it's like we're returning to the real world."

"I know," Annica said. "It's the spell of Forever."

She fell silent, still attempting to create a map in pencil that would make future trips easier. I slowed after every turn, making sure not to lose sight of Brent, and watched for a landmark of yellow flowers. At last we sighted the bridge, and I drove across, thinking about spells. Forever no longer seemed alien to me. It beckoned like a second home.

Clearly the town cast its spell on Brent. Having crossed the bridge in our wake, he parked in front of the Forever Diner and stood as if mesmerized, gazing down the Main Street, while Lucy lifted a picnic basket out of the back seat.

"It's true," he said. "A real live ghost town tucked away in this wilderness."

"Not so lively," Annica said, "but it's real."

"All those stores… Are they empty?"

"Most of them. The dime store's counters are fully stocked, but there are no salesclerks, no customers."

"And the houses?"

"The ones we looked into were abandoned," Annica said. "The people left heavy, bulky furniture but took smaller possessions with them. At least, that's what it looks like."

Lucy pulled her long black cardigan closer around her. "It was so hot a little while ago, and now it's overcast."

"You're wearing sunglasses, Lucy," Brent pointed out. "It looks pretty bright to me, and it must be around ninety."

"Not to me."

"It's a supernatural darkness," I said.

"The town was doomed," Lucy added. "The townspeople fled in terror. What I feel and see reflects that."

"Our job is to find out what doomed it," Brent said. "Let's plan to stay together. I promised the sheriff I'd watch over all of you, and I can't do that if you go your separate ways."

Annica objected. "But we won't cover as much territory that way."

"We're not in a hurry," I reminded her. "You don't want to meet up with a snake when the rest of us are on the other side of town, do you?"

Predictably she didn't.

"We can have our picnic on the lake," Lucy said. "It looks so inviting."

Brent started walking. "I'd like to have a look in the hardware store. Then we can check out the rest of the houses. Could be we'll find something different."

"So far I feel optimistic about today's adventure," Lucy said. "It even seems a little brighter."

That was good. Brent considered himself our protector and our leader, which I found a trifle annoying. After all, Forever was my discovery. Brent was... I had to think... Brent was just our lucky charm.

~ * ~

The fifth house had plain lines with no extraneous ornamentation. Its peeling façade had faded to a greyish-beige color. Weeds grew up right up to the entrance, and the door was half open. Nothing about it looked inviting.

Annica glanced nervously at the overgrown yard. "It looks like an old barn."

"Whoever lived here didn't bother to close the door," Brent said as he pushed it open.

A deep growl broke the all-encompassing silence of the town.

Brent froze, his hand inches from the door. "What the hell…"

A large black dog burst from the side of the house, teeth bared, hair bristling.

Dog? Or wolf? It had a wolf-like head and blazing eyes.

"Back up, Brent," I said.

I thought I knew what to do when confronted by a dangerous canine, but in an instant all my knowledge slipped out of my mind.

Stare back at the animal? Ignore it? Pretend you don't see it, so it doesn't consider you a threat?

I could only retrieve one thread. Don't run from it. Never, never run, or you'll activate its prey drive.

The dog maintained its stance. Its lips seemed even higher, its teeth lethal.

"What should we do?" Annica asked.

Lucy spoke in a low, calm voice. "He doesn't want you to go in the house, Brent. That's all. Let's be on our way."

"I don't want to shoot it," he said.

"Goodness, no. There's no need to do that. Come back to us, walk slowly, and we'll be on our way."

"He'll think we're running away," I said.

"It'll be all right," she promised.

Twenty

When we reached the end of the street, I looked back. The dog was nowhere in sight. If he was smart, he had found a shady place to lie away from the burning sun. My heartbeat slowly resumed its normal rate, allowing a rational thought to filter through.

"That didn't look like a feral dog to me," I said.

"I disagree," Annica countered. "He was ready to tear us apart."

"But he didn't." Lucy, who so often saw threats everywhere, didn't consider the dog one of them. "He was only warning us away from his territory."

I didn't want to lose track of my point. "He was a good weight, and his coat was sleek and shiny. My guess is that somebody has been taking care of him."

"Someone in town?" Brent asked. "I thought we decided no one was living in Forever."

"He might belong to a nearby farm," I said.

"We haven't seen any farms or even a house," Lucy pointed out. "Just woods."

"A dog couldn't easily get to what little food there is left in town," Brent said. "It's all put away. He may be killing birds and small animals for his own meals."

"Snakes and wild dogs," Annica murmured. "What's next?"

"Lunch."

That was Brent, who was always hungry. Annica had packed an assortment of sandwiches and cookies from Clovers, and I had supplied the bottled water and soft drinks. After searching through several closed-up houses and shuttered stores, we all needed a break.

"You ladies go on down to the lake," Brent said. "I'll get the basket and blanket."

So saying, he sauntered back to Main Street, and we headed for the beach.

It was a short walk, and the lake was larger than it had appeared when I'd first noticed it, shining beyond the town.

The first people in Forever must have built their houses with the view in mind, and it was spectacular. Deep blue water under an azure sky with pine forest beyond the lake. The sand was pristine and inviting. Best of all, we had the whole area to ourselves. How often does that happen in the summer?

"You're right, Lucy," Annica said. "The lake is inviting. I'd like to go wading and cool off a bit."

"Don't," Lucy said.

"What?"

"Don't go any closer to the water. We're close enough as it is."

"Why not?" she asked.

"I sense a darkness hovering over the lake. There might be danger."

"You mean I might drown? I'm a good swimmer."

"It isn't that," she said. "The danger is undefined at present. I'm sorry I can't be more specific."

While Annica accepted Lucy's pronouncement without further questions, a perverse spirit rose up to taunt me. Now, more than anything, I wanted to splash water over my face, to feel it cascade down my bare arms and sooth my burning skin.

Danger? What danger could there be? Lucy was always crying, "Danger!"

"I wasn't really going in the water. It was just a thought." Annica smoothed back her red-gold hair and set her silver bell earring a-twirl. She wouldn't want to disarrange herself with Brent so near. "It's so infernally hot."

"I feel it's for the best," Lucy said.

Still, she drew her phone out of her tote and took three pictures of the lake. Her expression was grim.

"Is this where you want the blanket?" Brent's booming voice dispelled the apprehension that had settled over us.

"This is good," Annica said.

She and Lucy began to unpack the contents of the picnic basket. When all the selections were spread out on the blanket, I selected a turkey sandwich from the stack.

"If that dog was starving, he'd be able to smell our food from a mile away," I said.

"Did you see anything suspicious, Brent?" Lucy asked.

"Where? At the cars? Everything is the way we left it." He grabbed a sandwich and plopped down on the sand.

His answer appeared to satisfy her. Suddenly, however, I felt uneasy. It seemed that eyes were trained on us from an invisible lookout. I tried to concentrate on eating, but the sense of being under surveillance intensified, probably inspired by Lucy's talk of danger. And it was so hot. I felt battered by the sun's rays. In and out of stuffy houses, in a town where air conditioning didn't exist, I hadn't realized how uncomfortable the heat was, and I was so thirsty.

Which reminded me of the dog. "Where does the dog get his drinking water?"

They were all looking at me. I realized I'd said that out loud.

"Good point, Jennet," Brent said. "He'd need water to survive, that's for sure."

"He has the whole lake," Annica pointed out. "Speaking of which, what does everyone want to drink? We don't have a lot of choices. There's bottled water, ginger ale, root beer, something orange...?"

"Water," I said.

Brent settled back with a root beer. "I think we did a good day's work. One more street and a few stores to go, and we'll call it good."

Annica passed me a bottle of Pinewoods Pure. "But we haven't learned anything new."

Lucy smiled. "This town likes to keep its secrets."

"Well..." I took a bite of my sandwich but found all I wanted to do was drink water even if it wasn't ice-cold. "Maybe it's saving the best for the last."

~ * ~

The last house was the smallest one in town with a diminutive front porch piled high with dried leaves from past seasons. It would have been at home in one of those new "tiny house' communities. It was attractive, too, and, from the outside, in better condition than its neighbors. The sage green edifice blended into the overgrown yard, and the unscreened windows were open, inviting dust and airborne debris to blow in.

The door, like those in most of the other houses, was unlocked.

Lucy laid her hand on the porch post. "One person lived here. She didn't want to leave but had no choice. She could hardly stay when everyone else had gone."

"Can you tell us anything else?" I asked.

"Only that this house absorbed the same emotions I've felt in the others. Fear, sadness, loss, panic. I see images, but they're blurred and constantly changing."

Inside, the little house was cluttered. Too much furniture had been crammed in too small an area. Figurines, mostly china and wood horses, occupied a shelf above a desk.

"She liked horses," Lucy murmured. "I think at one time she had a horse named Cinnamon."

Why hadn't she taken her collection with her? I wondered.

"Let's see what's in the kitchen," Annica said.

Brent had gone back outside on a mission of his own.

Left alone in the living room, I looked around. The surfaces were dusty, and some of the leaves had found their way inside. The top of the desk had been swept clean except for a long white envelope. Apparently it had fallen to the floor and gone unnoticed.

Maybe here was our elusive clue. I stooped to pick it up and for a moment knew a pang of disappointment. It was empty and bore only three lines of heavy black writing in the top left corner: *Camelia Yardley, 5 Willow, Ashton, MI.*

It was as if the writer had been interrupted in her task and never returned to it or started a new envelope.

And something was wrong.

Ashton.

On my first visit to the ghost town, I had made an assumption, and I'd been wrong.

"I found something," I said. "Everyone, come look at this."

~ * ~

"Ashton?" Brent said.

"This changes everything."

Annica peered over my shoulder. "Changes what? I don't understand."

"The name of the town isn't Forever. It's Ashton."

"Where did 'Forever' come from?" Brent asked.

"It's the name of the diner. The first day, we didn't realize we'd come to a ghost town. We were going to stop in the Forever Diner for a snack."

.   "And we just started calling the town Forever," Annica said. "It made sense."

"No wonder I couldn't find any information on the town. If I type 'Ashton' in a search box, I may find all sorts of information."

I could hardly wait to do it. "Just to be sure, the name of the street is Willow, right?

"Five Willow," Brent said.

Lucy touched the envelope. "Camelia Yardley was the single woman who lived here. She must have been writing to tell a friend what was happening or where she was going. That letter was sent long ago in another envelope."

"You're right. Darn. If we had the letter, it might answer all our questions."

Quickly I opened the other desk drawers. They were all empty, save for shelf paper.

"I can't shed light on the missing letter," Brent said, "but I found something else. When did it last rain?"

"Here?" Annica asked. "How would we know that? In Foxglove Corners it rained about a week ago."

"I found large footprints outside, leading up to the house. Whoever made them walked in mud, and the mud hardened. I think they're recent."

"That means someone else has been here," I said. "I suspected someone was spying on us."

Annica moved to the window and looked out. "He's awfully quiet and good at keeping out of sight."

"I didn't see anyone," Brent said. "Not even our wolf-dog friend."

"The mystery deepens," Lucy murmured. "But now we have a clue."

I nodded. "Ashton."

Twenty-one

Crane sat down to the bacon and eggs breakfast I'd fixed for him, with a basket of Camille's blueberry muffins close at hand. I didn't feel particularly hungry and could have slept longer, but more than sleep I wanted to be up and alert before Crane left for his shift. For my own breakfast, I was happy with a muffin and orange juice.

"That ghost town will be the death of you," he said.

He was looking at my arms. I had acquired a sunburn during yesterday's excursion. Entirely my fault. I'd brought a linen shirt to wear over my blouse to protect my skin from the sun, but I'd left it in the car. For that bit of vanity, I was paying. Dabbing on a baking soda and water mixture—Camille's remedy—wasn't working.

My nose was red, too, a bright cherry red. I felt decidedly unglamorous in my pink silk nightgown and hoped my complexion would be back to normal for Leonora's wedding.

"You may be right," I said.

I had told Crane about our discoveries: the real name of the town and the footprints that Brent believed had been made recently; and I'd downplayed the appearance of the aggressive black dog.

He remembered Annica's encounter with the snake.

"I knew that town was dangerous," he said. "I'm glad to know Fowler took care of you. Now in the future…"

"It was Lucy who knew how to react to the dog, and we didn't see anybody there," I said quickly. "The footprints could have been made ages ago."

"Or last week. I'm not comfortable with you visiting that place anymore, not even with Fowler."

"Then come with us," I said. "We still don't know why the town was abandoned, and I'm dying to find out... Oh, wrong word choice."

Last night while searching the Internet, I'd learned a few basic facts about Ashton online, for example, its location, which I already knew, and the population, at one time five hundred. If you were to believe the written word, you'd expect to find a drowsy lakeside town in rural Michigan where nothing momentous ever happened.

Why couldn't I find up-to-date information that reflected the Ashton of today?

"You should stay home and rest," Crane said. "It's going to be hot again."

"Hazy, hot, and humid with a chance of thunderstorms," I said, quoting the weather forecaster. "Home sounds good."

Whether or not I'd do that remained to be seen. The first day of school was right around the corner, and I couldn't afford to waste even one free day.

As I drank my juice, I spared a thought for the black dog in Ashton—if the ghost town was indeed his home. I hoped he had access to fresh water—not from the lake—and shelter from the heat, along with food. Not a small animal he'd caught himself.

Then, however, I'd have to add a human with a dinner bowl to the picture.

"I'll just take the dogs for a very short walk when you leave," I said.

I'd said the magic word, *walk*, and only Candy reacted. Candy, the dog who was so rambunctious that she had to walk with Crane. Usually. I didn't mention that I'd taken her out myself one time.

Our other collies didn't need to hear the weather forecast to know that their air-conditioned home was the only place to be on a sweltering August day.

"Instead of cooking, I may pick up dinner at Clovers," I said. "If that's all right with you."

"Whatever you decide will be fine, honey."

I gave him a smile. "Clovers it'll be then."

I had the most obliging husband in Foxglove Corners. If I didn't find a dessert worthy of him at Clovers, I'd bake his new favorite, Camille's orange chiffon cake, even though it meant inviting more heat into the kitchen.

~ * ~

Brent was having a steak sandwich lunch at Clovers, while Annica fluttered around him as if he were her only customer. She reminded me of a butterfly with her bright orange dress and long coral earrings. A happy butterfly. Brent's presence had that effect on her. She hadn't gotten burnt in yesterday's sun, or her compact contained magical powder.

Whenever I came in, one of Annica's fellow waitresses, Marcy or Evie, covered for her, allowing Annica a chance to visit with me. Brent invited us to join him and I ordered iced tea. We'd talk first, then I'd place my dinner order.

Evie brought two tall glasses of iced tea with lemon slices on the side as Annica said, "What do we do next about the ghost town, Jennet?"

"I have to think. I came across some old information about Ashton last night. Whoever wrote the account didn't know that Ashton had been abandoned."

"I'm starting to think it's a big secret," Brent said. "A cover-up."

Annica tossed the lemon slice into her tea. "Maybe we should tell the F.B.I. and leave it in their hands."

"That would be okay unless the F.B.I. is doing the cover-up," Brent said. "I'm for keeping Ashton under wraps for now."

I agreed with Brent. I still thought of the ghost town as our personal project, and we were far from knowing what had gone on there.

"Maybe I'll have a look through Miss Eidt's vertical file," I said.

Brent scoffed. "In the computer age? I can't believe she still clips newspaper articles."

"Well, the computer doesn't always keep up with changing times."

Finding the information I needed would be like looking for a needle in the proverbial haystack, but I thought it might work. I remembered that Miss Eidt had files labeled 'Catastrophies' and 'Natural Disasters.' Where better to look for what had happened in Ashton?

If such a record existed, that is.

~ * ~

With two roasted chicken dinners for tonight stashed in the trunk, I drove to the Corners and parked in the library's lot under the largest tree on the property.

The library, housed in an old white Victorian house on Park Street, was like a second home to me. Once it had been belonged to Miss Elizabeth Eidt, a longtime resident of Foxglove Corners. She had donated it to the town, together with many of her own books, and stayed on to serve as librarian, in recent years with the help of her young assistant, Debbie.

It was a pleasant blend of modern (a computer and printer in the librarian's office) and old time facilities like the vertical file.

As I climbed the stairs, Miss Eidt's cat, Blackberry, stared at me from the wicker rocker where she lay on a plump cushion, apparently quite comfortable on the porch. I opened the door and let the rush of cooled air wash over me.

Miss Eidt sat at her desk, wearing a pink suit, looking cool and professional as always. Shades of pink were her color choices this summer, from her rose-tinted strand of pearls to the carnation bouquet at her elbow.

"Jennet! What a surprise!" Her face lit up with pleasure. "I was hoping to see you before you went back to school. Look what I found at an estate sale."

She drew two tattered Phyllis A. Whitney books from a shelf behind the desk. *Thunder Heights* and *The Trembling Hills.* I may have read them once but it was so long ago, I'd forgotten the stories.

They weren't destined for the shelves. Knowing my love for old Gothic novels, Miss Eidt snapped them up wherever she found them. To reciprocate, I often brought her doughnuts or a coffeecake, and she treated me to tea in her office.

I wished I'd thought to bring her a dessert from Clovers.

"I've come on a mission," I said. "May I use your vertical file?"

She smiled happily. "Of course. You're the only one who ever does. Are you on the trail of a new ghost?"

"Not this time, at least I don't think so. I'm researching a ghost town."

She looked puzzled. "That's an unusual request."

"Ashton is an unusual place."

I hesitated for only a moment before I told her about the ghost town. I was sure the story would go no further.

"I can tell you now," she said. "I never came across a story like that in a newspaper. I'd remember it."

"I'm looking for a catastrophe, something serious enough to make the entire population abandon the town."

"Our part of Michigan has been fortunate," Miss Eidt said. "Offhand I can't think of any major disasters. You're thinking of floods? Fires? Tornadoes?"

"I remember one tornado," said, "the one that brought me to Foxglove Corners."

"Ah, yes. That was a blessing in disguise. I thought ghost towns died out slowly, like when there was no more silver or gold to mine," she added.

"That was the case in the West. In Ashton it was different."

"Well, I wish you luck," she said. "You know where the files are."

I did. I only hoped my search proved fruitful.

Twenty-two

Miss Eidit's office was as quiet and peaceful as if it were located in a separate building. She had made me a pot of tea and brought out a tin of maple cookies from Canada. As I searched through the most likely folders, I felt as if I'd stepped back in time.

She was right. Our part of the state had been fortunate indeed throughout the years. In Michigan we didn't have to worry about hurricanes or annual wildfires driving us out of our homes. The mayhem recorded in the painstakingly clipped articles, for the most part, originated with man rather than nature.

Of course there were exceptions like an historic flood, a blizzard that buried Foxglove Corners under fifteen inches of snow, and a deadly ice storm in which a man had stepped out onto his front porch, slipped on an ice patch, and fallen to his death.

Finally in a folder labeled 'Accidents' I came across a familiar name: Ashton. The article's headline was *Plane Crashes in Ashton, Pilot Killed.*

It had happened almost two decades ago. Apparently thrown off course in a developing thunderstorm, the pilot had gone down in Ashton Lake, in the rural community of Ashton, Michigan. He had perished in the crash. Investigators suspected sabotage. Therefore it seemed that the crash wasn't necessarily attributed to the storm.

I searched in vain for a follow-up story, but there was none. Nor did there appear to be any other happening of note in Ashton. Which I knew couldn't be true.

There was so much more I wanted to know besides the cause of the crash. The name of the pilot who was killed, for example, and whether the downed aircraft still lay at the bottom of the lake.

Here was something I wouldn't find in any news story. When Lucy described the lake as dangerous, was she reacting to the plane crash or some other tragic event?

There had to be additional stories on this major happening in the little town of Ashton, and, logically, it would be in the same folder; but I didn't find it. It occurred to me that I could search through the files of the *Banner*. That would be a project for another day.

My tea had grown cold. I closed the folder and sat back, thinking about flying. I always thought it was a dangerous way to travel, although the same could be said about driving, especially on the freeway. When you were in the sky, the fall from plane to earth was incredibly far. Furthermore, as a passenger, you had no control over life or death.

Well, plane crashes happened. Sometimes innocent people on the ground were also killed. Usually, though, as was the case with any tragedy, people mourned their loved ones and moved on. They had no other choice.

As traumatic as a plane crashing into their lake must have been for the people of Ashton, I didn't think it would have forced the entire population to leave their homes.

I printed a copy of the story, rinsed my teacup, and rejoined Miss Eidt in the library.

"Did you find what you were looking for?" she asked.

"I don't think so."

"Over the years I may have missed a few important stories," she admitted. "One summer I went on a cruise. Then one year I had pneumonia. I actually had to close the library that month. A lot of times I simply didn't see any news story worth saving."

"I have this article," I said, indicating my printed copy, "and a date. I may come back. This mystery won't solve itself, and I'm running out of time."

"Ah yes. School rears its head. You *did* have a good summer, though, didn't you?"

"The best. Now I have Leonora's wedding to look forward to. Will you be there?"

"I wouldn't miss it," she said.

"I'll see you before then."

I said goodbye to Miss Eidt, and, taking my two Gothic paperbacks with me, went back outside, into the scorching afternoon heat. I had a cake to bake.

~ * ~

Brent visited us that evening, not for dinner, but in time for dessert. The orange chiffon cake had turned out well. Instructed by Camille, I had mastered the art of decorating it with orange blossoms. I thought it was too pretty to eat. The dogs and the men had other thoughts.

We sat in the living room over coffee and cake while I told them about the Ashton plane crash.

"There's no way that made the people abandon their homes," Brent said.

Crane broke off a chunk of cake with his fork, trying to ignore Candy's bold stare. "I admit I'm getting curious about it myself."

"I've been thinking about all the 'For Sale' signs," I said. "People wanted to sell their houses, possibly to get away from something, but apparently there were no buyers. Why was that?"

"Isn't it obvious?" Brent suggested. "Who in his right mind would move to Ashton if the people who already lived there wanted to escape from it?

I pictured a steady stream of people fleeing from the dying town. Whatever the cause, it would have been next to impossible to keep it a secret. The disappointed sellers had left in such a hurry they didn't remove the signs.

"All right," I said. "We're back to the basic question. What was wrong with the town?"

"After all this time, who would know?" Brent asked. "Unless we could dig up a survivor and talk to him."

"Like the woman who left the envelope behind," I said.

"There's only one way to find out," Brent said. "We have to go back to Ashton. The answer must be there. Look at what we've found so far."

"Not that much. Let's see. An apple, some stores still stocked, others cleared out, the real name of the town, an aggressive, apparently well fed dog. Add to that Lucy's feeling of danger when she came near the lake, but we have to keep looking."

"When will the next expedition be?" Crane asked, apparently resigned to the inevitable.

"As soon as we can all get together again."

"I can be free anytime," Brent said. "Don't forget, I have to go to the collie rescue meeting tomorrow."

I'd almost forgotten. Sue and I planned to attend as well, with our filled-out applications.

In recent days, I'd tended to let the mystery of the rogue rescue group slip to the back of my mind. To be sure, it was important, but it lacked the glamor of the ghost town.

"We'll pretend we don't know you, Brent," I said. "Just in case they're suspicious of our intentions."

"Sure thing." He winked at me. "From now on, we're strangers."

Twenty-three

Sue pointed out a sign tacked to a weeping willow tree whose long drooping fronds cast eerie shadows on the road. *To the Collie Rescue Meeting.* The arrow pointed straight ahead.

"I've been here before," I said. "Sapphire Lake Estates. No one came to the door."

"I hope there's someone here tonight."

"There will be. The sign says so."

As I slowed down, trying to remember how far the house was from the road, Sue rustled the application papers. "If someone recognizes me as the president of the Lakeville league, we're in trouble," she said.

"If they do, we'll say we like rescuing collies so much we want to belong to two groups."

"Who's going to believe that?" she asked. "They'll be suspicious. We won't accomplish anything."

"We're pinning our hopes on Brent," I reminded her. "Nobody will associate him with collie rescue."

I remembered the house from my previous visit, found a parking place on the street, and we walked up to the door. Although plenty of sunshine remained in the day, the house was lit up inside and out. Sue rang the doorbell.

The girl who opened the door was young, in her late teens, I'd guess, with blue streaks in her dark brown hair and, I couldn't help but notice, sparkling blue fingernail polish. She wasn't my idea of a collie rescuer. But then what was?

A matronly woman with graying hair, dressed in denim and a shirt with a clever quotation or picture across the front? Young people tended to be busy with their careers and families, and women more than men were drawn into rescue work. In general, women were the nurturers of the world.

The girl greeted us with a warm smile. "Hi. I'm Jackie. You must be here for the meeting."

I said, "I'm Jennet and this is Sue. We plan to join the group."

"That's wonderful. You won't regret it."

Jackie led us to the living room where about a dozen women sat silently in chairs, some brought in from a dining room set. They reminded me of mannequins, unmoving and for the most part unsmiling. No one was wearing denim, and I didn't see Geneva, the girl from the fair.

One of the women was the author, Byrony Limon. She recognized us, greeted us by our names, and Jackie brought two additional chairs out of the dining room for us.

"Welcome, ladies," Byrony said. "We're just getting started. As you can see, I'm filling in for Ann tonight. Unfortunately she's under the weather."

So the elusive Ann was gone again. Interesting.

I for one didn't feel particularly welcome. The room was cool and well-appointed with elegant, classical furniture, but the atmosphere seemed strained to me; and the members of the league, the mannequins, appeared to be detached. Except for Byrony. She was effervescent, her eyes communicating enthusiasm.

She looked at me. "Will you please tell us how you learned about our organization?"

That was easy enough to answer truthfully.

"I saw the poster in Pluto's Gourmet Pet Shop and told my friend, Sue."

"I had hoped the right kind of people would notice our poster," she said. "We always ask prospective members to tell us a little about themselves, specifically why they want to join us."

Sue glanced at me. 'You first,' her look said.

"Well, I love dogs. After moving to Foxglove Corners, it seemed I was always finding abandoned collies. I figured I might as well join a group."

"I see." Byrony's gaze shifted to Sue.

"Sue Appleton here. I live on a farm. Abandoned dogs keep finding their way to my doorstep. I can't turn them away, but there's only so much I can do. I'd like to help find them good homes."

Byrony nodded. "In today's economy, pets often find themselves dispensable."

No one argued with her.

"We'll have coffee after the meeting," she added. "You'll have a chance to get to know everyone then. Now, I'd like to call your attention to our next fundraiser. The Carolotte Collie Club is hosting a fun match on Labor Day. Our artist, Amy, who couldn't be with us tonight, has volunteered to draw pictures of the participants' collies."

Someone asked, "Will she draw pictures of our dogs, too?"

"For a donation. In view of the fact that vet bills keep going up, we need every penny we can lay our hands on."

I tried to cover a yawn. What organization didn't need money? Wasn't one of these women a treasurer with a report to make? By the way, where was the secretary? I didn't see anyone jotting down notes.

"We're also planning an auction. We're looking for collie-themed memorabilia and books…"

And where was Brent? I needed coffee, or a Coca-Cola, anything to keep my mind on the meeting.

~ * ~

I might have known Brent would make a grand entrance. All eyes turned to him as he sauntered into the room, escorted by

Jackie. Byrony appeared to be thunderstruck, and the mannequins promptly came to life.

As he stopped beneath an overhead light fixture, his dark red hair took on a mesmerizing glow. Brent often wore green, and tonight was no exception. His forest green shirt was rolled up to his brawny elbows, and his lord-of-the-manor demeanor was obvious even though he was no lord and this was no manor.

"Sorry I'm late," he said. "What did I miss?"

Byrony hesitated, then regained her composure. "Nothing much. Just notification of fundraisers. And you are…?"

"Brent Fowler, ma'am," he said. "I have stables… and other interests."

The master of understatement accepted the chair Jackie brought into the room for him and bestowed one of his winning smiles on her. A faint blush tinted her face.

"What do you hope to accomplish by joining us, Mr. Fowler?" Byrony asked.

"Call me Brent."

"Okay…Brent."

"My philosophy is that the smallest things you do can make the greatest difference to all the creatures that share the earth with us. That's what I want to accomplish."

How sensitive! How profound! How unlike Brent.

But he'd voiced a similar sentiment before. Once… No, Caroline Meilland, the late animal activist had said that. Brent, the fox hunter, had joined her group, M.A.R.A., solely to pursue Caroline. Brent had an excellent memory.

"That's beautiful, Brent, and so true," Byrony said.

"Now I'd like to ask a question," Sue said. "How many collies has the league rescued since you've been in business?"

She paused. "I can't give you a definitive answer, but I can tell you about one, our latest rescue." With a flourish, Byrony produced the picture of a sable collie from a stack of notes and pamphlets.

"This is Lady. She's an older girl found tied to a random car in the Farmers Market."

Lady was the poster dog whose sad eyes had caught my attention in Pluto's Gourmet Pet Shop.

"We took her to our vet, had her groomed, and found a lovely foster home for her in the country."

"What about your other rescues?" Sue asked.

"You have to understand, our collies come to us in waves, so to speak. It's not a question of a dog a day or even a week. When our people come across an abandoned collie, they contact us. Tomorrow we may have a half dozen dogs to take care of."

"I have a question," I said. "Why are there two collie rescue groups in a little town like Foxglove Corners?"

Byrony looked startled. "As you know, anyone can take in a stray dog and call himself a rescuer."

"All right, but what's the difference in the two groups?"

"We're the official organization," she said. "I'm not going to talk against the other league, but we're not about politics or filling our pockets. Our priority is on helping collies in need. Only that."

She might as well have said, 'That other league is all about politics and raking in money for themselves.'

"So you'd advise us to join your group?" I asked, knowing it was a foolish question with an answer I could have anticipated.

"That goes without saying."

Brent rolled his eyes in my direction. He was enjoying himself, and was well aware of the admiring glances that came his way.

"Thank you for that overview," I said.

After announcing a string of additional fundraising events, Byrony called an end to the meeting and invited us to have coffee in the dining room.

The mannequins moved. I took a moment to sum up what I'd learned. This rogue rescue league had saved a single collie, Lady, from her dismal fate, and was dedicated to raising enough funds to take care of a hundred. In the meantime, their supposed founder, Ann Clarke, was once again indisposed.

"Are you in the mood for coffee?" Sue asked.

"Not really, but now's the time to hear the real story," I whispered.

Alas, I was wrong.

The women arranged themselves into their own little groups, drinking coffee and exclaiming over plates of store-bought cookies. No one invited Sue and me to join them; nobody even acknowledged us, but I noticed Brent managed to move smoothly from clique to clique, dispensing compliments and goodwill and spreading his own brand of rugged charm.

He was in his element, which was good. If anyone were able to delve more deeply into the rescue league's inner secrets, that person was Brent.

I had chosen my spy well.

Twenty-four

The next day found us together again, crossing the bridge to the mysterious town that had cast its spell over us. Brent was the driver, navigating through the secretive green world that surrounded Ashton while I directed his turns from the passenger's seat.

He brought the vintage Plymouth to a stop in front of the Forever Diner, our usual parking place.

"I wish they'd left some food behind," he said. "I could go for a bowl of nice hot chili and a piece of pie."

"Ugh." Annica's response left no doubt as to her opinion of years-old food. "Do you want to poison yourself? We have fresh sandwiches in the basket. Clovers' best."

They would be warm by the time we were ready for lunch. The sun blazed down on the quiet street, and eerie shadows fell across the pavement. Beyond the houses, lake water, impossibly blue, promised a respite from the August heat. I pushed my bangs to one side, wishing I had a band to keep my hair back.

"Before we embark on our expedition, let's make a plan," I said. "What exactly are we looking for?"

"Signs of life," Annica said. "Human or other."

Apple, dog, footsteps encased in mud. The words kept playing in my mind.

"I want to know why people abandoned Ashton en masse," I said.

"And where did they go?" Brent added. "All we need to do is track down one of the former residents."

"Good luck with that," Annica said.

I recalled the envelope with the return address. "We already have one name. It would be helpful if we were to find a diary or journal, but that's not very likely."

Lucy pulled her long black cardigan closer to her body. It was one of those new open styles, without buttons, not meant for warmth. But why would she need warmth with the temperature at eight-nine degrees?

"I'd like to find the source of the danger," she said. "For there is danger in Ashton. Great danger. Never doubt it. We are quite literally meddling in the unknown."

"Jeez, Lucy." Sometimes Brent couldn't resist chipping away at Lucy's Gothic rhetoric. "You make it sound so sinister. We're just a bunch of amateur sleuths looking to solve a mystery."

"A sinister one," Annica said. "What should we look for again, Jennet?"

"Something like that envelope in the house on Willow Street. You'll know when you see it."

Our previous searches of the shuttered houses had been superficial. We needed to look in desks and drawers, in bookcases and…

In medicine cabinets.

Where did that come from? Wouldn't people running away from an untenable situation take their medication with them? I knew I would.

"This time let's work in pairs," I said. "We won't cover as much ground, but we'll still be safe. Annica, you and I can go together."

"I never made it to that house where I saw the snake," she said. "Let's start there."

"Okay, but first we'd better check outside in case the snake has a nest in the yard."

"Do they make nests?"

I didn't know. It didn't seem relevant. Still, I brushed away an alarming image of a monster serpent coiled in front of the door, blocking our exit. Ghost towns and their denizens weren't for the faint-hearted.

~ * ~

"Their refrigerator is empty," Annica called. "There's an opened box of Special K in the cupboard and a loaf of super moldy bread. Yuk."

I was in the bathroom, opening and closing cabinets. The shelves held a jumble of bottles and tubes left behind. A half empty can of hairspray, sunscreen, cologne, baby powder, a bottle of aspirin, and a well-squeezed tube of ointment.

I didn't recognize the name on the ointment label, but it appeared to be a remedy for burns and skin disorders.

"But here's something strange," Annica said.

I closed the cabinet and the bathroom door. Annica was in the living room, holding a picture.

"What?"

"Someone left a personal possession behind."

The girl in the portrait was lovely, dressed in blue, with long dark brown hair that fell beneath her shoulders. The table appeared to be a memorial altar with rosary beads, a holy card, and a glass vase in a surround of dry brownish powder that had once been stems or leaves or flowers.

An altar for the dead.

I turned the card over, hoping to find the name of the deceased with birth and death dates, but on the back was a prayer.

Remember O most gracious Virgin Mary... A reminder to Mary that she never refused a plea for help.

Had the prayer been answered? I could only hope so.

"You'd think they'd want the picture," Annica said.

A wave of sadness stole over me. Yes, why hadn't they taken it? Hastily I replaced the card.

I heard the jingle of the silver bell bracelet that Annica had worn to complement her favorite earrings. She was scratching her arm.

"Something bit me," she said. "I thought it was too hot for mosquitoes."

I frowned. Below her elbow a patch of angry red marred her lightly tanned arm.

"Did you bring any bug spray?" she asked.

"Mmm, no." And there hadn't been any in the bathroom. "Maybe the dime store has some."

"But wouldn't it have lost its strength?"

"Maybe not. We can look."

"I hate mosquitoes," she said.

~ * ~

Brent unwrapped a ham sandwich and bit a chunk out of it. "It's funny. Some of the houses look like their owners might return at any minute. In others, everything that could be easily carried away is gone."

"What does that tell us?" I asked.

"Darned if I know."

"It suggests haste to me," Lucy said. "A family that didn't have time to pack. They left town with the clothes on their backs. Nothing else."

Annica reached for a bottle of water. Opening it, she took a long drink. "Like they had an hour's notice to evacuate?"

"Something like that. Other people had more time. They were the ones who took the warning seriously. But all this is just speculation."

I gazed at the lake, imagining a possible future situation. If I had an hour or a half day to gather my own necessities and treasures, what would I take?

I couldn't begin to decide what I couldn't live without.

But if I *had* to make choices? I had too many possessions.

"They say that people who don't have a lot of stuff are happier," Annica said. "For sure they can move from place to place easier."

"Who's they?" I asked.

"The author of a book I read."

"Just think of everything abandoned along with the town. I wonder why the people never came back for their property. There must be a fortune in the dime store alone."

"For some reason they couldn't," Lucy said.

"But why?"

No one hazarded a guess.

Ashton was the town of a thousand questions. If only I could have one answer. Just one.

~ * ~

By late afternoon we were ready to end our day of searching and begin the short walk back to Main Street. I began to fantasize about a hot shower and clean clothes and a regular meal that I'd have to cook, of course. Anything but a sandwich.

Great minds think alike.

"What do you say to dinner on me?" Brent asked. "I know of a good restaurant on the way to Foxglove Corners. They specialize in seafood."

I should go home, but Annica and Lucy had already accepted Brent's invitation with an exuberant display of enthusiasm. Besides, Camille was taking care of the collies, and Crane wouldn't be home for a couple of hours.

What could I say? "It'll be fun. Thanks, Brent."

Lucy gasped.

She had come to an abrupt stop and was staring at a small house half hidden by encroaching evergreens.

"Did you see that?" she asked.

"See what?" Brent said.

"Somebody walking." Lucy pointed. Her hand was shaking. "There, between the houses."

"Stay here," Brent ordered and took off in the direction Lucy indicated, only to return moments later.

"There's no one there. What did you see?"

"A figure," she said. "A man, I think. He was wearing a black cloak."

"Cloak?" I echoed.

"It happened so fast. Like the speed of light. I barely had time to register his presence. Then he was gone."

"Are you sure?" Brent asked. "That hot sun is getting to all of us."

"I think so."

"Well, I didn't see anyone. I wonder if this was one of your visions or whatever you call them."

"I don't think so," she said, appearing to waver. Then in a stronger voice, she said. "He was there. I know what I saw."

"But a cloak?" I said. "Who wears a cloak?"

Annica ran her hand along her arm, widening the red patch. "Nobody in this heat."

Heat? Annica was right. It must be over ninety degrees. Why did I suddenly feel cold?

You know why.

"I think we'd better get out of here while the getting's good," Brent said. "Hurry, everybody. Back to the car."

No one gave him an argument.

Twenty-five

Coffee and a hot meal in a normal place—the Mermaid's Cove—brought color back to Lucy's face. Her hands had stopped shaking, and when she spoke her voice was steady and resolute.

"Whether the man in the cloak was real or one of my visions, as Brent calls them, his appearance is significant," she said. "He's trouble."

"But he ran away from us," I pointed out.

"He didn't want to be seen."

Annica dipped a French fry in ketchup. "Do you think he's real then, Lucy?"

"I'm not a hundred percent sure, but I'm leaning towards 'yes'."

"I'll trust Lucy's perception," I said. "From time to time I've sensed someone watching me."

Annica looked up in alarm. "You never said anything."

"No, because it was just a feeling. I didn't have any proof."

Brent shook his head. "I'll swear we were the only people in town today. If there were others, why didn't we see them? Where could they hide? Why are they there?"

"They could stay out of sight in any one of the many houses," I said. "Why they're there is anyone's guess."

"I did see one," Lucy reminded us. "I've been reliving that moment in my mind. His cloak was long and full, and it swirled around him when he rushed past that house. I didn't see his face, but he was tall and dark."

These details told me that Lucy must have seen something of substance.

"Like Dracula?" Annica asked.

"Like Hollywood's idea of Dracula."

The introduction of that unholy name into the conversation added a shivery element to the sighting.

I turned back to my salad, a simple mix of cottage cheese, blueberries, and bananas on Romaine lettuce. I'd discovered that I wasn't hungry, but my lemonade, half gone, was a satisfying drink after hours in the sun.

"I thought we should get out of Ashton quickly today," Brent said, "but we'll have to go back soon."

"We will." I scooped up a spoonful of cheese. "I can't remember when a mystery intrigued me so much. I have to know what went on... and what's going on now."

Annica scratched her arm vigorously. "We left so fast I didn't get a chance to see if the dime store had any anti-itch spray. Speaking for myself, I'll be glad to get back to civilization. I need about a ton of the stuff."

Her rash appeared to be spreading. It couldn't be a simple mosquito bite, or even two bites, but I didn't say anything. She'd be getting worried about herself soon enough.

~ * ~

Although my thoughts were still on the ghost town and the figure in the black cloak, I, too, was glad to be back in my own civilized part of the world, playing with my collies and trying to decide what to cook for dinner tonight.

Dogs and dinner I could manage, but I couldn't rid myself of the notion that Ashton's secret lay at my fingertip. If only I could recognize it.

One or two families might have left their homes for greener pastures, but not an entire town. Why, oh why hadn't at least one person kept a journal or written a letter, then forgot to mail it?

Think, Jennet.

You leave a place because it turns on you. Staying isn't an option, and, if you delay, panic sets in.

And my time was running out. I glanced at the calendar. The days of August were rushing by. Leonora's rehearsal dinner, the wedding, and school all were rapidly approaching. I had to work quickly, and the only place to search for answers, other than Ashton, was the library.

~ * ~

"What did your team find in the ghost town today?" Crane asked that evening.

"A picture of one of the young inhabitants," I said. "It was part of what looked like a memorial. We left it there."

"I hope so. You shouldn't remove anything from Ashton. Technically it's theft."

Lucy would say, 'It's bad luck.'

I thought of the wood violet toilet water on my dresser, the scent that Misty had so strenuously objected to. Perhaps I ought to take it back, but… No, I'd paid for it.

Paid ten dollars for bad luck?

"Anything else?" he asked.

"We left in a hurry. Lucy thought she saw a figure in a black cloak."

Crane's voice sharpened. "What was he doing?"

"Disappearing around one of the houses. She said he moved with the speed of light."

"It's about time I saw this ghost town," Crane said. "I'll be home early tomorrow. We can go together. Just us."

"I'd love that."

Would Crane fall under Ashton's spell? I doubted it. Although he was receptive to my tales of supernatural experiences, he was still anchored firmly to the real world.

"Afterward we can have dinner out," he added.

Something to look forward to! I could hardly wait.

~ * ~

I lay beside Crane, wide awake, reliving the strange dream I'd had. It had swept me back into the past, about twelve hours ago.

We were having an early dinner in the Mermaid's Cove again... Annica, Lucy, Brent, and I. At first I thought everything was the same. Then I became aware of subtle differences. For instance, the name of the restaurant had changed. It was the Merman's Cove.

I couldn't remember a time when I'd been so hungry at this hour. I was eating a cheeseburger and French fries and eyeing the small dessert menu between the salt and pepper shakers. Cream puff hot fudge! I hadn't had one of those for years.

Like one of my favorite restaurants, the Adriatica, the Merman's Cove had an indoor fountain into which fanciful diners tossed coins and made wishes. The sound of falling water was soothing but at the same time intrusive.

"This is one of my favorite restaurants for seafood," Brent said, which didn't make sense as he had ordered filet mignon.

"I understand now." Lucy unbuttoned her long black cardigan. "The man in the black cloak wasn't real. He was one of my visions. He symbolizes death."

"Death for the town?" Annica asked brightly. The silver bells on her bracelet jangled, sounding like an alarm. She rested her arm on the table. It was toned and lightly tanned without a single blemish.

"No, death for us," Lucy said. "We intruded where we shouldn't have. We should never have searched those abandoned houses. We shouldn't have touched anything."

"Lose the doomsday rhetoric, Lucy," Brent said. "I'm trying to enjoy my steak."

"Enjoy your food while you can, Brent," she said. "Our days are numbered."

The sound of falling water was so loud we could hardly hear one another's voices. The silver bells on Annica's bracelet rang out vigorously although her arm was still.

Well, that was all right. I didn't want to talk. All I wanted to do was finish my cheeseburger and maybe order another. It was too small, more like a slider than a regular burger.

Without any prior sensation of discomfort, my left arm began to itch.

~ * ~

I turned on the miniature flashlight on my night stand and stared at my arm. There was nothing on it that could have caused it to itch, and yet I felt it still. Idly I scratched at it and pulled down the sleeve of my nightgown.

Misty woke up, stared at me for a moment, and closed her eyes again.

Dreams. It seemed that scarcely a night passed without my having a dream, often multiple dreams bleeding into one another. Curiously I could remember them, for a while anyway, before they dissolved. They were seldom pleasant dreams.

I believed they were trying to tell me something I needed to know.

But what?

Good grief, Jennet, you're even finding a mystery in dreams.

If Crane were awake, I'd tell him about it. But what is more boring than listening to another person's dream?

Go to sleep, I told myself.

Tomorrow was going to be an exciting day. When Crane came home we'd drive out to Ashton. My handsome deputy sheriff husband would certainly scare away the specters.

Twenty-six

The next morning I took a dozen jelly doughnuts from the Hometown Bakery to the library for Miss Eidt, anxious to get them back into an air-conditioned environment before their icing melted. Before *I* melted.

These were truly the dog days of summer. My collies had turned up their pretty noses at my suggestion of an early morning walk while it was still relatively comfortable. Five minutes in the heat and humidity were sufficient for their needs, then it was back inside where they retired to their special places. Even Raven broke with her habit of lying in front of her house and slipped into the kitchen with the rest of the dogs.

The sun was hot, burning merrily through my light cotton sleeves. My sunburn had faded, and I didn't want to acquire another one so close to Leonora's wedding. It was strange, though. There wasn't a mark on my left arm other than a stray freckle or two, but it itched. It wasn't intolerable, only annoying, as it tried to convince me that something was there, even though I couldn't see it.

Could it be the power of suggestion?

Miss Eidt's cat, Blackberry, had left her beloved wicker rocker on the porch, no doubt to find a secluded resting place among the stacks. At times animals can be smarter than humans.

Inside the old white Victorian, it was blessedly cool with the whir of ceiling fans, turned on to help the air conditioning along.

Miss Eidt, looking crisp and professional in a pastel blue shirtwaist dress and pearl necklace, stood at the carousel adding paperback books to the revolving shelves.

"Good morning, Miss Eidt," I said. "I have jelly doughnuts. Blueberry, raspberry, and strawberry." I set the long white box on the main desk.

Her face lit up. "All my favorites. You're a lifesaver, Jennet. I skipped breakfast this morning. It was so hot, I didn't fancy cereal or an egg when I got up, but now I'm hungry. For pastries," she added. "Will you join me in the office? Debbie can take care of the crowd."

Miss Eidt's idea of a crowd was approximately twenty people, all of them engrossed in books or newspapers. "Now where's that girl?"

Blackberry peered out from behind the carousel, jewel-green eyes shining.

"Over by the secret room," I said.

"Ah, that."

At one time Miss Eidt had treated the Victorian's long hidden room as an Exhibit 'A', reveling in the appearances of the library's ghost. These days for some reason she didn't mention it, and few people knew it existed. Only those of us who had been in Foxglove Corners for a while knew that once the library had been haunted.

Debbie wheeled the return cart over to the desk, glanced at the box from the Hometown Bakery, and smiled. Apparently a box of doughnuts was the ticket to practically anywhere.

"There you are, Debbie," Miss Eidt said. "Will you sit at the desk for a few minutes? Then you can take your break. Jennet brought us doughnuts."

"Sure, Miss Eidt," she said.

Debbie loved to be in charge of the library. She was studying library science, and I hoped when she earned her degree, she wouldn't leave Foxglove Corners for a job downstate.

In her office, Miss Eidt filled the teakettle with fresh water and cut the string on the box.

"Did you read about the radioactive waste another state is planning to dump in Michigan?" she asked.

"No, I haven't seen the paper."

Or listened to the news on television or paid attention to the issues in my own world. I'd been too involved in the mystery of the ghost town.

"Well, apparently there's nothing to stop them," she said. "They claim it's legal and safe. Who believes that?"

"Not I. Where is this?"

"It isn't in our backyards, but close enough. I already wrote to our representative. I tell you, Jennet, it makes me ill to think about how humans have ravaged the earth. I wish I could do something about it instead of just lending books."

I heard the echo of Caroline Meilland's philosophy in Miss Eidt's words, about small things making a difference. True, Caroline's focus was on animals, but they were also victims of ravaging humans.

It occurred to me that I'd never heard Miss Eidt so passionate about a subject.

"You bring together readers and books, and reading allows people to cope with the world," I told her. "If you want to do more, keep writing letters. You can take part in a protest, if there is one. I'll do the same."

She laughed softly. "Can you see me carrying a picket sign?"

"Well, no."

In fact, in my view, Miss Eidt was a personification of her library. Elderly and dignified, but young in her ways, she blossomed among her precious books. Aside from helping Debbie maintain the grounds, she was very much an inside person.

"Our world is poisoned," she said. "Our air and water, even our food. The climate is changing. Whole species are dying out. No place is safe. I'm glad I'm at the end of my life rather than the beginning."

"You're a long, long way from the end."

"Well, I'll do what I can," she said. "Are you going to use the vertical file today?"

"I thought I'd look for books on Michigan towns, on their history and any legends associated with them."

In this whole library, there must be at least one mention of Ashton.

"You're not having much luck with this new mystery, are you?" she asked.

"It seems like I'm at a standstill."

She poured boiling water over the tea bags and lifted the top of the bakery box to an array of doughnuts topped with powdered sugar or glaze. At the moment I couldn't imagine anything more appealing. Then I remembered what we'd been talking about.

Berries. Strawberries from California, Michigan-grown blueberries and raspberries. Were they poisoned, too?

~ * ~

Research is thirsty work, especially when you haven't found what you're looking for. Apparently Ashton was too small a community to warrant a write-up in a book. It was a mere speck on the map.

I left the library, once again frustrated, and instead of heading for home, I made a stop at Clovers. The bright green plants that decorated the restaurant's border made me think of mint...which made me think of chocolate peppermint pie.

Annica greeted me as if we hadn't just been together yesterday and ushered me to my favorite booth by the window. She wore a navy blue skirt that brushed her ankles and a white long-sleeved blouse.

She didn't usually cover her arms.

She handed me a menu.

"I glanced at the dessert carousel on the way in," I said. "You wouldn't happen to have a chocolate mint pie in the kitchen, would you?"

"Not today."

"Darn. I've been craving one."

"I guess you'll have to make it yourself. But cheer up. We have chocolate mint ice cream."

That would do.

"I'll have two scoops of that with iced tea," I said and leaped to another subject that might be considered indelicate if Annica and I had not been friends. "How's your rash?"

"The same. It may be spreading a little."

"Didn't the anti-itch spray or whatever you used help?

"I used Benadryl," she said. "It didn't help much. I'm keeping my arm covered. I don't want the customers to think I have poison ivy."

Could that be it?

"Did you touch a suspicious plant?" I asked. "You know, one with three leaves?"

"My ankle may have come into contact with one in all those weeds we tramped through, but it's my arm that itches."

"Maybe you should see a doctor," I said.

"That'll have to wait. I have my class and a paper to write."

"Don't put it off too long."

"I drove out to the wildflower field to see the violet this morning," she said. "I've been neglecting it."

She tended to speak of the mysterious violet as if it were a sentient being. As if it had missed her.

"How does it look?" I asked.

"Beautiful. Tall and healthy and its flowers are the color of sapphires. I don't have the heart to cut it."

"Then don't. Let nature take its course."

"You mean, let it die?"

"The whole wildflower field will die in a few months."

"Wouldn't it be amazing if it bloomed in the snow?"

"That won't happen," I said.

But if it did, it wouldn't surprise me. All of us half-believed there was something unnatural about the violet, that it was in some way connected with Violet Randall.

It would be interesting to see what happened when the snow came.

Twenty-seven

We stood between the Jeep and the Forever Diner gazing at a dead world. Nothing stirred, no wandering creature scampered out of the wilderness, and not a single leaf spiraled through the air. Only the clouds moved lazily, languidly, across a deep blue sky.

Crane hadn't changed into civilian clothes, which meant he still carried his gun. Good! Let the giant snake slither up to us. Let the man in the black cloak creep out of his hiding place.

It was so quiet I could hear our breathing magnified in the hot, dry air.

"I can see why this place fascinates you," Crane said. "By rights it shouldn't exist."

"Not on this planet. Nor in this century."

He took my hand, and we walked down Main Street toward the silent houses, toward the lake that rivaled the sky for pure blue color.

We passed the dime store.

"It's truly weird," I said. "The store is fully stocked. All that merchandise was abandoned by the owner. You'd think somebody would have cleared it out."

"The owner?"

"Or some enterprising thief."

"Is that where you found your perfume?" he asked.

"Yes, and Annica bought a lipstick. She's been wearing it."

I frowned at the thought that had dropped into my mind. Riding Hood Red, a luscious shade from another era. Annica had applied it to her lips with a heavy hand.

Could the lipstick possibly be the cause of the rash on her arm?

I could almost hear Miss Eidt's voice. "Our world is poisoned."

Sometimes I thought Crane could read my mind.

"Do me a favor, honey," he said. "Pour that perfume down the drain. If you like the scent of violet so much, I'll find another brand for you."

"It's toilet water, not perfume," I said, "and Misty hated it."

"I remember. Our Misty is a perceptive pooch."

Now that I thought about it, I couldn't help worrying. I had sprayed the toilet water on my wrists and behind my ears one time only, when we were paying one of our early visits to Ashton. I hadn't used it since then.

I glanced down at my arm. Was that a bit of redness just above my right elbow?

Surely not.

Don't obsess about it.

"Just think, Crane," I said. "All those old abandoned houses. It's unreal."

"Let's walk down to the lake, honey. That water looks mighty appealing in this heat."

Hand and hand, we strolled through the silent streets to the lake. I had never felt so safe in Forever. Never so comfortable.

It's Ashton, I reminded myself. *Not Forever.*

"You know what I think, Jennet?" Crane said.

I waited for him to tell me, although I thought I knew what he was going to say.

"It's time you told someone about your ghost town," he said. "Let's start with the police."

"You *are* the police," I said. "You've known from the beginning."

"Technically, I'm a deputy sheriff. I'll rephrase that. Start by telling the proper authorities."

"You may be right, but I hate to share Ashton with people who might swoop down and change it."

"That probably won't happen."

"You can't be certain."

"You *do* want to know why the inhabitants left," he said.

I couldn't deny it.

"That may be the only way to find out."

He was right, of course, but I didn't have to do it today.

On the beach I contemplated the color of the lake. Viewed from this close perspective, it was almost too blue, almost as if a careless hand had tipped a vial of cobalt dye into the water, turning it an unnatural shade.

"It's funny having a nice lake and no one to enjoy it," Crane said.

"Not a bit like our Sagramore Lake."

A beach needed sunbathers, children building fanciful sand castles, watercrafts skimming over the waters. It needed people.

Crane wiped his forehead. "Wish it would cool off. This has been the longest hot spell I can remember."

He put his arm around me, and we headed back to Main Street. Past the house where Brent had found footprints and I'd discovered the envelope that gave me the town's correct name. Past the place where Lucy had glimpsed the figure in the black cloak, past that part of the street where I'd found the apple.

Everything was peaceful, the ghost town showing its innocuous side for the benefit of the lawman in its midst. The sun was high in the sky, and our shadows moved with us as we passed the shuttered stores. Friendly shadows.

It should have been a pleasant walk, a stroll down a street frozen in time, but gradually a feeling of unease came upon me, a suggestion of hidden eyes trained on us, marking our progress. All was not as it seemed.

Yes, that's the way. Go back to your vehicle. Out of the town. And don't come back.

""Do you have the feeling we're being watched?" I asked.

"No, more like we're walking through a graveyard. Where is this person who's supposed to be watching us?"

"In one of the stores or on the top floor of a house?"

"It's possible, but I'd swear that you and I are the only humans within thirty miles or so."

That was encouraging. Crane was the realist. I was the one who always let my imagination take me to unexplored heights. I should let his assurance that we were alone in Ashton comfort me.

I should, but I didn't.

~ * ~

Over dinner at the Adriatica, a restaurant with an abundance of continental ambience and good Italian food, I tried to concentrate on my ravioli and our rare date night. Instead, I kept wondering if I had inadvertently poisoned myself with the wood violet toilet water from the Ashton dime store.

I thought it unlikely that a single application on one occasion could have such a dire long-lasting effect. But what if there were something tainted about the toilet water?

All right. What if there were?

A few drops landing on a few parts of my body. One time.

Misty following me downstairs, barking all the way, refusing to be quiet or come near me when we were eating pancakes.

"Don't you like the wine, honey?" Crane asked.

My glass was full.

"It's fine," I said. "I'm not used to having wine with dinner."

On second thought, I should have ordered a soft drink or iced tea.

"The ravioli is delicious," I added.

Eventually I remembered Annica. She loved makeup, especially different shades of lipstick. I imagined her painting her lips Riding Hood Red every day. Twice. Three times. Maybe more.

I had to warn her.

What had Lucy taken from the dime store? I couldn't remember, but I didn't think it was a product she would use next to her skin. A tea towel, maybe? An apron?

Memories of previous visits flooded back. I had suggested that we look in the store for anti-itch ointment when Annica first complained about a bite, but we'd hurriedly left town instead.

I'd phone her as soon as we got home.

Crane said, "They have one of your favorite desserts, crème caramel."

I remembered.

Miss Eidt believed that our food was poisoned, along with our air and water.

No! I refused to be afraid of food. Not of my ravioli, not of a special dessert.

Makeup was another matter. So was toilet water.

Twenty-eight

That night I emptied the bottle of toilet water into the bathroom drain and let the cold water run for five minutes. The air filled with a light, sweet scent reminiscent of meadow flowers on a spring morning.

Was it necessary? I didn't know, but it didn't matter now. Wood violet was gone.

The next day I had a second breakfast of tea and apple muffins at Clovers.

Annica was wearing red lipstick, several shades lighter than Riding Hood Red. She'd seemed incredulous yesterday on the phone when I told her my theory. Apparently she'd had second thoughts since then.

"I hated to throw it out," she said. "It felt so creamy when I put it on and lasted longer than my other lipsticks, but it's better to be safe than sorry. I may be sorry already."

She had covered her arms again with a white vintage-inspired blouse embellished with lace.

"I'd rather have a light case of poison ivy" she added. "I could treat that."

"Isn't your rash any better?" I asked.

"About the same. I hate it. I like to wear sleeveless tops in the summer."

"You still can."

"I wouldn't. Not in a restaurant."

"Did you make a doctor's appointment?"

"I will next week as soon as I finish my paper. In the meantime, I'll rely on Benadryl. Jennet…"

She glanced around. Marcy was passing by, carrying a tray of breakfast dishes, and no one was close enough to overhear our conversation.

"Do you really think there's something harmful about the ghost town?" she asked.

"I'm not sure, but I agree with you. It's better to be safe than sorry."

"But Lucy seemed to think it was okay. I mean, she was there with us."

"That's true, but she *did* see that cloaked figure."

"And she warned me away from the lake when I mentioned I'd like to go wading. She didn't give a reason."

"Remember when the sun was so bright and Lucy thought it was dark out?"

"Putting everything together, I'm ready to believe there's a good reason for us to be leery of Ashton," she said. "I'm not going back. It was fun while it lasted, but…"

She scratched absently at her arm. "You succeeded in scaring me."

"Crane thinks it's time we alerted someone higher up about the town," I said.

"Who's higher up?"

I shrugged. "The proper authorities. The F.B.I.? We'll figure it out."

"Brent will be disappointed," she said. "He's already planning our next expedition."

"He'll survive. Or he can go alone."

"We *did* have fun, though, didn't we? Now the fun's over."

"And the bill has come due," I said.

~ * ~

Brent pulled a rolled-up poster out of a shopping bag from Pluto's Gourmet Pet Shop while the collies circled him in anticipation. Wondrous meaty scents wafted around them.

"What do you have, Fowler?" Crane asked.

"The latest from the rogue rescue group."

He unfolded the poster and presented it to me. This one was mainly an advertisement for an auction fundraiser. The winsome face of a collie puppy named Nugget adorned the entire top half.

"Did somebody give it to you?" I asked.

"I took if off Pluto's board. They can put up another one."

"I hope no one saw you. We want to keep a low profile."

"No one was around when I took it," he assured me.

I studied the picture of the puppy, wondering where I'd seen it before.

"This must be a pup they rescued," I said.

Nugget was a baby, all legs and caramel fluff, with one ear tipped and one straight up. Her little head was tilted in a manner to beguile the beholder.

Who doesn't melt at the sight of a collie puppy? Who wouldn't stop the read the text below?

Royal Doulton collie figurines, original watercolors by a renowned animal artist, first editions of Albert Payson Terhune's books, DVDs of the original Lassie movies, sterling silver collie jewelry, and original collie greeting cards.

"It's a treasure trove for collie lovers," I said. "We have to go."

"Let's see." Crane studied the poster. "The auction is being held at Chanticleer Farm."

"Where's that?" I asked.

"North of Spearmint Lake."

"I'll be there," Brent said. "I have an inkling of what they're up to, but I need to ingratiate myself with Byrony."

"What do you think is going on?" I asked.

"I'll tell you when I'm sure. Byrony loves to hear herself talk."

"What about Ann?"

"I asked if Ann was ever going to be at league event, and Byrony ignored me."

"Ann is supposed to be their founder," I said.

"Maybe there's been a bloodless coup."

"Maybe."

But I didn't like to think of a coup and the rogue league in the same sentence.

Brent handed out the treats he'd bought, many flavored bones, and watched them disappear. When he sat in the rocker, Misty leaped onto his lap and nudged his pockets with her long nose.

"What's this Annica tells me about our ghost town being off limits now?" Brent asked.

I hesitated. It wasn't easy to explain without telling him about Annica's rash, and somehow I knew she wouldn't want him to know. He thought she had a mosquito bite, long since gone. But I had to say something.

"We're afraid some of the products we touched may be contaminated."

"Based on what?"

"Some makeup. I used toilet water from the dime store. It may have adverse effects."

"What happened?"

"Redness. Irritation." I glanced at Crane.

"What does that have to do with the town being off limits?" Brent asked.

"I checked out the place with Jennet," Crane said. "We decided it was time to let the authorities know that it exists."

"But we're not finished with our exploration yet. We still don't know what happened there. We don't know who's prowling the streets wearing a black cloak."

All true. Brent wasn't going to allow himself to be convinced.

"It'll soon be out of our hands," Crane said.

"Did you tell anyone yet?"

"Not yet, but we will," I said.

"Hell! I'd better do some more exploring on my own then. Annica will want to come. I'm not sure about Lucy. She's ambivalent about the town."

I doubted that Annica would risk acquiring another rash or worse. I wasn't sure about Lucy. She didn't seem overly curious about the cloaked figure.

"If you go, be careful," I said. "Don't touch anything."

"You're serious about this, aren't you?" he asked.

"Very serious."

"You never leave a mystery unsolved, Jennet. What's really the matter?"

"It's what I told you. I don't want to come in contact with anything if there's the slightest chance it may be contaminated. I don't want my friends to take any chances either."

"That's too vague," Brent said. "I'm not afraid, and if there's a person living in Ashton and wearing a cloak, I want to find him."

"We can't stop you," I said. "Just remember, though. There may be danger."

Twenty-nine

After Brent left, I looked at Nugget's picture again. It's true that many collie puppies resemble one another, but because of the glimpse of pink foxgloves in the background, I felt certain I'd seen this same picture before. Where? And how could this precious little creature have been abandoned?

I paused over the fine print. 'Nugget is enjoying play time with her new family in the country.'

Hadn't Byrony said something similar about the first poster collie?

Where I had seen Nugget? It was going to bother me until I remembered.

At present my mind refused to cooperate. *Let it go*, I told myself. *It'll come in its own good time.*

Crane said, "Fowler is the most stubborn man I know."

"I didn't give him much of a reason to stay away from Ashton. He loves an adventure."

"I'll tell Mac about the ghost town tomorrow and take him out to see it. He'll know what to do next."

And that would be the end of Ashton as we knew it.

"We had fun… at first," I said.

In a rush, memories flooded back. The thrill of discovering a town hidden for decades in the midst of a green forest; secretive houses whose abandoned possessions yearned to tell their stories, and mystifying suggestions of present habitation. In other words, a mystery never to be solved.

"I'll miss it," I said.

Crane rose. "It's for the best, honey. Now let's take our girls for a walk in the moonlight."

Candy leaped up from her nap and raced to the hook where her leash hung, just waiting to be attached to an eager collie body. The other dogs clustered around us, excited to be going out as a pack with both Crane and me.

The mystery of the puppy's picture slipped out of my mind. It fell behind my memories of Ashton and lay there quietly.

~ * ~

Before school began, I wanted to visit Lucy at Dark Gables. She didn't know about Annica's rash or that I'd poured the wood violet toilet water down the drain.

I finally remembered what Lucy had taken from the dime store. It was an apron meant to be worn over a dress or skirt. As long as it didn't touch her body, she should be safe. Also, I wanted to bring her up-to-date about the Ashton development and Brent's refusal to be kept away from the town.

She and I had a lot to talk about. Also I was eager to learn what the tea leaves had to say.

We sat in her sunroom with Sky, drinking tea and eating the pineapple muffins I'd brought. Brent had already informed Lucy of his intent to return to Ashton. He might be there already.

"I hope we don't have to extricate him from another tangle," she said, offering a bite of muffin to her patient blue merle.

"What kind of tangle?" I asked.

"I'm not sure, but remember when he was determined to go back in time? That could have ended badly."

"I'll never forget it. Did you try to talk him out of going to Ashton?"

"I did, but he wouldn't listen."

"Well…" I let the tea slide down my throat. It was the perfect temperature and had a slightly different taste. A hint of mint. "Do you have any premonition of disaster?"

"Not at this time," she said. "The question is, do you think Annica will be okay?"

"She isn't sure what's causing the rash. I hope I'm wrong about the lipstick. It's just that she was using it every day for a while."

"You'd think the rash would be on her face then. Around her mouth."

I shuddered. "She would hate that."

"Unfortunately I already wore my apron when I was making breakfast this morning," Lucy said.

"Do you feel all right?"

"Perfectly. So far. But in the spirit of being proactive, I'm going to cut it up for the rag basket."

"I sort of regret spilling my toilet water out," I said. "Crane promised to find me another brand, something comparable. I'll have to remind him."

"I agree with your decision to report the existence of Ashton to the authorities, but, like you, I wish it could stay the way it is."

"Imagine that quaint town razed. Condos built higher than the treetops. The lake crowded with swimmers and watercrafts. Everything that's wonderful about it gone."

Lucy was quiet for so long that I looked up. Had her mind drifted to the story she was currently writing? She was gazing out the French doors at her yard with its fountain and backdrop of wooded acreage.

"What is it?" I asked.

"That isn't going to happen, Jennet. I see Ashton as it will be several years from now. It looks the same, a shadowy ghost town asleep in the sun."

~ * ~

My visit, as always, ended with Lucy reading my tea leaves. When the muffin basket was empty and I'd drunk all my tea, I drained the excess liquid into the saucer and turned the cup three times toward myself as I made my wish.

That was the ritual. I knew it by heart.

Hokus-pokus, part of me thought, while the other part anxiously awaited Lucy's interpretations of the leaves' patterns.

"I don't see the ghost town," Lucy said.

"What would it look like?" I asked.

"A tiny house. Maybe two of three of them in a row. Anyway, they're not here. It looks like that chapter in your life is finished."

"Well, I expected that."

"Mmm. I don't see your wish."

"But you always see it," I protested. "Three little dots. They aren't there?"

She turned the cup around. And around and around.

"I don't see them today."

"Did you open a new tin of tea?" I asked.

"Yes. Didn't you like it?"

"It was wonderful. I thought maybe the leaves weren't powdery like they are at the bottom of the tin."

Lucy smiled. "The leaves would find a way. I usually see your wish, Jennet. Just not today. You don't have to believe this, you know."

I was being ridiculous. My wish was always the same, for a continued happy life with Crane. "Maybe the leaves are having an off day."

"Do you want me to continue?" she asked.

"Please."

"All right. Let's see…"

Quietly she studied the patterns in the cup. "I see a challenge ahead of you. It's fraught with danger. She paused. "You're going to receive a gift. Oh, and here's an initial. *V.*"

V? Oh, no! *V* for Veronica. She was the female deputy sheriff in Crane's department who I believed had set her cap for Crane. She'd been lying low, so low that I forgot about her existence for long periods of time.

"Really Jennet," Lucy said. "I don't want to distress you."

"I'm okay. Just surprised."

"Well, you look devastated. Let's do this another time. And I want you to remember this. Only you are in control of your fate. Your future is in your hands. No one else's."

Thirty

Sue Appleton leaned against the fence. She had a new foal, only a day old. I couldn't believe how big he was for a newborn and wished he'd come closer so I could touch him. He stayed near his mother, both graceful animals silhouetted against the sky and rolling grass.

Halley and Misty were enthralled at the sight of the small creature, no doubt wondering if it were a dog, but Sky was unsure of his intentions. She lay at my feet, content to watch from a safe distance while Icy, Blueberry, and Echo chased one another around the fields.

Sue brushed her strawberry blonde bangs off her forehead. "Come over to visit him anytime, Jennet. He'll only get larger. I haven't decided on a name for him yet."

She turned to the poster Brent had given me. "What's this? Oh, the league's auction."

"It's a hot property," I said. "Brent took it from the board at Pluto's Gourmet Pet Shop when no one was looking. Don't you think the puppy looks familiar?"

She held it up to the sun. "I don't recognize the puppy, but I see what you mean. This doesn't look like the kind of picture you expect to see on a rescue site. With the flowers in the background, it looks carefully staged."

"Of course they wanted the most appealing model and the best photograph possible for their poster," I said. "Hence, a collie puppy and pink foxgloves."

"I'd like to bid on some of these items, especially the collie figurines for my collection. They should rake in a fortune with all this pricey merchandise."

"Annica and I are going unless she has to work. It's at a place called Chanticleer Farm, which isn't too long a drive. I hope you can come with us."

"I wouldn't miss it. So, little Nugget has a new home in the country. Ideal. Just like that other poster collie. Lady was it?"

"I suppose Byrony could have found two country families to adopt the collies."

"I can't help being suspicious. When I asked her about the number of collies her group saved, she didn't give me a direct answer. I'll bet it's only those two."

"She never told us why the mythical Ann Clarke decided that Foxglove Corners needed another rescue group either," I said.

Sue slammed her hand against the fence, startling Sky who moved back as far as the leash would allow.

"We didn't learn anything we can trust at that meeting," she said. "It was a total waste of time."

"Maybe not. Brent caused quite a stir among the female members."

"I wonder what he's been doing," Sue said.

"He's pursuing another mystery these days."

"Is it more important than infiltrating that bunch of rogues?"

"They're both important. Right now, he's involved in this other matter."

"With his horses?" she asked.

She was certainly curious this morning. I wondered why.

"There's something else," I said.

Should I tell her about Ashton? Well, why not? After today, after Crane and Mac visited the ghost town, it would no longer be a secret.

"There's something else. Do you remember when Annica and I went up north to bring Echo back to Foxglove Corners? We got lost on the way…"

Every time I repeated the story of Ashton, I relived the wonder of it.

The tale fascinated Sue. "I've never heard of a town named Ashton, and I've lived here all my life," she said.

"It's way off the beaten track, hard to find, and completely deserted. Well, we think so, but that's another story. As I said, we more or less ran into it after we left the freeway."

"And you and Annica have been back there several times?" she asked.

"With Brent and Lucy Hazen."

"I wish I'd known. I would love to explore a real ghost town. Can we go together sometime, you and me?"

"It's still there, but…"

All right, Jennet, you'd better tell her everything.

"I suspect there's something unhealthy about Ashton. Maybe it's in the atmosphere, maybe it's absorbed in the very walls. I don't know. I didn't even think of contamination at first, but one of us has developed a troubling skin affliction. I bought a bottle of toilet water in the dime store and was so concerned I threw it down the drain."

"You're saying I'd better stay away?"

"I'm telling you to go at your own risk. Crane and I won't be returning. Brent doesn't agree with us. He may be there today."

"Do you think he'd take me with him some day?" she asked. "I'm busy with my horses and lessons and the dogs, but I could find time for something like this."

"You can ask him," I said. "He may want a companion. I really don't want to go back. Lucy doesn't either."

"Well, it'll be something to look forward to. You know, Jennet, if you listen to the naysayers of the world, you'll be afraid to eat or drink or even take a breath. Everything is out to get you. I can't live my life that way."

I gazed at the newborn foal cavorting in the grass and thought about what Sue had said. There was so much beauty in nature and in life. I didn't want to live in a constant state of fear either. But continuing to expose oneself to the possible poison in Ashton was tempting fate. I had done that long enough.

Sue returned the poster. As I looked at it, yet once again, I had an idea. As soon as I was back home, I'd check it out.

I gave a gentle tug on the leashes. "Brent is going to ask Byrony to have dinner with him some night this week. He'll tell her he wants to know everything about the Foxglove Corners Rescue. Let's hope she's sufficiently charmed to give up her secrets."

"Good old Brent," Sue said. "He has no scruples. That's exactly the kind of man we need on our side if we're going to take down the rogue collie rescue group."

~ * ~

Every December I bought at least two collie calendars. At the end of the year, I couldn't just throw them away, not with all the gorgeous illustrations. My collection, which spanned about twenty years, was stored in the basement with college notes and past lesson plans.

Sue's remark about Nugget's picture being staged reminded me of all the collie pictures I'd seen over the years... collies posed in gardens and among autumn color and in the snow.

At home I embarked on a new project.

Foxglove... summer.

Starting with the previous year, I worked my way back to 2008--and found puppy Nugget, sitting in an English garden. She was the illustration for June of that year, meaning that she wasn't a baby any longer. In all probability she hadn't been abandoned and never found shelter in the rogue league.

Byrony, or whoever designed the poster, had helped herself to a picture from the old calendar, almost certainly without permission. It was a bold move, but the culprit must have figured that no one would go searching through calendars from previous years or even be suspicious.

How could we believe anything this rogue group said? And what about Lady?

I didn't have the older collie's picture, but I suspected the number of dogs the League had rescued was zero.

If they had only omitted the information about Nugget's rescue, all they'd be guilty of was violating copyright laws. But someone associated with the group had been blatantly dishonest, supplying a fictitious account for an illustration.

All right. What should I do with this information?

First, pass it on to Sue. Tell Brent, of course. He was in a position to question Byrony. After that, what?

Wait and give them enough rope to hang themselves? As we still didn't know their purpose, it would be best to keep our new knowledge quiet.

I took one last sad look at the calendar girl. Sweet little Nugget would be a geriatric collie today, if she were alive.

As soon as I shared my discovery with Sue, I had to fix dinner. From the thrill of discovery to the mundane.

Thirty-one

Crane wasn't the kind of man to embellish an account. That afternoon he gave me three details about his visit to Ashton with Lieutenant Mac Dalby. First, Mac had been suitably impressed by the existence of a place he'd never heard of. Second, he was going to bring the ghost town to the attention of the parties who should know about it...whoever they might be. And third, nothing unusual had occurred during their brief tour.

"You could hear a pin drop on Main Street," Crane said.

If Brent had gone adventuring in Ashton, he might have a story to tell. It was near our dinnertime. In anticipation of his visit, I had baked a chocolate peppermint pie, roasted two chickens instead of one, and had plenty of potatoes ready for mashing.

I reminded myself that Brent was a civilian. The watcher in the black cloak might well have been intimidated by the appearance of two armed lawmen in his territory and kept out of sight.

I hoped that Brent would stop by tonight. If he had already taken Byrony out to dinner, I was anxious to hear if he had learned anything relevant about the rogue group. I also wanted to tell him about Nugget's picture in the old calendar.

Crane locked his gun in its cabinet and set a box illustrated with purple violets on the kitchen table. "This is for you, honey. I hope you'll like it as well as the one you threw away."

Woodland Violet eau de parfum. I'd seen it advertised in a catalog. It was expensive, far more so than the bottle I'd bought, so to speak, at the dime store in Ashton.

"I'll love it and thank you. Let's see."

I sprayed my wrist. Instantly the light fragrance of violets in early spring surrounded me. Calling Misty, I waved my arm under her nose. She licked her chops. Candy pushed her aside with her head and nudged my hand.

Crane laughed at my little experiment. "Misty is okay with it. Now we know for sure the old perfume was bad."

"And I'll stop regretting I poured it down the drain."

"Is Annica's rash any better?" he asked.

"She still had it the last time I saw her. She's going to see a doctor."

I made a mental note to visit Clovers tomorrow. Annica was the only one of us who'd had such an adverse reaction to an Ashton product.

"Lucy cut up her apron into rags," I said. "She's being proactive."

"You ladies are seriously worried."

"Aren't you?"

"I'll be more worried if they find something harmful in the town," he said. "We won't know anything for a while."

And there we left the Ashton matter, at least for the present.

~ * ~

After an early walk with Halley, Sky, and Gemmy, I drove to Clovers for a light lunch. Since waking to a hot and humid morning, I had been craving a salad. Crisp lettuce leaves with fresh fruit. I could have created one at home, but on a day like this one it was easier to have a salad handed to me. Besides, I wanted to talk to Annica.

She was working today, wearing sleeves again. That alone told me the rash still bothered her. She wore an aqua midi dress with one of those linen shirts in a darker shade of the same color. Crystal teardrop earrings sparkled through flyaway strands of reddish-gold hair. She had a talent for dressing to showcase her moods.

After taking my order, she said "My skin problem is the same. I saw a doctor. He recommended a dermatologist and gave me a script for a new ointment."

"Is it helping?"

"It's too soon to tell. Brent was in for breakfast today, and a little later your nemesis came in."

"Who's that?" I thought I knew but asked anyway, even though I was loath to hear the answer.

"You know, that hussy who's interested in Brent."

Veronica the Viper. I waited for the brick to fall.

"Did she ask about Crane?"

"Oh, yes. She said she loved her job in the sheriff's department. Everyone is so friendly to her, one person in particular."

"My husband?"

"She didn't say."

Crane hadn't mentioned Veronica lately. Was that significant? In truth, he never said much about his life as a deputy sheriff.

Lucy had seen the Viper coiled in my teacup, but I didn't have to believe that she was poised to enter my life.

What else had Lucy seen in past readings that never made the leap to reality?

That trip around the world. The surprise inheritance. I had no one to leave me anything. But Crane did.

"Are you listening, Jennet?"

Annica had left the table to retrieve a pitcher and poured water over the ice cubes crammed into a tall glass.

"Listening? Sure. Veronica was trying to trick you into telling her something about Crane."

"Well, I didn't fall for it. I said I hadn't seen him in ages. Now about Brent…"

Obviously I had missed something.

"He's going to invite us to dinner at the Hunt Club Inn, all of us. He went back to Ashton and apparently made a discovery. He wouldn't even give me a hint."

"Brent hasn't been over lately," I said. "Not since we told him we're staying away from the ghost town. Lieutenant Dalby knows about Ashton, too," I added.

"Brent looked okay, good as always, but he was complaining about a sore throat. He actually ordered cream of wheat instead of his usual big breakfast. He never gets sick. Do you think…?"

She didn't finish her question, but I knew what she meant.

"I hope not. How's *your* throat, by the way?"

She swallowed. "Oh, dear Lord."

"What?"

"It's a little scratchy. I've been poisoned."

An image of myself spraying the toilet water from the Ashton dime store on my wrists and ear lobes rose up to enlighten me.

Ears are close to the throat.

I took a long drink of ice water. There. I was all right.

At the moment.

~ * ~

Brent came to visit at the dinner hour that evening, bringing a variety of flavor bones for the dogs and a bouquet of pink and white carnations for me. Rather, for my table, as he said under Crane's watchful eyes.

"I see you survived your solitary trip to Ashton," I said.

"You've been talking to Annica?"

"She told me you made a discovery."

"I did."

He sank into the rocking chair and motioned for Misty to join him, which she was only too eager to do.

"How is your throat?" I asked.

"How did you know about that?"

"Annica mentioned it."

"You women sure know how to gossip."

"Well, how is it?"

"A little sore. It doesn't hurt when I eat, though."

"You missed roasted chicken yesterday," I said. "We're having stew tonight and there's half a chocolate pie left."

He smiled. "Your good beef stew should take care of a little sore throat."

Apparently that was all he was prepared to say about his health, for he launched immediately into an account of his day in the ghost town.

"I walked down to the lake and didn't see anybody, but I had the strangest feeling that somebody was watching me. The kind of feeling you talked about. I picked a house at random and looked around. That's when I found it."

He paused... for dramatic effect, I imagined.

"Found what?" Crane asked.

"An empty pizza box and pop cans in the kitchen. It looked like somebody had just gotten up from dinner."

"Could it have been there all along?" I asked.

"The box was still warm."

"Well... It's so hot out. I'd expect everything inside to be warm, too."

"And it was right on the table in the kitchen with a pop bottle beside it. I don't think the box has been there for decades. One corner looked like it had been chewed."

"By a rat?" Crane asked.

"How could I tell? I think it may have been that mad dog we saw earlier."

"And he couldn't find anything better to eat than cardboard?"

"You know our dogs are captivated by boxes of all kinds," I reminded Crane. "I stopped Gemmy from eating a bar of Dove soap once. Then I found Misty chewing the box it came in."

"What do you make of your discovery, Fowler?" Crane wanted to know.

"That's easy. I think someone is still living in that house. Maybe one of the people stayed behind."

"Remember we didn't find any working vehicles in Ashton," I reminded him. "Did this person walk miles through the woods to buy a pizza?"

"You can't expect me to find out everything," he said. "You're the famous detective."

"Hardly that."

"If we're ever going to know what's going on in Ashton, we need you," he added.

I swallowed again. Was I completely sure that my throat wasn't sore?

Thirty-two

After we'd finished yesterday's chocolate pie, we moved to the living room with our after-dinner coffee. With a contented sigh, Brent sank into the rocker. Sky lay at his feet and Misty in his lap. None of the pack disputed their shared ownership of Brent, the bringer of treats.

I showed Brent the old calendar.

"That's Nugget, the puppy from the poster!" He held it under the lamp. "Or does it just look like her?"

"They're the same," I said. "The same foxgloves in the background, too."

"This means the rogue group's model is famous."

"Not quite. Look at the date. Two thousand eight."

He stared at the picture. "What the hell?"

"Exactly. The puppy in the poster isn't some waif they rescued last month or even last year. They helped themselves to the picture."

I watched as he put it all together.

"You got them, honey," Crane said.

"Did you ask Byrony out yet?" I asked.

"Not yet. I thought we'd all go out to dinner first and talk about the ghost town."

"Dinner's okay," Crane said, "but what else is there to say about Ashton?"

"Plenty. Did you know that Annica's mosquito bite turned into something worse? She's really worried."

I didn't know that Annica had confided in him. I'll admit I was surprised. She tried to maintain an illusion of perfection in Brent's company.

"You and Crane think the town might be contaminated," he said. "Where else will we find out what happened there and maybe a cure?"

It took me a minute to marshal an argument.

"You're overlooking the fact that there might not be a cure. If there were, Ashton would be a thriving resort town."

"Here's something else," Crane said. "If some sickness infected the townspeople, what's to stop *us* from getting sick?"

Brent nodded. "That's possible. It may already have happened to Annica."

And to him, but misplaced pride kept him from seeing himself as a victim. On the other hand, he'd eaten dinner with his usual enthusiasm for food and hadn't asked for cream of wheat or oatmeal.

"You have a point, Brent," I said. "And I have an idea."

Crane speared Brent with his sharp deputy sheriff's voice. "I won't let you drag Jennet into your latest scheme, Fowler. Besides, Mac Dalby knows about Ashton now. He'll take care of whatever has to be done."

"My idea won't take me any farther afield than the library," I said. "I'm going to do research on contaminants."

"Good luck. There must be millions of them."

"All I need is one. The right one."

"Hope you find it," Brent said. "Oh, if it's okay with you two, dinner's on me tomorrow at the Hunt Club Inn."

At that moment, I remembered. "Sue Appleton is going to call you. She wants you to take her to Ashton."

"There's one more thing to do," he said. "Well, maybe Sue will bring me luck."

~ * ~

The next morning, after taking the dogs a little way up Jonquil Lane, I drove to the Corners and walked to the library under a smoldering sun. It seemed as if the August hot spell was going to last forever, but I knew it would be comfortable inside the old white Victorian with its modern air-conditioning and ceiling fans.

Blackberry the cat dashed across my path out through the open doorway. Foolish creature.

Miss Eidt looked cool and crisp in a mint green dress with the requisite strand of pearls. She glanced up from the book she was reading and set it aside.

"Good morning, Jennet," she said. "I hoped I'd be seeing you today. I have a dozen jelly doughnuts in my office."

It was never too hot for doughnuts and tea. "I have to do some quick research. May I use your vertical file again?"

"Of course. You're the only one who does. Oh, I think I already told you that. Are you still looking up ghost towns?"

"Indirectly."

"Because a brand new book came in on that very subject. *A Guide to Michigan Ghost Towns*. It has some wonderful photographs."

"I'm more interested in contaminants and pollutants today."

"There's no fun in that."

"I guess not."

"That's what we were talking about the other day," she said. "I try not to think about it in the interest of keeping my sanity. Have you read *The Silent Spring*?"

"Yes, years ago."

"Well, I'll leave you to it. I'll get that book for you, and when I'm through, I'll make us a pot of tea."

I let myself into her office and browsed through the vertical file, looking for different folders to search. A sense of urgency tugged at me. I had a feeling that time was running out… not only for me, but for Ashton. Perhaps for the entire world as well.

~ * ~

Contaminants. We couldn't escape them.

They were everywhere. Present in the air we breathed and in our drinking water, creeping insidiously into the very food on our tables.

Oil spills and radioactive waste befouled our lakes and rivers. Harmful chemicals lurked at every corner, even in our medication. You could search for the most pristine, most unviolated place on the planet, and it may still have been subtly altered. Every minute someone, somewhere, launched an attack on the earth, or so it seemed.

That thick juicy steak might well contain a deadly ingredient. What about that glorious basket of just-ripened fruit? That tall glass of water from the tap? Fields of wheat, the apple orchards, the cherry crops. Fish from the lake. Eventual death lay everywhere, often hiding behind a pleasing facade.

The situation was beyond discouraging. What should a concerned citizen do? Surrender to the inevitable, live his life, or fight the slow destruction of our precious earth?

I remembered what the slain animal activist, Caroline Meilland, had said and, years later, repeated by Brent.

Always remember that the least thing you can do can make all the difference to the animals who share the earth with us.

To the animals. To that phrase, I added *to the people and to the earth itself.*

That quote held a message meant for me. I should be doing more to help save the world for the next generation. I should at least be doing my part.

Before I reached the point of being overwhelmed by the many ways in which man laid the world to waste, I found an old, yellowed newspaper clipping. The folder had a curious label, *Essays and True Stories*, which was why I had previously overlooked it.

The title of the article was *The Murder of a Town* by Margaret M. Lawson, reporter for the *Banner*.

When did we realize that our hometown had been murdered?

Slowly. After the fact. Some people never knew. Some didn't remember the day a pilot crashed his plane, losing his life and releasing his cargo of pesticides into the crystalline water of Ashton Lake.

It wasn't until sometime later—years in fact—that a connection was made between the plane crash with its lost load and the high rate of illnesses experienced by the inhabitants of Ashton, Michigan.

Colds and cases of influenza that occurred on a regular basis. Respiratory problems and unexplained rashes plagued the townspeople. An untoward number of people died, supposedly by natural causes...or by causes the doctors couldn't identify. As is usually the case, the youngest and oldest among the population were the most vulnerable.

All this time, the state's government that should have been responsible for the welfare of the people who elected them, concerned itself with other, often trivial matters.

At first and for a long time, rumors spread that the town was unlucky. The superstitious fringe believed in a curse of indeterminate origin. Gradually the feeling spread that Ashton was an unhealthy place to live.

In the early years, no one could have guessed the reason. Those who were financially able to move tried to sell their houses, but who would be foolhardy enough to move into an area that forward-thinking people wanted to leave?

By the time Mason Guilford, teacher of science at Louisa May Alcott Middle School, traced the source of Ashton's woes to the pesticide spill, the town was beyond saving. The last families moved out, leaving behind the ghost of a once vibrant town. It was too late for Ashton. But what about its people?

There followed case histories of three Ashton residents who had been forced to leave the town after a family member had succumbed to the 'Ashton malady.'

Here was the answer then. I made a copy of the article, recalling the story of the plane crash. I, too, had been slow to make a connection.

I looked askance at the box of doughnuts. Surely no contaminant hid inside those glorious exteriors? I *loved* doughnuts.

Don't let yourself be afraid of food, I told myself. *Especially the food you love.*

But there was much to fear.

Thirty-three

"Are you ready for the wedding, Jennet?" Leonora asked.

We sat on her patio under a green-striped umbrella drinking peppermint sun tea. Leonora's collies lay under a tree whose leaves were slowly turning a dark shade of red, the color of Brent's hair.

"I can't decide what jewelry to wear," I said. "I may choose my crystal heart and bracelet."

"That would be lovely," she murmured. "Crystals or rhinestones go well with pale green."

"Are *you* ready?" I asked.

"Pretty much. I made my hair appointment. I still have to check on the cake and flowers. I hope nothing goes wrong."

It was a maid of honor's duty to reassure the bride-to-be. "It won't."

I was picking up the flowers, and Camille was in charge of the wedding cake.

"What if it rains?" she asked. "That's unlucky."

"We can't control the weather," I reminded her. "Anyway, you're marrying the man of your dreams. Sunshine would be nice but not essential."

Unlucky would be a deadly lightning strike or a bride left at the altar or a murder at the wedding, that classic mystery novel dilemma, or...

I brought that train of thought to an abrupt halt.

All of the actors had their costumes, knew their lines, and the wedding was going to go down in history as the premier social highlight of Foxglove Corners.

It was a pleasure to talk about something other than the ghost town.

"What have you been doing?" Leonora asked.

"Some library research and a little sleuthing."

I told her about the stolen picture on the rogue league's poster, and she asked what was new in Ashton.

So much for taking a break from the ghost town.

"It isn't right," she said when I finished. "You're happily living your life, not bothering anyone and a plane crash turns a lake toxic. Then everything changes." She shivered. "Whenever I see a plane in the sky, I say a prayer that it stays there."

I could empathize with Leonora. Ever since the tornado had broken my life in Oakpoint apart, I found myself studying the sky whenever it turned dark during the day.

"Are you going to try to find the people who moved out of Ashton?" she asked.

"I could, but that isn't my first priority. Annica was using a lipstick she found in the town's dime store. Now she has a rash on her arm. I'm hoping to find a way to help her."

I decided not to mention Brent's sore throat, which might have disappeared on its own.

"The rash might be unrelated to the lipstick," Leonora pointed out. "Maybe it's some other skin condition or even an infection. Something curable."

"That would be wonderful," I said. "Anyway, I'm glad the ghost town mystery has been solved."

Do you really think so?

Had I said that aloud or was it my pestiferous inner voice speaking?

"I'm glad, too," Leonora said. "Now you can save all your energy and time for my wedding."

"Absolutely," I said.

The near future for both of us was decided, and at the moment I considered the distant future too far away to fret about.

"Nothing's going to spoil your big day," I said.

~ * ~

Annica was wearing a pretty French blue tunic with long sleeves and teardrop sapphire earrings. She looked beautiful... and unhappy. As she poured my water, I noticed her fingernail polish. Soft blue. Her appearance sent out a clear message.

"Isn't it any better?" I asked.

She sighed. "Not really, and it's on my other arm now, high up. Thank heavens it doesn't show."

"Well, don't despair. I'm going back to Ashton. Maybe this time I'll find a cure."

"We don't even know what caused it," she said.

"True, but I know what happened now. Can you take a short break?"

Instantly her face lit up. She glanced at Marcy who nodded. Marcy was always so agreeable. I'd have to do something nice for her.

"Tell me," Annica said.

"I found an old clipping in Miss Eidt's vertical file..."

As she listened to the tale of a downed plane and a pesticide spill, the light in her eyes dimmed.

"I could have anything under the sun then," she said. "What am I going to do?"

"What you're *not* going to do is give up. The answer may lie in Ashton. Brent is looking for a cure, too."

"You said you were through with the ghost town," she said. "Crane thinks you are."

"I changed my mind."

Marcy stopped by the table. "Can I get you two something to drink?"

"Please," Annica murmured. "Is iced tea all right, Jennet? I owe you, Marcy," she added.

"I'm afraid to go back to Ashton," she admitted. "I might pick up something worse."

"You don't have to. Just try to be positive and let your friends help you."

~ * ~

Sue Appleton was an enthusiastic addition to our team. By then, Brent knew the way to Ashton by heart, and we arrived at the bridge before noon. It was another in the never-ending string of hot and humid August days.

The abandoned stores on Main Street unfolded before us in a rolling haze. From the Forever Diner beyond them rose the houses at the edge of the street and a glimpse of the lake.

That beautiful lake that had always seemed too deep a shade of blue to be natural. The toxic lake. Had the pesticides ever been removed from the water? I wondered. Could that even be done? For that matter, was the plane still there, leaking its poisons into the lake and the adjacent town?

"It's just the way you described it, Jennet," Sue said. "I feel like I'm about to step into another world." She pulled her pink sun hat lower over her strawberry blonde bangs.

"Ground rules," Brent announced. "Whatever you do, don't touch anything. Not even a stone or flower. Keep your eye peeled to the ground. Annica almost stepped on a snake. Don't wander off on your own. And you may see a figure in a long black cloak. Lucy did."

"Good grief, Jennet, you didn't say anyone lived here."

"We don't know for sure that he does, or even that he exists," I said.

"Oh, and I almost forgot the dog," Brent added. "He's aggressive, but if you don't bother him, he should leave you alone."

Anyone listening to us would think we were crazy to come willingly to this place.

"Aye, Captain," Sue said. "Noted and agreed. I loaded up on Vitamin C this morning," she added. "Just in case."

"Okay, let's roll."

He drove the vintage Plymouth across the bridge into the town and parked in front of the Forever Diner. I knew what I was searching for and was aware of the stakes, but how to proceed eluded me.

The cure?

I was imagining those old mystery staples, a journal or a diary. Failing that, a newspaper clipping that hadn't seemed worth keeping in the library file. Perhaps another true account by a reporter. Letters. An album or scrapbook, maybe?

The best place to search for this kind of evidence would one of the many untenanted houses.

Thirty-four

As we headed down Main Street, once again doubts about our search began to taunt me. Looking for a cure to an unidentified illness, perhaps a new strain borne of the pesticide spill?

It turns mosquitoes green and renders them incapable of flying. It turns humans red and ultimately kills them...

Ours was a next-to-impossible undertaking.

I shook off the bizarre thoughts. My inner voice woke up and yawned.

Admit it, Jennet, you're not one hundred percent altruistic. You just don't want the adventure to end.

What an awful accusation! If it weren't for Annica's distress, I would be happy never to enter this accursed town again. It could keep its secrets.

We passed the dime store which looked innocuous, not unlike any dollar store in the 'outside' world. Sue stopped to peer in at the window display. It was decidedly, genuinely, vintage.

"Is this where Annica found the bad lipstick?" she asked.

"That's the place."

Where I'd seen a bottle of wood violet toilet water and made a snap decision to buy it.

"We'll give it a wide berth then," Sue said.

"It's hot already." Brent mapped his forehead and looked longingly at the sheen of blue barely visible through the light haze. "That lake water would sure feel good. Too bad it's poison."

"It's weird not to hear a single sound," Sue said. "Not even a bird chirruping."

I had to agree, but I was used to the unearthly silence of the town.

"Either the birds all died off or they know better than to fly over forbidden territory," I said.

"Remind me," she added. "What exactly are we looking for?"

"Anything written by a resident."

"Got it."

"Let's start here." Brent pointed to a one-story beige bungalow rising out of a field of waist high grasses. The very walkway was covered by invasive ivy. I stepped carefully to avoid tripping in the wandering vines.

"Something written," Sue murmured when we were inside. "How about this calendar?"

It hung on a kitchen wall. August's illustration was a prosaic basket of sunflowers. Each day had been X'ed out in black magic marker except for the twenty-seventh. In that space were two words: Last Day.

Yes." I pulled my notebook out of my pocket. "I'm assuming the people in this house left on that day."

The large room contained minimum furniture: two chairs and a matching sofa with twin end tables on either side. There was an unplugged floor lamp and a square of space on the wall where a picture had been.

One of the tables had three drawers. I opened each one. All empty except for shelf paper. This job was going to take forever and, in the end, might prove futile. Oh, well, a tedious and dusty search was the only way to achieve our goal.

~ * ~

No one wanted to have a picnic on the beach. Knowing what had happened in the lake detracted notably from its allure.

Without one of Annica's custom Clovers baskets, our choices were skimpy. Brent had made three sandwiches with stacks of lunch meat piled between slices of plain white bread. We sat on the steps of the next house on our list, devouring the unappetizing fare quickly, anxious to return to our search.

As I ate, I intercepted the surreptitious glances Sue cast at Brent. Not another conquest for the flamboyant lord of the manor! On second thought, why should I be surprised? Few women, no matter what their age, could resist Brent.

"Is everyone done eating?" he asked.

Sue looked with yearning toward the door. "I suppose the water is shut off."

"You suppose right. Anyway, you wouldn't want to drink it."

"All of a sudden I'm *so* thirsty."

"That lunch meat was on the salty side," I said. "What was it, Brent?"

"Olive loaf, I think. I have a six pack of root beer in the trunk, but it'll be warm."

That sounded about as appealing as the sandwiches. Really, I should have packed lunches for us with bottled water.

"Don't think about it, Sue," I said.

Brent rose and gathered discarded bags and plastic wrap. We'd agreed not to leave anything behind in Ashton… nor take anything away from it.

"Let's try the house across the street," Brent said.

The door was ajar, a sign that the inhabitants had considered it futile to lock the house. Inside on an otherwise bare table sat a liter bottle of Pepsi-Cola with the cap missing.

"What the heck?" Sue said.

I touched it and instinctively drew my hand away. "It's cold. Ice cold."

As cold as if it had just been taken out of the refrigerator, which, in this town, was an impossibility. About a quarter of the drink was gone.

"Is this the house where you found the pizza box, Brent?" I asked.

"No, that was on the other side of town."

"We're not alone in Ashton," I said. "Lucy was right. There are at least two people roaming around."

"I think I know what happened." Brent hurried through house. We followed, coming to a small landing at the end of three steps. A door led to the outside. It was also ajar.

"He must have seen us coming and took off," Brent said. "I don't see anyone now."

"That sounds likely, but why would he leave his drink?" I asked.

Brent took the bottle from my hand and stared at it. "Who the hell are these people? We don't see them, we don't hear them, but they're here, leaving their stuff."

"Skulking in the shadows," I added. "Why the compulsion to keep out of sight? They have as much right to be here as we do."

"What do you mean?" Sue asked.

"We're all interlopers."

She reached for the liter, kept her hand on it. "This feels divine. I love Pepsi. I wish I dared..."

"Don't even think about it, Sue. You might as well drink water from the lake."

"I know. But there's a chance it's okay."

Nonetheless, she replaced the bottle on the table.

Suddenly I had a good feeling about our day's expedition. One discovery might well lead to another. I wondered if the Pepsi's owner would return...if he was even now watching us from an unseen vantage point. Would we ever see him? And would he be wearing a black cloak in this heat?

Whatever the outcome, we were ready to move on. Across the street.

~ * ~

It was a young girl's bedroom, pink with white French Empire furniture. The room was dark with low-growing branches cutting off the sunlight. The twin bed had been stripped and a small bookcase swept clear of books, but several dolls were crammed into an open toy chest. The curtains, once white and ruffle-edged, were yellowish and topped with cobwebs.

The room had been deserted for a long time.

In the top drawer of the single nightstand lay a book that had been apparently overlooked when its owner emptied the drawers. A blue unicorn and gilt lettering graced the cover: *My Diary*. Exactly what I had hoped to find... and never thought I would.

This wasn't the first time a diary or journal had helped me unravel a puzzling mystery, revealing facts I couldn't have otherwise known. In the case of the ghost town, a written record was a necessity.

But how strange to leave something so personal behind.

I flipped through the small book. The pages were covered with writing in turquoise ink and tiny pencil sketches that were drawn quite skillfully. This wasn't as valuable as an adult's diary would be, but it was more than we'd found to date.

"I found a diary," I announced.

Brent and Sue joined me in the bedroom before the echo of my voice died away.

"Finally," Sue said. "Let's read it right away."

Why not? We'd read it and leave it here, as agreed.

"Out in the sun, though," I said. "It's too dark inside."

We returned to the porch and made ourselves as comfortable as possible on the jagged-edged wooden steps. I opened the diary to the first page.

"It belonged to a girl named Dorinda," I said. *"Dorinda's Diary."*

Thirty-five

July 28—I felt sick this morning and now I'm stuck in bed. Mom bought me this diary and told me write a few sentences every day. She said this is a crucial time but didn't say why. I'll start tomorrow.

July 29—My name is Dorinda Jane Stockwell and I live in Ashton with my mother and dad and little brother, David. I like to swim and go camping in the summer and in the winter we go ice skating on the lake. I also like to read and draw. When I grow up, I'm going to be an artist. I already have my art school picked out.

July 30--I read The Sign of the Twisted Candles today but now my head hurts. I don't know what's wrong with me.

August 3—Still sick. Mom brought me a heating pad. I'm supposed to put it on top of my pillow and lie on it. She called the doctor, but he didn't come. His nurse said he's out of town. When I try to get out of bed and walk, I get dizzy.

August 4—Nothing to write about. Just I'm <u>so</u> thirsty. I wanted a drink of water but Mom brought me a glass of orange juice instead. She says we shouldn't drink the water.

August 5—I'm so tired of lying in bed. "Here's a game you can play," Mom said. "Pretend the whole family is moving to Mars. You can take all your clothes but only ten of your personal possessions. Which ones will you choose? They should be light enough for you to carry."

I have to think about this.

August 6—Here is my list. My cross and chain, ruby ring, charm bracelet, Grandma's music box, Teddy's picture, Easter bunny figurine, skates, my camera, photo album, sketch book with pencils. Each one is light. I packed them in a tote. The album and sketch box are the heaviest, but I can carry them.

August 8—I don't have anything to write about, so I'll draw the unicorn on the cover.

August 9—We have an appointment next week with a new doctor in another town. I hope he can fix whatever's wrong with me. I'd give anything to go swimming. Mom says I'm too weak. She made pancakes for breakfast and brought me mine on a tray. They tasted different.

August 10—We're going to move. Dad told me this morning. I asked him when. He said before school starts. I don't want to leave Kathy and Marjorie but it turns out I won't have to. The Simmonses are moving, too. Nobody will tell me where we're going. Mom said they don't know yet. Maybe up north somewhere. I asked Aunt Brenda, who's going with us, where we were moving to. "Away," she said. "Just away."

August 11—Mom and Dad are talking in the kitchen. I can't make out what they're saying. I thought about getting out of bed and eavesdropping but I'm too tired.

~ * ~

Lightning flashed in the sky. Startled, I look up from the page. The sky had darkened. The smell of rain hung in the air. I studied the clouds, remembering the weather forecast. Late afternoon rain, heavy at times. But it was hardly late afternoon.

"Where the heck did that come from?" Sue asked, rising. "We'd better get inside."

"No way." Brent pushed the door shut. "I don't like the looks of that sky. Let's hightail it back to the car."

I looked upward, always on the alert for a developing funnel cloud. So far I didn't see anything to worry about. The suddenness of the storm was a red flag, though.

"Wait!" I winced as a high wind whipped the tall grasses back and forth. A branch sailed through the air, and raindrops landed on my arm.

"What?" Brent was already on the sidewalk.

"Should I put the diary back? We weren't going to take anything out of Ashton, remember."

"Change of plans. You only started reading. Here's our chance to know what happened."

"I'd like to know why Dorinda didn't take her diary with her," Sue said.

I slipped the little book into my pocket. "Okay. I don't suppose one little thing will hurt."

"It's pretty much a coincidence, that diary just lying there, waiting for us to find it," Sue said.

She was right, but there was no time to think about it. Chalk it up to one more ghost town mystery. "Let's hurry then."

We hadn't gotten much farther than Main Street before the cloud burst. In the short distance to the Forever Diner where Brent had left the Plymouth, rain pelted us, and the wind whipped us along as if we were as light as the overgrown grass in front of Dorinda's house. I felt vulnerable, felt that the wind could blow me off my feet, and there was nothing to grab onto.

Brent reached the car first and held the door open for us.

"Is it safe driving in a storm?" Sue asked. "There are all those trees that could come down."

"I'm not going to be a sitting duck. We'll take a chance. Get in."

With no further conversation, he sped over the bridge, and we raced down the narrow road that led away from Ashton while lightning fired the sky.

"It's like the town chased us away," Sue said.

Her fanciful comment fitted with a vague notion that had been lurking at the edge of my subconscious mind.

"Yes," I said, "we're getting too close to the secret."

It was pure fancy. No one, certainly not a town, controlled the weather.

Brent swerved to avoid a rock that had somehow rolled to the middle of the road. "Well, we have the diary."

I only hoped the secret lay hidden in Dorinda Stockwell's sickbed ramblings.

She would be an adult now, that is, if she had survived the malady that had decimated her town. Where had the family gone? Along with Sue, I wondered why Dorinda hadn't taken her diary with her.

The storm had turned into light rain by the time we reached Foxglove Corners. Brent turned onto Jonquil Lane and parked the Plymouth behind my car.

Home. Safe. The town had gotten rid of us.

Collie faces appeared in the window. Candy, Misty, Halley... Raven ventured out of her house and dashed up to greet us. Her paws were muddy, and rain water flew off her coat. There was enough barking inside the house for twenty dogs.

"Everyone, come in," I said. "I made a big pot of beef stew yesterday. We can wait for Crane and all eat together. Then we'll finish reading the diary."

Quickly I reviewed the food items on hand. I had plenty of salad makings, and I'd bake cornbread muffins.

Meanwhile, the collies outdid themselves to be charming. Even Sky emerged from her safe place under the dining room table. Misty ran out of the living room and returned with her toy goat while Halley offered her paw to Sue.

They had been alone, left in Camille's care all day, but all was forgiven. We were home, and good times and treats were guaranteed.

Gradually they settled down and Misty claimed her place on Brent's lap, which enchanted Sue.

"I wish I had a picture of that," she said.

"I have one," I told her.

"Do we have to wait for Crane?" she asked. "He didn't hear the beginning."

"I guess he can read through it by himself," I said.

Crane. It occurred to me that he had no idea where I'd gone today. He thought I'd ended my association with Ashton.

Oh, well, he'd be happy to know I'd found a diary written by one of the residents. Wouldn't he?

I made my guests comfortable with sandwiches and coffee and opened the diary.

"When we left off, Dorinda's parents were talking in the kitchen. If only she hadn't been too tired to get out of bed and listen."

Tiredness was a symptom of Dorinda's illness, along with headache and vertigo. 'I felt sick' was vague. Sick in what way? Was it the sort of illness that causes unspecified aches before it announces itself? Was it debilitating enough to keep a young girl in her bed on a summer day?

I glanced at the page and turned to the next one. "All right," I said. "The next two entries aren't words. They're drawings. The second one was done in colored pencil. "

I handed the diary to Sue who passed it to Brent.

On one page, Dorinda had drawn a rocket ship. (To Mars?) It looked like an illustration from a science-fiction movie, circa 1950. The other page contained a depiction of a rather ugly woman with a tall peaked hat and long black cloak.

"Nice," Sue murmured. "She was talented."

Apparently seeing what I saw, Brent said, "Since when do witches wear cloaks?"

Thirty-six

A witch in a black cloak? While it wasn't traditional witch garb, why not?

"Maybe this is just a drawing," I said. "The artist figured that a black cloak would complete the picture."

Sue finally grasped the significance. "That means the cloaked figure that Lucy saw was prowling around the town in Dorinda's time. Do you think witches were responsible for the sickness that ran through the town?"

That was too far a reach.

"We know what caused the sickness," I said. "The pesticide spill. There was nothing supernatural about it."

Brent studied the drawing in the diary, a frown on his face. "This doesn't look like any witch I've ever seen."

He couldn't have meant that, and I couldn't resist teasing him.

"Do you see many witches, Brent?"

He had a ready answer. "At Halloween, sure. Everybody does. They're all over the place. You were a witch at Miss Eidt's Halloween party."

I nodded, remembering. I'd been a glamorous witch, though, and not, I trusted, as hideous as the one depicted in the diary.

"It stands to reason that Dorinda knew what a witch looked like," I said. "Except for the cloak. I'll admit that's strange."

I couldn't recall ever seeing anybody, male or female, wearing a cloak except on stage during a play.

"I've been wondering if what Lucy saw was a ghost," Brent said. "Nobody else saw that figure."

For some reason I'd never considered that possibility. Where would a witch-ghost be more comfortable than in a ghost town? At one point, Lucy had been afraid that her powers had deserted her, but that couldn't apply in this case. Besides, *I* was the one who saw ghosts, and I'd been walking alongside Lucy the day she saw the cloaked figure.

"Let's get back to the written entries," Sue said.

"Yeah, before the sheriff comes home." Brent looked a trifle uneasy, which was unusual for him. He added, "He's going to blame me for taking you back to Ashton."

"Nonsense," I said. "You didn't kidnap me. And Crane will be excited about our find."

I hoped.

"Let's see if we can finish reading the diary before he gets home," I said. "Then we can give him a summary of the contents if he doesn't want to read it."

I turned the page. "We're still in August. Let's see what happens to Dorinda next."

August 15—I'm afraid I'm going miss the whole summer. I don't feel any better, but the new doctor says there's nothing wrong with me. He gave me a bottle of nasty tasting tonic to drink. It isn't helping. I'm not going to drink it anymore.

August 16—Mom gave me a little white kitten today. She said, "I found her lying in the garden all alone, and she came to me when I brought her a saucer of milk. I think she was sent to keep you company." I named her Cottonball.

August 17—Mornings are the best time of the day. I started reading The Whispering Statue. It isn't as good as The Sign of the Twisted Candles. I'd rather be swimming. Aunt Brenda came over in the afternoon with a chocolate cake. I forgot. Today is my birthday. *How could I forget that? The book was my present. Mom says we'll have a real celebration in our new house. I asked her where it was. She said, "In Alpena, Michigan. Your aunt is moving in with us until she finds a place of her own."*

August 18—I looked Alpena up in the Atlas. It's way up north. The Simmonses haven't found a house yet.

August 19—The news is bad. Aunt Bremda died. I don't know why. I don't understand. She wasn't sick. Mom cries all the time. I heard her tell Dad that we have to get away from here.

August 20—I dreamed I was swimming in our lake all by myself. It was a nice dream. Over too soon. I'm so hot I could die. Cottonball stays close to me. I'm so glad I have her.

August 21—I drew a picture of Aunt Brenda this morning. I don't ever want to forget her.

August 23—Mom says Marjorie is sick, too, and Kathy can't visit me.

August 24—David is gone. Mom sent him to her cousin in Foxglove Corners for a vacation. We'll pick him up on our way to our new home.

August 26th—I want Teddy.

I turned another page, then another.

"She started drawing instead of writing," I said, flipping through the pictures. "She drew one of her aunt. How pretty she was! And the kitten, Cottonball. The beach, the way it looks today without any swimmers or sunbathers. There's a sketch of her house. A car."

I passed the diary to Brent. "It looks like my Plymouth!"

"I wonder who Teddy was," Sue said. "She doesn't say. A boy she liked? Another pet? A Teddy Bear?"

"We don't know, but Teddy's picture is one of the possessions she was going to take to Mars."

Dorinda seemed to be an unusual girl. We didn't even know her age, but I'd guess she was twelve or thirteen.

Sue and Brent didn't seem to be particularly moved by that last entry, but I found it sad. Dorinda wanted Teddy. Had anybody given it (him) to her? Last wishes should be granted if possible, and I was certain that Dorinda had passed away. The rest of the pages were blank.

"This doesn't tell us much," Sue said. "One person died, and Dorinda's friend was sick, too."

"There was one death that we know of," I added. "Dorinda couldn't know what was happening in the town." I closed the diary, considering how to apply its revelations to the mystery. "The family was moving to Alpena. I should see if there are any Stockwells living in the area."

"Her clothes were gone and everything else except this diary," Brent said. "I wonder if we're right that she died."

"Who knows? If Dorinda were my daughter, I wouldn't leave her possessions behind."

"We still haven't found a cure," he said. "I say we try to search the doctor's house or office. His nurse claimed he was out of town. Maybe he didn't plan on coming back to avoid dealing with the sickness and left his records behind."

The cure. That was what kept luring us back to Ashton in spite of the unlikelihood of its existence. Fortunately, Annica's rash sounded nothing like whatever had ailed Dorinda. On the other hand, Dorinda's aunt had died, apparently without being sick.

"How can we tell which house belonged to the doctor?" I asked.

"Simple. We have to search all of them again. This time we'll look for medical stuff like a plastic skull or skeleton."

"I was surprised we were able to enter Ashton today," I said. "I expected yellow caution tape to block us. Crane was going to tell Lieutenant Dalby, who would inform the authorities. If that happened, it appears that Ashton isn't as important to them as it is to us."

"That's good. For us. Hey, then we have more time to look around. I keep thinking about a big gray house I saw. It was so cluttered inside that I didn't spend much time there. I'd like to go back."

"If we *do* go back, I'll return the diary," I said.

A car door slammed. As if they'd suddenly grown wings, the dogs flew to the back of the house to wait for Crane to open the side door. Even Misty leaped down from Brent's lap to follow the pack. Together they created an unearthly amount of racket.

When you live with dogs you can count on a raucous welcome home.

"We have company for dinner," I told Crane as he appeared in the midst of jumping collies with wagging tails.

He locked his gun in the cabinet. "This looks like a conspiracy. What's up?"

"We found a young girl's diary in Ashton," I said.

He looked at me.

"I've been reading it out loud. The girl who wrote in it was sick. It's possible she died."

All he said was, "That's a deadly town."

"It isn't off-limits, is it?" Brent asked.

"No. I don't know if it will be."

He sat beside Brent as the dogs, calmer, drifted back.

"So what's new on the roads?" Brent asked.

"Not much," Crane said. "It was a quiet day."

I rose. "I'd better get dinner together."

"I'll help you," Sue said.

There wasn't much to do. While I heated the stew, I mixed the muffin batter. Sue began tearing lettuce leaves for a salad.

"I guess we'll be going to back to Ashton," she said.

I nodded. "As long as we can.'"

"It can't be tomorrow. We have the collie auction."

Thinking it was later in the week, I glanced at the kitchen calendar. No, Sue was right. It was tomorrow, and I remembered Annica saying she had to work at Clovers that day."

"I hope we finally meet up with Ann Clarke."

"Don't count on it," I said. "I don't think there is such a person."

Thirty-seven

Handmade signs posted on trees served as a guide to Chanticleer Farm where the rogue rescue league was hosting the summer auction.

Sue read: "*Five Miles to Collie Auction.* They want to make sure nobody gets lost."

"That's a good idea. It'd be easy to do."

I glanced to my right. Farmland baking in the sun, no houses in sight. To the left, the same. Another sign warned *Deer X-ing.* We were in unfamiliar territory, and the road, North Lyon, was deeply rutted.

"Hold onto your hat." I slowed for a mammoth depression that stretched across most of the road but still managed to give the Focus a thorough shaking. I hoped the tires would stay attached.

"My hat's in my lap, not on my head," Sue said. "And this road is a nightmare."

"There's another sign. *Keep Going Straight—You're Almost There.*"

"How cute," she said. "I hope the elusive Ann Clarke makes an appearance today. I know you don't think she exists, but for the life of me, I can't see the point of having a make-believe woman in the group."

"We don't know enough about them yet."

Before we'd parted yesterday, Brent had announced his intention of inviting Byrony Limon to have dinner with him at the Hunt Club Inn the next day. He was going to present her with a bouquet of roses which, combined with his legendary charm, should turn her head and inspire her to confide in him. Meeting Ann Clarke and finding out the purpose for the extraneous rescue group topped his agenda.

Sue gasped. "Jennet! Look out!"

A black spotted dog running free dashed across my path. Instinctively I braked, praying the car would stop in time. Miraculously it did. The dog cleared the road and bounded off into the brush. But my heart was pounding, and I'd veered too far to the right, squashing a lovely patch of purple coneflowers. Fortunately mine was the only vehicle on the road.

"That was close." I straightened the car and drove at a slower speed than usual. "People think because they live in the country their dogs are safe. My dogs don't run free."

"Neither do mine."

"Well, except for Raven," I added.

We'd never been able to leash our bi-black collie or even keep her in the house unless she wanted to be with us.

That was, of course, a lame excuse. If some motorist were to run over her…

Don't think about that. Not now.

Raven preferred roaming in the woods to crossing roads. All I could do was try to convince her that home was best and leashes were good. And I'd better do it soon.

The next sign caught and held the sun's rays with its splatter of glitter. It instructed us to *Turn Right*. A few miles down a road in even worse condition than Lyon brought us to Chanticleer Farm— and another sign, this one permanent.

CHANTICLEER FARM CIDER MILL

Apples. Cider. Doughnuts. Apple Pies. Fudge. Antiques

"It's a multi-purpose enterprise," Sue said.

It was bustling with activity. A sprawling red farmhouse sat back from the driveway with a large barn, also red, far to the left. It seemed to want to distance itself from the house. People milled around the auction tables set out in front of the barn, and red, white, and blue balloons splashed patriotic colors in the still air.

Outside the air-conditioned car, the heat struck us with full force. Sue tied the ribbon of her hat under her chin, and I draped a sheer blouse over my tank top to ward off the sun's rays.

"We'll have to come back next month," I said, imagining the first ripe apples of the season and cold cider.

I wished I had a drink of cider now, I thought, as we blended into the crowd.

"Maple-nut Fudge," Sue murmured. "That's my favorite. I haven't thought about fudge all summer."

While we were here on behalf of our rescue league, I was eager to explore the collie wares. Byrony Limon sat at a prominent table signing her books. Aside from her, I didn't see any members of the rogue league, but several women dressed in black circulated through the crowd. They must be Byrony's minions. Could one of them be the mysterious Ann Clarke?

Sue wandered over to talk to Byrony while I examined the books on another table, all of them about collies.

It was an impressive collection: Albert Payson Terhune classics like *Bruce* and *Treve* with smudged covers and yellowing wartime paper, stacks of collie-themed periodicals from previous years, more copies of Byrony's *Heart of Lassie*, and books for young readers featuring Lassie in dozens of harrowing adventures. I could happily drown in the wave of literature devoted to my breed.

Sue came up behind me holding a figurine, a standing tricolor with a remarkably realistic face for a china collie. "It's seventy-five dollars. What do you think?"

"That you should buy it. Where did you find it?"

"Over here." She led me to a table nearest the barn where a sign cautioned prospective buyers not to touch the merchandise. "That white puppy looks like your Misty."

Luckily I'd brought my credit card.

"Oh, look at that!" She pointed to a collie figurine on top of a music box. According to a tag on top, it played the theme song from the old *Lassie* television show.

Lucky indeed. "That's mine," I said, taking possession of the music box.

"You'd better see if it works first."

"Good idea." I turned the key and the familiar tune tinkled out into the air.

"That's a marvelous find," Sue said. "Let's see what's in the barn."

There, more people were crammed into a dim place that smelled faintly of hay and apple. They were snapping up collie items while black clad League members kept a hawk eye on them.

Brent Fowler stood out from the crowd with his dark red hair and forest green shirt. He saw us and waved, and we headed toward one another. He was eating a hot dog and had a shopping bag with the League's logo emblazoned on it in his free hand.

"They put together a nice selection," he announced. "If they sell out, they'll make a mint."

"What did you buy?" Sue asked.

"Notecards and stuff for gifts. One of Byrony's books. Gotta get on her good side."

"Did you see anyone familiar?" I added.

"Just Byrony. Other than that, no. This is a different bunch of people from the ones that were at the meeting. They look like a bunch of crows."

He'd raised his voice and garnered curious looks from a pair of elderly shoppers. He intercepted them with a wide smile.

"The rogue league must be larger than we thought," I said. "I wonder if one of the ladies in black is Ann Clarke."

"I don't think so," he said. "They wear name tags. You have to get close to read them. Hey, are you girls hungry? The hot dogs are great. My treat."

Sue nodded. "Now that you mention it, a little."

I wasn't. We had stopped for a quick breakfast at Clovers. At eleven o'clock I couldn't look mustard in the face. They should have set up an indoor café with mid-morning tea and muffins. Then I'd be interested.

"You two go ahead," I said. "I'm going to look around."

Left to my own devices, I discovered a display of collie cookies with tinted frosting for distinctive markings. What wonderful Christmas presents they'd make! Now where could I find a custom cookie cutter?

I saw the dog meandering down the makeshift aisle. She was a sable collie, older, with white around her eyes and muzzle, and she resembled the dog from the calendar. Had I been wrong in assuming that one of the rogues had stolen her picture?

I stared at her. It was hard to visualize the winsome puppy grown into a mature dog. But I had a feeling… I did a swift calculation. The dog was about the right age.

Her collar jingled merrily, but she wasn't dragging a leash, and I couldn't see an owner with her. I followed her progress as she came to a stop in front of the cookie table where she lingered, eying the baked treats with that irresistible begging gaze that hardly ever fails. She licked her chops.

I wished I could buy a cookie for her, but I didn't. I'd never let my dogs accept food from a stranger. Still, she desperately wanted a bite, the perennial hungry collie, and she was unsupervised.

That doesn't matter. Do what's right.

I turned away for a minute. In that sliver of time, she was gone.

As I looked for Sue and Brent in the crush, I noticed an attractive woman wearing jeans and a bright red sweater. She was coming toward me, walking rapidly. She wasn't wearing a name tag.

I knew her!

From somewhere. I'd seen her somewhere. Where?

I gave her a tentative smile.

She ignored me and vanished in the crowd streaming through the barn door.

I almost followed her, but what would that accomplish? Instead, I tried to remember where I had seen her. Not recently. She wasn't anyone I knew well. But I felt certain that she had once walked in and out of my life, wearing that same red sweater or one like it.

At a meeting of our league, maybe, when I'd first become a member?

Could it be Ann Clarke?

I made my way to the door and scanned the immediate area, but, like the calendar collie, she was gone.

Thirty-eight

Brent and Sue were sitting on a bench still eating their hot dogs... or maybe they were different ones. I walked up to them.

"Did you see a collie without a leash wandering around the barn?" I asked.

"A couple of them," Sue said. "A sable and a tri."

"I think the sable looks like the collie on the calendar, Nugget."

"It's a good idea to show people where their money's going," Brent said. "Collies are a draw."

He had missed the point. "I accused them of stealing that picture to use on their poster, but maybe someone in the group owns Nugget."

"How can you possibly tell if it's the same dog?" Sue asked. "The calendar girl was a puppy."

"It's just a feeling." I knew I sounded like Lucy, but that was all right. I couldn't think of a better role model.

"If the rogue league had been in existence ten or eleven years ago, I would have heard of it," Sue said.

Or, during my shorter sojourn in Foxglove Corners, I would have come across them before.

"I'm not saying the group is that old," I said. "Just that I may have seen the real Nugget when she was a puppy."

"Sure you won't have a hot dog, Jennet?" Brent asked.

"Thanks, Brent, but no."

I would have liked something lighter like a chicken salad sandwich with lettuce on white bread, a lunch you'd more likely find at Clovers.

"I want to look around," I said. "Maybe I can find something else to buy."

Brent had the right idea. It was months until Christmas, but all of my friends had collies and would appreciate a collie-themed present like the Lassie music box. This one was for me.

I had almost forgotten to ask them about the woman in the red sweater.

"I thought I saw someone I recognized," I said. "Did either of you see anyone familiar?"

"Not me." Having finished his hot dog, Brent looked for a waste container. Spying one, he walked away from us for a few minutes.

"Where do you think you know this woman from?" Sue asked.

"I have no idea. I tried to catch her eye, smile at her, but she just walked past me."

"It'll come to you," Sue said. "Or not. Lots of people look alike. They say everybody has a double somewhere in the world."

I didn't believe that. Surely not everybody. But I had another feeling. Knowing who the woman in the red sweater was could be important.

Was she Ann Clarke? Probably not. I was convinced there was no Ann Clarke, although why the rogue people said there was escaped me.

I made a final sweep through the auction, ending up at the collie book table, and added Terhune's *Treve* to my collection. I didn't have that one. Then I visited other displays, buying my gifts.

I looked for Nugget again but didn't see her. I hoped her owner had showed up and bought her one of the cookies she'd longed for. And speaking of cookies... I went back to the barn and bought a dozen for myself. Purely in the interest of copying them in my own kitchen. Honestly.

~ * ~

The heat wrapped itself around us as we left the cool comfort of the barn with its many fans circulating the air. We stood together in the lot of Chanticleer Farm, laden with our purchases and ready to go home.

"This was a perfect day," Sue said.

"Not as exciting as a day in a ghost town, though," Brent countered.

"We'll have to go back soon to Ashton soon," I said. "I don't know when these so-called 'proper authorities' are going to make their move."

"If ever. It's like what's happening with those unfinished French mansions off Jonquil Lane."

We had tried to get rid of them. "We should revive our petition to raze the whole development and not let anything interfere with it this time," I said.

"Maybe next spring. No one's going to do anything about it in the winter."

"How about scheduling another trip to the ghost town tomorrow?" Brent asked.

"Oh, I can't," Sue said. "I have two riding students. When school starts, I'll have mornings free."

"And when school starts, I'll be in my classroom all day, but I can go tomorrow."

"I keep thinking about the house I want to explore," Brent said. "Our new goal is to find the doctor's office and look for his files or something. See you tomorrow, Jennet."

On that note, we parted.

"I wonder if there's any chance of wrapping up the mystery this month," I said, as I drove out to the road in Brent's wake.

~ * ~

Sue's perfect day ended on a somber note. Sometime during the hours we'd been at the auction, Echo had disappeared. I couldn't understand how it had happened. Sue was always so careful with her animals. And that it had happened to Echo, the collie we all thought was too beautiful to end up in a shelter. I'd suspected from the first there something mysterious about her.

"How could that happen?" I asked.

"Somebody unlocked my front door and took her from the house."

"Wait! Wasn't the door locked?"

"I kept a spare key under my birdbath," she said. "The key is gone."

"I can't imagine separating Echo from Icy and Blueberry. They would have raised a fuss."

"They were anxious when I came home. I could tell something was wrong. Bluebell tried to leave the house. I wouldn't let her.

"Who knew where you kept the key?" I asked.

"No one."

Well, somebody had known or gotten lucky when searching for one.

"We were gone five hours," I said. "That was plenty of time for anything to happen. But how would anybody know you'd be gone so long?

"I don't know."

"They must have worked quickly."

"I guess." Sue wasn't her usual sharp self. I supposed she was still in shock at having her home invaded and a collie under her care snatched by an unknown dognapper.

I knew where all of my dogs were but had to count them again. Raven had come dashing out to meet me when I came home. From the sofa, Misty and Candy sat side by side watching the activity, or lack thereof, on the lane. Gemmy, Halley, and Star were in the kitchen waiting for dinner, and Sky was under the dining room table. All accounted for. All safe. This time.

What happened to Sue's collie could happen to me or anyone, although I never left a house key in an outside hiding place.

"I drove all around looking for Echo," Sue said. "Then I called the police and Lila Woodville at the Animal Shelter and every shelter I could think of. It's like she vanished into thin air."

In Foxglove Corners, home of the strange, that was a logical first explanation. However, in Sue's case, her house had been entered illegally and Echo taken out of it.

"Let's go out and look for her again," I said. "If we don't have luck, I'll help you make 'Lost Dog' posters.

"Stolen dog. Lieutenant Dalby stopped by," she added.

"This sounds personal to me, Sue," I said. "It's a direct attack. If you want to hurt somebody, the best way is to hurt your dog. Now, who are your enemies?"

Thirty-nine

Sue continued to look for Echo, covering the same territory three times. She mobilized her riding students to post 'Stolen Dog' flyers around town. It seemed as if the collie had been spirited away and well hidden. Meanwhile, Sue had her locks changed and hid spare keys inside the ranch house. She couldn't give me the name of a single enemy.

"I'm nice," she insisted. "I live a quiet life and never hurt anyone."

"I wish I could say that. I have enemies galore."

"That's funny. You live quietly and try to help anyone in trouble, especially collies."

"I suppose the few villains I've brought to justice might conceivably hold a grudge against me."

"What do you suppose whoever took Echo will do to her?" she asked.

I didn't want to plant disturbing images in Sue's head.

"First we have to find out who stole her and why. I think the culprit wants you to know he has her."

"He or she. We can't be sure. But then why doesn't he send me a ransom note?"

I couldn't answer that. In any event, I didn't think the dognapper wanted money. From the first, I'd felt that the theft of

Echo was a personal blow directed at Sue. Sometime, somewhere, she would have had to antagonize somebody. Everybody did.

With time and luck, Sue would remember a past incident that could have inspired this attack. Either that or Echo had dropped into one of the black holes that were as common as ponds in Foxglove Corners.

But I didn't believe that. Not this time.

Crane promised to watch for Echo as he navigated the roads and byroads on his shifts. As I couldn't think of anything further I could do to bring Echo home, I went ahead with plans to visit Ashton again the next day, packing sandwiches and bottled water.

I had wondered if we could wrap up our two mysteries before the end of the month. Impossible goals. Now we had a third one.

~ * ~

It seemed that the sun was always shining on Ashton, hot rays burning down on unprotected heads, chasing secrets out of hiding, luring parched wayfarers to the cool water of Ashton Lake.

Neither Brent nor I were tempted to wander on the beach today. Brent had brought along bottled water, too. I hoped it would be enough.

Before entering the town, we stood at the bridge for a moment. Shining water beneath, darkness beyond. Once we crossed that bridge and entered the town, anything could happen. It didn't look wholesome. At the same time it looked quiet enough. I imagined hordes of living persons clothed in black, waiting in the silent houses.

Obviously Brent didn't share my fancies. He was in an optimistic mood, positively exuberant.

"Let's check out the big brown house first," Brent said. "I can't get it out of my mind."

"I've never been inside that one. This was Annica's street."

I paused on the sidewalk. A linden tree root grew under the pavement, raising it to a dangerous height. The windows on the first floor were bare of shade or curtain. But upstairs, perhaps in a bedroom, I saw the edges of curtains, hanging like narrow ribbons.

The overgrown landscape communicated a dark and stealthy ambience to its non-existent neighbors.

"I don't think the town's doctor lived here," I said.

"Why?"

"It doesn't look clean to me."

"An impoverished doctor then. Let's see who did."

Brent was right about the clutter. A baby grand piano occupied the whole of one corner. Elsewhere in the room stacks of books covered end tables and other surfaces. We made a hasty search of the first floor. Apparently the homeowner had left all but his most personal possessions when he fled the town.

It looked as though he had come home one day, packed quickly, and abandoned the house, not bothering with sheet music and nonessential items such as vases and baskets. It would probably take months to sort through the accumulation of memorabilia. I couldn't imagine anyone with only a passing interest taking the time to do so.

"Let's see if we can find an office or study," I said.

"With a file cabinet," Brent added, still believing in his doctor.

If there was such a room, it wasn't located downstairs.

The kitchen table was bare except for a white pitcher containing the dried remnants of what had once been a summer bouquet, along with an empty cup, further testimony to the person who had left the house without preparation.

Why didn't he take the cup? That would have been useful.

He probably had a set of china in the cupboard. I opened the door and stared in amazement at the contents arranged neatly on the shelves: several bottles of light green liquid resembling dishwasher soap.

"Bug juice," Brent added.

"Let's hope not. What a noxious display."

There were perhaps thirty tall bottles, all the same, all sealed with labels and prices: Ashton Elixer, $12.95.

"This isn't a doctor's work," I said. "A mad scientist lived here."

"Am I mistaken in thinking that elixir is another word for cure?" Brent asked.

"Well, obviously it isn't a cure or everybody would have bought a bottle and Ashton's story would have a different ending."

"I'm out of my depth," Brent admitted. "What are you thinking?"

"Snake oil."

"Is that a more refined kind of bug juice?"

"Someone must have made a bundle selling this concoction, preying on the fear and desperation of the victims."

I wished Brent hadn't planted those words in my mind because they created unholy images of squished insects. Centipedes. Double yuk.

"I know we agreed not to take anything out of Ashton, but I'm helping myself to a bottle of this stuff," I said.

"You're not going to give it to Annica."

"Heavens, no, not to drink, that is. I'm going to have it analyzed."

That reminded me of Dorinda's diary. I took it out of my pocket and replaced it with a bottle of the Ashton elixir. If I held the little book in my hand, I wouldn't forget to put it back in Dorinda's house.

Could this have been the nasty-tasting drink Dorinda didn't want to take? Then I remembered that the tonic had been provided by her new doctor.

Before crossing the brown house off our list, we searched the basement where we found a refrigerator and stove and various kitchen implements like a food processor. More bottles of the Ashton Elixir covered an old table; still more filled the first shelf of an enamel cabinet.

"This is where they made the elixir," I said. "Maybe a doctor lived here after all. Or an amateur chemist?"

"Then they left all of it here?" Brent asked.

"I imagine people were moving to different places where they could get real help."

These bottles with their hideous liquid. Could I force myself to drink a dose if I thought it would cure me of the Ashton malady?

Possibly. Not everybody looked at green liquid in a bottle and thought of squashed bugs. I was so squeamish. So impressionable.

All right. I wasn't going to be sick, and, sick or well, I wasn't going to drink the bug juice. Still I'd better have the elixir analyzed.

"Let's stop at Clovers," I said. "Annica knew a botanist at the university. Maybe she has a chemist friend, too."

"What are you going to tell her?"

"The truth, of course. If Mac Dalby is interested, he can conduct his own search."

"I hope she won't want to drink it," Brent said.

"She's smarter than that."

I'd like to look around a little before we leave," I said. "I'd like a general idea of how many people fell for this elixir scam."

Forty

Annica stared at the bottle with distaste.

"It looks disgusting. Put it out of sight, Jennet. I don't want people to think we use something like that in our kitchen."

Never one to let a good joke die, Brent said, "It's bug juice." Unfortunately this was neither a joke nor good.

I slipped the bottle into my shoulder bag... temporarily.

"I hoped you'd take it with you, Annica," I said.

"Why on earth would I do that?"

"To see what it's made of."

She dropped into the third chair at the table and crossed her arms. Today she wore a long-sleeved blue and white striped blouse with a blue pencil skirt, a decidedly nautical look with long coral earrings. She was still dressing to conceal her rash and draw people's eyes up to her face.

"Let me guess," she said. "It came from Ashton."

"Apparently they had an illegal operation going on while people were getting sick and leaving town. This was supposed to cure them at twelve ninety-five a bottle. We found their workshop," I added.

"So we want to know what's in it," Brent said.

"I saw bottles like this in some of the kitchens and bedrooms I visited," Annica said. "I assumed it was fingernail polish remover, so I didn't mention it."

"I thought you might have a boyfriend in the physics or chemistry departments at the university who wants to impress you," I said.

"Boyfriend?" echoed Brent.

"I'd like to have this analyzed by someone who's discreet," I said.

Annica cast a coy glance at Brent. "Actually I do. It isn't poison or anything like that, is it?"

"If I had to guess, I'd say it's food coloring mixed with some soft drink like Sprite and a few other ingredients to give it a bite."

"I'll ask my friend," she said. "I'm pretty sure he can help us. Now, what can I get for you two?"

"A drink," I said. "Speaking of Sprite, I'd like a Vernors Float."

Brent suddenly remembered the other reason for our stop at Clovers. "Yeah, I'll have one of those, too."

"I thought you might be coming in for take-out dinners, Jennet," Annica said.

Oh, my goodness! I'd forgotten dinner! And it was getting late.

I could never admit that, not even to myself. This was for my husband without whom I couldn't go on living if I had access to eternal life and he didn't.

"I'll decide after we've had our floats," I said. "Right now, I'm thirsty."

~ * ~

In the end, Annica took the loathsome elixir, bringing her tote over to the table and dropping the bottle inside when she thought nobody was looking.

"All this intrigue," Brent said. "It'd be funny if it were just peppermint-flavored soda water."

"This is the same guy who helped me try to identify the violet in the wildflower field. He has two majors."

"How did he help?" I asked. "We still don't know what the flower is."

"Process of elimination."

"Is he one of those nerds?" Bent asked.

"Not at all."

"Ask him if he thinks the ingredients could kill," I said. "Also, how much a person would have to drink before it killed him?"

"Jennet! Lower your voice!"

When had Annica become so paranoid? No one was interested in our conversation, nor were they close enough to hear it.

"Okay," she said, "I'll do it, but it had better not be illegal for me to have this."

I had never thought of that. "Don't worry. I'd better check out the menu."

~ * ~

That evening, over roasted chicken and mashed potatoes from Clovers, I contemplated my earlier Eternal Life question. With or without the world's best husband at my side, would I want to live forever?

No.

Life, however wonderful it could be when you experienced it for the average number of years allotted to a person, would inevitably get boring. Like summer in a state where it seemed to be summer all year long.

I'd settle for a 'happily-ever-after' with Crane and perhaps when we left the earth, we would go together—with all of our collies.

"You look like you have a secret," Crane said, following that comment with, "Did you visit Ashton today?"

"How did you know?"

"You look guilty."

At the observation—which I didn't think was true—I felt a rush of warmth spread over my face. Probably I was blushing. But why should I care? It was best to plow on.

"I found something interesting today," I said.

Now I had to try to convince him how sinister a find this was, describing the elixir without the bottle to show him. No easy task, and I didn't feel I did it justice.

Still he asked, "Can I see it after dinner?"

"Not for a few days. I gave it to Annica to have it analyzed."

"She can do that?"

"Not exactly. She has a friend…"

"I thought you were going to abandon Ashton," he said.

"Like the townspeople did?" I hurried on before he could answer. "Little mysteries keep cropping up. The diary and now the elixir. We found the lab they used to manufacture the stuff, except it isn't a real lab. It's the basement of that old brown house Brent wanted to investigate."

"You took something else out of the town?" he asked.

"But the diary is back in Dorinda's bedroom."

Apparently Crane was willing to let the matter drop. Why? Because it really wasn't that serious?

I seized an excellent opportunity to mention a future excursion to the ghost town, to pave the way for it, so to speak. "Brent still wants to find the doctor's house. Neither of us believes he was the one who made the elixir."

"Mmm," Crane said. "In other news, I haven't seen Sue's lost rescue collie. Mac Dalby is looking for her, too."

"Echo isn't a typical lost dog. She was taken for a reason."

And tonight Brent was going to grill Byrony Limon about the rogue rescue league, its history, and perhaps its never-seen founder, Ann Clarke.

I hoped he'd be subtle and charming. If he gleaned even a little information from their conversation, perhaps we'd be able to make another plan.

Later that evening, while Crane walked the dogs on the lane, I looked up 'Ashton Elixir' on the internet. Not surprisingly, it didn't exist, although a band, Ashlyn Easter, came close with a slightly similar-sounding name. Next I looked up 'elixir.'

What a mishmash! I could scarcely understand what I was reading. The best I could do with this information was to find a source slanted for a person who wasn't blessed with a scientific mind. I'd been thinking of an elixir as a magical drink, perhaps one that contained the secret of eternal life.

Slow down, I told myself. *Eternal life is a myth. A fairy tale.*

Still, I was right to ask Annica to have the Ashton Elixir analyzed. I only wondered why Crane wasn't more curious about it.

Forty-one

"I've been thinking about Echo," Sue Appleton said the next morning. "You're right about her theft being a personal attack on me."

We were having tea and blueberry muffins at my house. The collies knew muffins were superior to the bones spread on the floor for them. Sue, whose own dogs were better behaved—make that better trained—than mine, didn't seem to know how to respond to the row of furry beggars who were demonstrating their right to the refreshments. Candy practically sat in Sue's lap.

"Back!" I ordered. "Everyone."

They rose, shuffled themselves around, and regrouped, ending up an inch closer to the table.

What unmannerly creatures!

"Would you like to move to the porch, Sue?" I asked. "It'd be more peaceful."

"This is fine." She broke off a piece of muffin but didn't eat it. "I've come to the conclusion that I do have at least one unknown enemy out there. I must. I overlooked the rogue league. What names come to mind when you think of people who would like to see them booted out of the breed?"

"That's easy. Yours and mine. Brent's, but they don't know that yet."

"And who is the Rescue League's president?"

"You are, of course."

"Therefore, I'm the one they've targeted because Echo is my dog now. I'm sure they know I'm not their friend," she added.

"I wonder why they stole Echo rather than Bluebell or Icy? They're all your dogs."

"Well, Icy would have given the dognapper a run for his money. If he could have stopped the thief in his tracks, he would have. Bluebell... I don't know about her. I keep coming back to what we know about Echo's history."

"There isn't much. All three collies were rescues."

"Yes, but we know the background of the River Rose collies. They were practically our neighbors. Echo was a mystery from the beginning. Do you remember?"

"Very well." Echo was so beautiful no one understood how she could have ended up in rescue.

"This may not be the first time Echo was stolen," I said. "If so, her real owner may want her back."

"*I* want her back," Sue said.

"Then we'll have to find her."

If I were right, it wouldn't be the first time a surrender had been steeped in mystery. One way or the other, Echo needed our help again. And maybe if there were a real owner in her background, that person would be mourning her loss.

~ * ~

To find a stolen collie.

Easy to say; not so easy to accomplish. We had taken all of the traditional first steps to make the county aware that Echo was missing. If her abduction were part of the rogue group's twisted plan, we had Brent in our corner.

I couldn't wait to see him again, to see if he had learned anything relevant from Byrony Limon.

Great minds travel on the same wavelength. Brent dropped over that evening, bearing a gift of liquor-flavored chocolates for the humans and liver-flavored bars for the canines.

"Don't get them mixed up," he said.

I thanked him. "That'll never happen."

As a pack, the collies paid more attention to the gilt decorated box than the tan and maroon package of dog treats. I'd always supposed liver smelled as good to them as chocolate did to us. Obviously I was wrong. I gave the dogs a sampling of the canine largess and relocated the candy to the mantel.

"What did you find out?" I asked.

"Really, Jennet, do you expect a progress report on my dinner date? I don't kiss and tell."

Crane laughed. I couldn't believe Brent was serious.

"Okay," he said, "I learned that Byrony is smarter than we thought. She may be suspicious."

"Of what?"

"Of me. She doesn't trust me. I must be slipping."

"You asked the wrong questions," I said. "Too soon."

"Nobody gave me a script."

"Sorry, Brent, I know you did your best. Where do we go from here?"

"I'm not sure, but I made another date with her. She does like to talk, mostly about herself. She's very self-centered. I'm not used to that kind of woman."

"That should work to our advantage," I said.

I made coffee, then opened the candy and passed it around. Chocolate cherries were delicious in themselves and irresistible when dipped in brandy.

Candy followed the progress of the box with feverish eyes. "Eat your liver bar," I told her.

To Brent I said, "Sue and I were wondering if the rogue league is responsible for stealing Echo."

"Why?

"Why do they do anything? Think of it as part of their nefarious plan."

"You want me to add Echo to my agenda?"

"If possible. You say Byrony is suspicious of you. First you have to change that."

"I can try. I told you I'm taking her out again. You wouldn't believe the sacrifices I'm making for the Cause."

"Most men wouldn't consider dating a beautiful woman a sacrifice," Crane pointed out.

"Who said she was beautiful?" I asked.

"Sue. I think it was Sue."

I sat back, wondering when she had done that.

"Now Sheriff, I'd like your permission to escort your wife to Ashton," Brent said. "We left a small matter undone."

He surprised both of us with this formal request. Crane was the first to recover.

"What gives, Fowler? You never bothered to ask for my permission before."

"Because I thought you'd give it automatically."

"You never thought that," Crane said.

"What's different about this time, Brent?" I asked.

"I had a feeling," he said.

Crane stared at him. "You, too?"

"Let me finish. This isn't like the kind of feeling Lucy has. It's more of a premonition that this is going to be our last visit. We have to make this one count."

"That sounds ominous," I said. "And it *does* sound like something Lucy would say."

Crane reached for the chocolates and passed them around again, causing Candy to awake from what I had presumed was a deep sleep.

"I'll be glad to see this obsession run its course," Crane said.

"Is that a 'yes'?" Brent asked.

"You have my permission, Fowler. One trip only for exploratory purposes. No side trips."

I couldn't be happier to see this most unusual confrontation come to a peaceful end.

"I'm glad you're finally on board, Crane," I said.

Forty-two

Lucy handed me a cup of Darjeeling in one of her plain white tea leaf reading cups. I'd brought the doughnuts for our morning visit. What a great way this was to start a summer day!

"Yesterday I had a premonition about you and Brent. It dealt with your forays into the ghost town," she said.

I took a sip of tea. Lucy had the air conditioning on already, and her new indoor fountain brought the music of falling water inside the sunroom. In spite of Lucy's rhetoric, I made up my mind to relax.

"Brent had a premonition, too," I said. "Was yours good or bad?"

"A little of both. You're going back to Ashton then?"

"Brent and I are, tomorrow one last time, and Crane approves. Will wonders never cease?"

"That astonishes me," she said. "I hope this isn't going to be the one time you'll run into danger."

"That," I said, "would be ironic. As you know, my husband tries to discourage my interest in mysteries, so I'm not going to look a gift horse in the mouth."

But she had spoken of danger. "I'm assuming there's danger waiting there for Brent and me then."

"No more than there's been all along, and so far it hasn't touched you. This foreboding of mine involves a discovery. The

216

details are fuzzy, but apparently Ashton isn't a town rooted in the supernatural as you've been telling yourself. The answer to what's going on there is really quite simple."

"Then where does the danger come in?" I asked.

"I think, through your choices. I wish I could tell you more."

"Brent had a feeling this will be our last visit to Ashton," I said.

"It *is* time to wrap it up."

I drained my teacup. Sky eyed the bit of doughnut left on my plate. It was plain with a dollop of maple frosting.

"Can she have it?" I asked.

Sky whimpered. *Can I? Please?*

I was teaching her incorrect usage. "Yes, you may." I laughed at my own private joke.

"You're in a good mood this morning," Lucy said.

"Well, yes, I'm happy."

Another free day, another trip to Ashton coming up, another chance to crack open the mystery of the century.

"But I guess I shouldn't let myself be too happy," I added. "Sue Appleton's collie, Echo, was stolen right from her locked house. The thief used the key Sue had hidden outside."

"My goodness. So we have another lost dog to find."

Lucy was quiet for a moment, watching Sky as she daintily ate her share of the doughnut. "Let's see if the tea leaves know anything about this theft," she said.

I prepared my cup for reading and gave it to her. She seemed to take an inordinate amount of time studying the patterns. I listened to the fall of water from Lucy's fountain and thought about Ashton Lake. How could the solution to the mysteries be simple?

"I see a dog," she said.

With a blue-tinted fingernail, she pointed at a light brown leaf that certainly looked like a tiny collie silhouette.

"It's Echo waiting to be rescued, wondering why this is happening to her all over again. She thought she had a home."

The chunk of doughnut I'd just eaten lodged in my throat. I hadn't told Lucy about Echo's background, only that Sue had adopted her.

Lucy simply knew, from looking at a simple little tea leaf for a second.

What else did she know? I waited for further enlightenment, but she grew quiet again.

The idea of Echo in distress, Echo waiting for deliverance, filled me with sadness. If only someone could point me in her direction.

Someone like Lucy.

Finally I asked, "What can I do?"

"You'll know when the time comes," she assured me, "and it'll be soon. Now this time I see your wish. That viper is still coiled too close to your home for comfort. I see a church, candles, flowers... You're going to a wedding..."

~ * ~

The sun was hot in a cloudless blue sky as we left Brent's vintage Plymouth. A wind blew through the town, stirring up the gravel, and keeping the heat at a tolerable level. Brent handed me a bottle of Pure Michigan and took one for himself.

I pulled my camera out of my shoulder bag. "I want to get a picture of you and the car with the diner in the background."

He posed obligingly, one hand resting on the Plymouth's graceful fin. This would be a good picture. The green of his cotton shirt matched the green paint on the car, and his dark red hair had an almost unnatural shimmer in the sunlight.

This was the way I always wanted to remember him, proud, sun-kissed, the lord of the manor and, incidentally, of this mysterious town.

Wait! The way you always want to remember him?

The strange thought, coming out of nowhere and wreathed in darkness, appalled me. It sounded like a memorial. It sounded as if, after today, I'd never see Brent again.

Just when I thought Ashton had lost its power to convey dark thoughts, just when Lucy assured me its mysteries weren't rooted in the supernatural after all, I felt as if I were taking a picture of Brent for remembrance. For posterity.

It was the town that inspired that thought. Somehow.

Just take the picture.

The wind blew my hair in my face, obscuring my vision. Impatiently I pushed it back. The darkness that had accompanied the thought faded, loosened its hold. Free of it, I snapped two more views of Brent from different angles.

"Can we start now?" he asked, taking a swig from the water bottle.

"Anytime you're ready."

"If this is going to be our last ghost town adventure, let's make it a good one," he said.

"Did you have anything in particular in mind?"

"I sure do. First I want to find the doctor's house and have a look through his files. I won't be satisfied till we do that. Then I plan to lay a trap for our cloaked friend."

"What kind?"

"The best kind. With money. I'm going to drop two twenties farther down on Main Street. I'll leave another couple of twenties in the heart of Ashton, then another two on the beach. If they're gone when we come back, we'll know someone else is living here."

"But if we don't observe anyone taking the money, what good will that do?"

"I may have a few kinks to work out."

"This is going to be an expensive trip for you," I said.

"Can you think of anything better?"

"Yes. Let's concentrate on finding the doctor's house, if that's what's important to you. And forget about the cloaked figure. What if he's a figment of Lucy's imagination?"

"Then he won't need money."

Leaving the kinks entrenched in his plan, Brent pulled a handmade map out of his pocket. "We left off the last time three streets over." He pointed. "Ash Street."

"That sounds right," I said.

"That's one of the nicer areas, and it's close to the lake. I can see the doctor living there."

We set out at a brisk pace for Ash Street. I followed, on the lookout for snakes in the grass, territorial dogs, and a glimpse of flowing black material rounding a building.

I was going to miss this place.

Forty-three

In front of the dime store, Brent pulled two bills from his pocket and opened his palm. The wind whisked them out of his hand and sent them flying down the street, mixing with the swirling leaves.

"They're going to end up behind something," I said. "No one will see them."

"I'm leaving it up to chance. No matter where I set them down, the wind will blow them. I may have to sacrifice more money to the Cause," he added.

"Wouldn't it be better to scatter dollar bills around instead of twenties?"

"I want to make a splash," he said. "Make it worth somebody's while."

Well, it was Brent's plan and his money. For anybody, forty or sixty dollars would be quite a find.

We turned onto Ash Street and zeroed in on a medium-sized beige house with white gingerbread trim. It would have been attractive if its paint hadn't fallen prey to the weather. The lawn was overgrown and the landscaping around the foundation dying, although tall, flowering weeds lent a bit of rosy color to the scene.

Brent dropped two more twenty dollar bills on the cracked sidewalk. The wind blew them into the branches of a scraggly cedar, part of a natural fence on the property line. It looked as if they were caught fast in the tree's prickly embrace, visible to whomever might pass on the sidewalk.

"This doesn't look like a doctor's house," I said.

"What kind of house would a doctor live in?" he asked.

"Something a little bigger, maybe with a front porch and a garage. He would need a car. I don't see him walking to visit his patients."

"Whoa! Your doctor makes house calls?"

"In a small town like Ashton, sure, but enough speculating. Let's have a look inside."

The door was slightly ajar. A fine layer of dust and debris carpeted the hall and living room. The owner had covered the furniture with white sheets and moved it close to the walls. The overall effect was ghostly and uninviting.

I took a deep breath. The interior wasn't as stuffy as that of other houses we had explored. Still, it was a struggle to fill my lungs with air.

I glanced at the staircase to the right. "It's bigger than it appeared from outside. There's a second story."

Brent peered into the kitchen. "Everything's covered with sheets in here too. It looks like they planned to come back some day."

"Let's look upstairs."

"You go," Brent said. "I'll check out the other rooms. A home office would be on the first floor."

I climbed the stairs to the upper level where three doors stood half-closed. One led to a small bathroom stripped of towels and toilet articles. The first bedroom was large and nondescript. In the second I found something odd. The bed was made, although not neatly, with a crumpled spread and a pillow lying half on the floor.

How recently had someone slept in it?

A night stand and dresser, both topped with white dust, completed the furnishings. The drawers were empty except for faded liner paper, but small off-white tiles had been attached to the wall above the bed. Each one bore a letter; together they spelled *Hilla's Room.*

Was *Hilla* the person who had slept here?

A loud crash broke the thick silence into pieces.

I rushed to the door.

"Brent! What broke?"

No answer.

"Brent?"

Heart pounding, I raced down the stairs, almost missing the last step. Desperately I grabbed the banister and stood for a moment trying to catch my breath and regain my equilibrium. My heartbeat slowed, but only slightly.

In the living room, the edges of the sheets moved fitfully in the wind that pushed its way in through the door. Dust moved through the stagnant air. I sneezed.

"Brent! Where are you?"

He didn't answer.

I had attempted to hold back the panic, but suddenly it broke through, turning my blood to ice-water. He wasn't going to answer. He wasn't here. I had stepped into the embodiment of all my nightmares, rolled into one. In peril in the ghost town. Brent and I should never have separated.

I tried to push disjointed images of black cloaks and slithering vipers out of my mind in order to think rationally, to make a plan. I had to find Brent. If he needed help, I alone could provide it.

First, what caused the crash? There should be shards of glass or china... A vase shattered on the hardwood floor... A brick thrown through the window... Brent somehow involved in whatever had happened. On the receiving end? I saw no sign of a mess.

I was certain the sound had come from inside the house.

The living room looked the same as it had when Brent and I had come through the door, filled with anticipation as we began our search for the doctor's house. How quickly that had changed.

I tore through the house, calling his name.

If he's here, he would answer, I told myself.

Unless he tripped over something, hit his head. He might be unconscious.

How could that happen to a man like Brent Fowler? He was too much in command of every situation he encountered. The environment worked for him, not against him.

It was my turn to be in command. To calm down. To act for both of us.

I made a second sweep of the ground floor. The house didn't have a basement. It probably had an attic, but Brent couldn't be up there unless he'd passed me on the stairs, and that hadn't happened.

Where was he then?

Gone. And I'd better get out of here myself while I could.

~ * ~

The sky had darkened to a dull metallic gray. Nothing moved except for a spattering of dirt, debris, and bits and pieces of leaves. The wind had acquired an eerie wail, almost a hum.

It can't rain now. Please!

I looked up and down the sidewalk, looked as far into the distance as I could see. Nobody was there. No assailant, no Brent. Which meant…

Dear God, what did it mean? Against all odds, something had happened to him. I had been spared—this time—and I was alone in the ghost town.

All the houses on Ash Street spread out before me. Brent could be in any one of them or in any other house in town. He could be a prisoner, perhaps unconscious. How could I possibly find him?

Absently I noted that the two twenty dollar bills stuck in the cedar were gone, either dislodged by the wind or taken. I couldn't worry about them now.

What *could* I do?

Call for help. I reached into my pocket for my cell phone and immediately remembered leaving it in my purse in the Plymouth. After all, Brent had his phone. Why did I need mine?

This is why, I told myself.

My thoughts turned to the car, my safe harbor in a world grown hostile. Had Brent locked the car? Usually he did, as the vintage Plymouth was his most prized possession, but we were alone in Ashton, or so we'd thought. This time he might have left it unlocked, planning to return in an hour or two for more bottled water. Maybe… I could hope.

I made my way back to the street, hoping the car would be where Brent had left it, in front of the Forever Diner. In an extension of my nightmare, the car would be gone, even as Brent was gone, and I would be stranded in Ashton with the sky growing darker every minute and an unknown menace waiting to pounce.

The wind pushed me along through silent streets to the edge of town. My breathing grew rapid, and a painful stitch erupted in my side.

In the distance I could see the Plymouth, its white and green shining in the gathering darkness. It looked like a vehicle from another planet, but it was Brent's car. With the shining fins, there was no doubt of that. My purse would be inside, and inside my purse, my phone… and deliverance.

If the car was unlocked with the keys inside—it had to be—I'd barricade myself inside, call Crane and Mac and wait for help to arrive. I'd never leave Brent behind. We'd come to Ashton as a team. We'd leave together.

Leave now. Save yourself.

Who said that?

No one, even though I could have sworn I'd heard something. Nothing spoke but the wind. I'd imagined Brent's voice, put words in his mouth.

Halfway to the Plymouth, I had to slow down, but I kept moving, looking neither right nor left, afraid of what I might see.

Finally I reached the car. On the back seat, I saw my purse lying on its side, open.

There was no key in the ignition.

I grabbed the handle and turned. "Open!" I cried.

Nothing.

Brent had locked the car. He had the key. The prospect of deliverance that had carried me this far abruptly evaporated.

Forty-four

I leaned back against the Plymouth, breathing heavily. What could I do now? Surely I must have exhausted all my options.

Think.

My mind might have been an empty stage, all lights out, the play ended, and the actors gone.

Think of something!

I looked behind me at the silent town, then at the bridge. The green beyond seemed to go on forever. It beckoned to me, solid wood above restless wind-churned water.

Walk across the bridge to safety.

I had a feeling—another one of those weird unaccounted-for feelings—that the danger was contained in the town. Still, endless miles of wilderness traversed on foot couldn't be considered safe. In Ashton I could find shelter in one of the abandoned houses if it started to rain or, if it became necessary, I could find a hiding place.

Wilderness or ghost town? There had to be another way.

How about the obvious?

Did I dare break Brent's window? In the circumstances I felt certain that he would understand. Then I could call Crane and Mac, the entire cavalry. The nightmare would be over.

Lucy claimed that the mysteries of the ghost town weren't rooted in the supernatural. That was somewhat encouraging. Nonetheless someone had attacked Brent and taken him away. There was still danger in Ashton, no matter the source.

One way or the other I had to access my cell phone.

Sorry, Brent, I'll make it up to you with a dozen chocolate meringue pies.

I retraced my steps, scouring the ground for a rock or a brick.

Once I left Main Street, I found all the rocks I could desire, embedded in the ground and extracted to use in landscaping. I chose a substantial one that would shatter glass but not be too heavy to carry back to the car. As I bent to pick it up, a branch snapped. The sound was like a gunshot.

Or was it a gunshot, sounding like a branch snapping?

Behind me something breathed, a rusty choked sound.

My hand still around the rock, I turned around. A flash of black dipped into my peripheral vision and vanished around a slanting wall. I still heard breathing.

Once again my heart began to pound.

Did I really see something?

Yes, and I heard it.

I picked up the rock and ran back the way I'd come, back to the car.

Was the rusty breather following me? I couldn't tell and didn't dare turn around. I kept my eyes on the Plymouth as if it were the one safe haven in a world gone mad.

But it seemed the closer I came to the Plymouth, the farther it receded, which was impossible.

You can make it!

A short, stocky man stepped heavily out of the hardware store, a figure in black with the bill of his hat pulled down low over his face. He stood for a moment, then advanced on me. He was close, about twenty yards away.

The other way. Quick!

I headed back to the heart of town, to Ash Street. In this direction lay the lake, which would bring my flight to a stop.

Duck in one of the houses, I told myself. *Through any open door.*

Then I'd be trapped. But I was trapped here on the street.

My right side felt as if a knife had flown into it. I couldn't keep running, had to stop. Just for a minute. Just a second…

Realization slowly struck. The sound of labored breathing, the pounding of heavy feet on the ground, had ceased. When?

It didn't matter. Ashton was steeped in a deep ominous silence broken only by the wind.

I leaned on a maple tree and let the world take a final spin before it limped to a stop.

The man in black had apparently given up the pursuit. I couldn't fathom why, but I was back where I'd started before my mad dash to the car. The house from which Brent had disappeared was across the street. The lake was closer than I'd thought.

I felt safe for the moment, but it was an illusion. I still didn't know where my pursuer had gone. For all I knew, he would spring out at me any minute. I had no idea what had become of Brent and had no way to make my call.

I headed toward the lake, that impossibly blue expanse of water that I now knew held sickness and possibly death. Could I walk around it? I could, but what was there on the other side but more woods? I had to come up with another plan.

Again, my mind was blank.

As if to taunt me, the wind whipped one of Brent's twenty dollar bills into the air where it caught in the low hanging branch of a tree.

~ * ~

The lake was farther away than I'd thought. As I drew nearer, I saw a man lying on his side facing the beach. His dark red hair had a familiar shine in the scorching sun.

Brent… Alive? He had to be alive.

He moved slowly, pushed himself up, and cradled his head in his hands.

Thank God.

I shouted his name and reached him before the echo of my voice died. Falling to my knees, I touched his forehead. A long gash above his right eye had bled and dried. That was good, wasn't it?

"Jennet," he tried to speak. Took a deep breath. Tried again. "Are you hurt?"

"No, you are. I've just been running—for my life."

He shoved his hand in his pocket, pulled it out again. "They took my wallet," he said. "I never saw him coming."

"There were two of them?"

"I heard two voices. No, three. One was a woman. Damn! They got all my identification. My credit cards. My money."

"Did you have a lot of money?" I asked.

"Not much. Eight or nine hundred dollars, but it's my ID. How the hell am I going to get duplicates of everything?"

"You'll manage," I said. "You're not going to worry about that now. Did they leave your cell phone?"

He felt in his shirt pocket.

"It's gone."

"How about the keys to the Plymouth? Please say they left them."

He rummaged through all his pockets. "They're gone too. But all is not lost. I have a spare. Somewhere…" Reaching into still another pocket, he pulled out two keys attached to a small silver horseshoe. "In case I ever lock myself out."

"Let's get out of here then," I said, helping him up.

"Not before I get my hands on that jerk who robbed me."

"Now, before they come back. My phone's in the car. Oh, no!" A horrible thought occurred to me. "If they took the keys, maybe they stole the car."

That galvanized him into action. He stood on his own, not too steadily on his feet, but he was standing. "If they did, they're dead."

We began walking back into the town. "A short guy in a black jacket was chasing me," I said. "Then he stopped. But he's still around."

"This isn't over," Brent said. "Not by a long shot. I'll get a cup of coffee, wash up, and I'll be back."

"Not until you go to Emergency. That gash on your head…"

"It's nothing."

As we entered Main Street, I saw the Plymouth in all its green and white glory parked in front of the Forever Diner. The car was there, Brent had the key, and we were as good as on our way out of town.

"What else could have gone wrong today?" Brent said with a grumble.

It wasn't a time for levity, but I couldn't resist. "Be thankful they didn't push you into Ashton Lake."

Forty-five

Brent started the Plymouth and turned the car around. "We're on our way. It won't be long now."

He headed for the bridge and, as soon as he drove across it, suddenly stepped on the brake. "Jennet, would you hand me a bottle of water, please?"

I reached in the back for two bottles, one for myself. Now that we were out of Ashton I could think about luxuries like water.

He squinted into the distance. "Did it get hazy all of a sudden?"

"No, it's clear. The sun is pretty bright, though."

"Maybe you'd better drive," he said. "Do you think you can?"

"Drive a stick shift? Sure." I glanced at him, still marveling that he was safe, sitting beside me. "Are you feeling dizzy?"

"A little," he said. "Maybe it's the sun."

A little dizzy was a danger signal. I hoped he'd be okay.

"Let's change places then," I said. "That settles it. We have to get you to a hospital."

"Let's just get out of Ashton."

I was happy to comply. I took my place behind the wheel and with a sigh, Brent settled back, resting his head against the seat. It seemed as if the Plymouth went on forever behind me and ahead of me as well. It was quite different from the modern day Ford Focus.

"I'm glad they didn't take the car," Brent said.

"If they had we'd still be there."

For a while I'd been certain that one of the natives had stolen the car, leaving us stranded, taking my purse and cell phone and the water.

"The sheriff is going to blow a gasket," Brent said. "I could have gotten you killed."

"He *did* give us his blessing."

"Yeah, well he'll never do that again."

"That's okay," I said. "I don't care if I ever see Ashton again."

"You don't mean that."

I steered carefully around a curve. The Belvedere's body was so long and sleek I felt as if I were dragging another vehicle behind it.

"At the moment I do," I said.

"I'll go alone then." He seemed to relax as we traversed the familiar route. "Do you want me to call the sheriff for you?"

I glanced at my watch. "He isn't even home yet. I'll tell him in person. It'll be easier."

"I'm the one he'll be mad at," Brent said.

It was best to take his mind off Crane who would realize that Brent was not to blame for what had happened.

"I heard a crash back at the house," I said. "Do you have any idea what they hit you with?"

"It felt like a two-ton brick, but I never saw anyone. Just heard their voices. There were two men, one with a southern accent, and a woman."

A woman? A glimpse of a black cloak, a man in a black jacket whose face I couldn't see... What else? I felt needles of ice jab at me, glad I could no longer see Ashton or the bridge in the mirror, wondering if the stocky man who had chased me had been part of the Brent's grim welcome committee.

"Who are these people?" I asked.

"I've been thinking," Brent said. "They live in the town but keep out of sight. Today I guess they saw the money and figured there was more where that came from."

"Could they be the original inhabitants?" I asked. "The ones who didn't leave?"

"Could be, but I don't think so. That was a long time ago."

"A cult that set up shop there then?

"Maybe." He held his hand up to his head. "Whatever, they're a bunch of crazies. Who knows? Maybe they stay out of sight because they're deformed."

I thought that was taking the mystery a bit too far—into the realm of science-fiction.

"Who on earth would live in Ashton if they had a choice?" I asked.

"My guess is a bunch of homeless people who banded together for mutual protection. Where else can they find shelter and not have to worry about the cops running them off?"

"But there's no water in the town," I said. "No electricity, and no food unless they shoot rabbits or pheasants."

"In spite of all that, they have it made."

"Do you think they know the lake is poisoned?" I asked.

He shrugged. "Maybe, maybe not. We won't know till we corner them and get them to talk."

I couldn't see that happening unless Mac rounded up the whole gang and interrogated them.

"I think there must be more to the story," I said.

"As soon as I know I'm okay, I'm going back and heads will roll."

Brent was in no condition to hunt down his assailant, but he was intelligent enough to know that. This was wounded pride talking. It would be better to send Mac and his men back to Ashton with guns blazing. With luck, Brent might get his wallet with his identification back, if not his money.

I wondered how many people made their home in the ghost town and if they shared their resources. Brent's hundreds of dollars would be well worth fighting over.

Brent slapped his sore head. "Ouch," he said, then "Damn, I forgot. I'm taking Byrony out tonight."

"You can call and cancel," I said. "Say you were mugged. She'll understand."

"That's not the point. I have a job to do. I don't want to fail at everything today."

"We didn't fail," I said.

Of course anyone hearing our story would think we had.

~ * ~

Brent tried to talk me out of stopping at the hospital, but I was in the driver's seat. In Emergency, after a long wait, he was pronounced in perfect health. The dizziness had passed, and he felt well enough to drive home and get ready for his next big adventure of the day... the date with Byrony Limon.

Safe at last, I marveled at the normalcy of my home and the pack of overjoyed collies who had been convinced I was never coming home. The usual sense of returning from an alien world lingered. Ashton was the place where unearthly things happened. This green Victorian farmhouse was my reality.

Fortunately I was home in plenty of time to get ready for Crane's homecoming. I had to shower off the dust of Ashton, change clothes, and plan dinner. Something easy, I decided, steaks and salads. Wearing a clean yellow dress, with dinner in the broiler, I sat in the living room longing to share my misadventures with Camille but lacking the energy to contact her.

Misty was particularly clingy. Of all the dogs, she was the one most affected by my absence. Or was something else bothering her? I remembered her reaction to the toilet water from the Ashton dime store. Locked in the house, had she somehow known about my desperate flight from an unknown pursuer?

I thought my psychic collie capable of any feat. It was too bad she couldn't sail through windows like Lassie.

With that whimsical thought, the fallout from the day's trauma caught up with me. The people of the town could have assaulted me along with Brent. They could have thrown both our bodies in the lake and stolen the Plymouth.

Good Lord! Crane knew where we'd gone, but how long would it take before it occurred to him to look in the lake?

I could almost feel the water close over my head, feel my last desperate attempt to fill my lungs with life-giving air.

Don't think about that, I ordered myself. *It didn't happen. Unlike Brent you didn't suffer a blow to your head, and everything in your purse is still there.*

I had to be content with that.

Forty-six

By the time Crane came home, I was myself again, calm and fresh in one of my favorite dresses. All traces of my frantic hours were ensconced in the past. I was able to tell my latest tale without histrionics. There was, after all, no point in wringing every last ounce of drama from the story. I had survived.

"Brent will be all right, except for his stolen identification," I said in conclusion. "He didn't seem to mind so much about the money."

Crane focused on the day's major dilemma, from my point of view. "But for a while you thought you might be stranded in Ashton. I wouldn't even know you were in trouble. You'll be the death of me, Jennet."

"I won't go to Ashton again," I said. "Today was my Ashton Farewell."

"I wish I could believe you."

"This time it's true. I swear it."

"Won't you want to know where the original people went, or if the doctor had a home office in town?"

"I can live without solving those mysteries. I thought Mac was going to cordon off the town," I added.

"He may still. He should." Crane locked his gun in the cabinet as he always did. Mine was there as well. I should have taken it with me today.

"I think Fowler is right," Crane said. "The homeless moved into your ghost town. Who knows how long ago? You and Brent are the invaders."

"They're not hurting anyone," I said.

Even as I spoke I realized that this wasn't true. One of their kind had struck Brent a serious blow and stolen from him, while I, by the grace of God, had escaped with a fright.

"From now on, Ashton isn't your problem," Crane said. "It isn't even Fowler's problem. Leave it to Mac." He glanced at the stove. "Do I have time for a quick shower?"

"Just enough."

The steaks were almost ready, the rice and asparagus done. I contemplated the remainder of the raspberry pie on the counter. It would have to do. I'd bake another one tomorrow.

Candy placed her paws on the counter and stretched; still, she couldn't reach the pie. The salad was closer to her but she never paid any attention to greens. Defeated for the moment, she retreated to the doorway to look pitiful.

Misty, on the other hand, insisted on weaving between my feet. She had been at my side while I'd told Crane about the day's trauma. She kept her bright eyes glued to me and occasionally whimpered and nudged me as if to say, 'You should have taken me with you.'

For a moment I was certain she'd understood every word I said.

~ * ~

I walked into Clovers the next day, savoring the waves of cool air that washed over me and the delightful smells that wafted out of the kitchen. The dessert carousel was filled with meringue topped lemon squares and frosted brownies.

Something was different about Annica, besides her natural radiance.

I had it! She was wearing a pale peach dress with cap sleeves. Her arms were a few shades lighter than her face and shoulders, but they were undoubtedly healed.

"The rash is gone," she said as she joined me in a booth. "I don't see any redness, and it doesn't itch. I'm so excited. I can wear my new dress to Leonora's wedding."

I couldn't be happier for her. "That's great news. Did you ever find out what it was?"

She shrugged. "The doctor did a biopsy and told me I had inflammatory hives. I guess I didn't get that in Ashton."

"Not likely," I said. "What brought them on?"

"They couldn't tell me. Now that they're gone, it doesn't matter." She signaled to Marcy who nodded. "I have other news. My friend at school found out what's in the elixir. It's really simple."

I leaned forward. It seemed that I was going to have one answer without any undue effort.

"It's a mixture of strawberry and avocado with a whole bunch of vitamins and a dose of castor oil for good measure."

"Yum."

"No, 'Ugh'."

I couldn't imagine how that concoction would taste. Like bug juice. I put it out of my mind. I planned to order a double chocolate soda and didn't want to think about insects.

"This concoction sold for around twelve dollars a bottle," Annica said.

"It couldn't have helped anyone."

"No, but it didn't hurt either. It was just a scam, giving people false hope."

"Psychologically it might have helped a little," I said. "If you're convinced some kind of medication will be effective, maybe it will be, a little."

We both ordered sodas and having exhausted the topic of the elixir, I told her what had happened to Brent and to me in Ashton.

"Will he be all right?" she wanted to know.

"He bounced right back. He took Byrony Limon out last night. I'm dying to know if he found out anything relevant about the rogue league or Echo."

I didn't tell Annica that Brent had vowed to return to Ashton. Did he plan to drive the Plymouth into town and challenge the homeless ones to a duel? He'd be one against who knew how many? I hoped he'd reconsider. His time and effort were better spent infiltrating Byrony's group, and he wouldn't be likely to receive any dangerous blows at her hand.

"We have to find Echo," I said, "and I think Byrony took her."

~ * ~

In some part of my mind, I must have been thinking about those weird, black-garbed denizens of Ashton, because they filled my dreams that night. Every time I woke up and fell asleep again, they were back, dozens of them, all in black, all with their faces hidden from view.

In the manner of dreams, I was then whisked off to my classroom at Marston, teaching a strange story to my American Literature class, one that wasn't in the textbook.

I remembered its title from my distant past: *Evening Primrose.*

I'd read it or perhaps seen an old television version of it but forgotten most of the plot. I only remembered that a group of people had taken up residence in a department store by night to survive during the Great Depression. During the day when the shoppers flocked to the store, they hid from sight and kept their secret. There was a grisly little detail about humans being turned into mannequins.

What a ghastly story! I couldn't remember how the gruesome transformation had worked, but here I was trying to teach the story on the first day of school. Never in my life had I attempted to teach a selection that I didn't know well.

Seamlessly the scene changed back to Ashton. I couldn't find Brent.

I heard Crane's voice, but I didn't see him. 'You'll be the death of me, Jennet.'

"I didn't mean to come back." I said that aloud.

People spilled out of ramshackle houses, gathered together, merging until they looked like one dark entity. They were chasing me, closing the distance between us...

If they caught me... When they caught me... They would turn me into one of the tall wooden Indians that stood sentinel in front of the dime store.

They were gaining on me...

I couldn't breathe... The pain in my side was severe... Unbearable...

'You'll be the death of me, Jennet.'

There was no place in town to hide, no hope...

I felt a hand close tightly around my arm...

And woke up. Thank God. Oh, thank God.

Moonlight flooded the room, touched every corner with light.

God bless the moonlight.

Misty was sitting by the side of the bed, her paw on my arm.

"Good girl," I whispered, giving her a pat on the head. "Do you have to go out?

No, I'm here to protect you.

That was what she would have said.

Crane was asleep by my side, Halley watched silently from the doorway, and Misty sighed and lay down on the rag rug at the side of my bed.

I let wakefulness float away, thankful that dreams weren't real, that the moon was bright, and above all that my Misty collie was faithful.

At last I slept.

Forty-seven

This was Leonora's day. I refused to let anything intrude on it. That meant Ashton, the town that wrapped its tentacles around the unsuspecting victim and wouldn't let go. It even meant the lost collie, Echo, but just for today.

I smoothed the folds of my green dress and turned in a circle for the pleasure of hearing them swish. It was time for finishing touches. A crystal heart on a sterling silver chain and a crystal bracelet, a touch of green eye-shadow and my wedding rings. A spritz of *Joy* and I was ready.

Halley and Misty watched me from the doorway. Both had worried looks on their faces. They were most likely afraid I'd leave again and this time wouldn't come home. To add to their angst, they could tell that Crane was also getting ready to go out. Well, it isn't every day that one's best friend gets married.

I hadn't heard from Brent yet. He had promised to let us know if he learned anything about Echo from Byrony. So much for promises. Calls to him went straight to voice mail. I didn't think he would have gone back to Ashton so soon. With Brent, however, one never knew.

He planned on going to the wedding but hadn't invited anyone to accompany him. We were giving Annica and Lucy a ride and driving them home.

Leave it to Brent to create a mystery wherever he went. On the other hand, this is how Ashton made certain I didn't forget her, by dangling Brent's fate in front of me.

Well, he had proved many times that he was capable of taking care of himself. Except that last day at Ashton. I'd probably see him at the reception.

Crane stopped in the doorway. "You look pretty enough to be the bride, honey."

His frosty gray eyes held a special gleam. In a sense this was also our day. I didn't have school, and he didn't have to patrol the roads and by-roads of Foxglove Corners. We could devote the entire day to revelry and romance.

How deliciously medieval that sounded!

"I remember when I *was* a bride," I said. "It wasn't so long ago." I patted the last strand of hair in place and turned away from the mirror. "Are you still happy, Crane?"

"What kind of question is that?"

"I just wondered."

About Veronica, the department's lone female deputy, also known as Veronica the Viper. I didn't think about her all the time. Only when she appeared in my teacup and Lucy began talking about the snake in my home.

"Well, stop wondering." He kissed me thoroughly. "Are *you* happy?"

"I've never been happier."

He kissed me again. "Then, if you're ready, let's go get Jake and Leonora married."

~ * ~

Everyone was in his or her place, and the fragrance of yellow lilies on the altar blended with the scent of burning candles. As best man, Crane stood beside Jake. Leonora's father waited in the wings, and the priest was about to make his entrance. I seized the opportunity for a few minutes alone with Leonora in St. Emerentiana's small dressing room.

Leonora ran her hand lightly over the shimmering veil that lay like mist on her golden hair in its elegant French twist. Her hair seemed brighter today than it had ever been.

"Do I look okay, Jen?" she asked. "Is the dress right? Is anything showing?"

"You look perfect," I said.

She wore a high-waisted creation with a bodice of delicate ivory lace and a cascade of white satin that molded to her form as if it had been made especially for her, which, come to think of it, it had. She wore her mother's pearls and her grandmother's earrings.

"Perfect," I repeated.

"I have such high hopes for Jake and me and our future," she said. "I don't know how real life can ever measure up to them."

What to say? I wanted to set Leonora's mind at rest without resorting to one of those dreary wedding clichés. I thought for a moment, and inspiration came to me. "I believe that love and real life are far better than any dream. Before I forget, I have a special present for you," I added. "It's both old and new."

I reached into my pearl clutch for the antique locket that I had dropped inside earlier. Embellished with fanciful scrollwork, it hung on a long gold chain. I had found it at the Green House of Antiques where Leonora and I had spent so many happy hours discovering treasures from the past.

I opened it to reveal our pictures inside, face to face for all time.

"This is for you to remember our friendship," I said.

"As if I could ever forget. I should have something for you."

"You're the bride."

"I love it, Jen. Can you slip it over my head?"

"I didn't think you'd wear it today. You already have your pearl necklace."

"I'll wear them both."

I did as she asked, and the locket lay against the lace, a pure gold symbol of our years together, a memento for the years to come.

Leonora closed her hands around it. "We *do* go back a long way," she said, "all the way to our first year at Marston. Do you remember I helped you move to Foxglove Corners after the tornado? I made up my mind then that I would move out with you as soon as I found the right house."

"And you did," I said. "Then we had one adventure after another. Do you remember that first winter? I got us stuck in the only snow bank on the road."

"Oh, I'll never forget Grimes, the dognapper. You smashed him like a pumpkin. How about the fire at the Lane's End cottage?"

"And all the ghosts. The poor lost woman doomed to walk the halls of the Spirit Lamp Inn."

As the first poignant notes of *Pachelbel's Canon* floated through the church, Leonora's mother rapped lightly on the door. "It's time, honey. Dad's ready."

"So are we," I said.

~ * ~

At the altar I said a prayer that Leonora would be as happy in her marriage as I was in mine. That was a tall order. I glanced at Crane, so tall and blond and handsome. He had swept into my life in the wake of the Oakpoint tornado, and nothing had been ordinary since that day. In like manner, Leonora had fallen deeply in love with Jake.

"He's like Crane," she'd told me, "a deputy sheriff, except he's tall, dark, and handsome."

If only every love story in the world could turn out like ours.

I wanted the best for my friend. Next to Crane, I suspected that Jake was the best, although I hadn't cared for him in the beginning. He'd had the audacity to give me a speeding ticket. Perhaps it was deserved, but still… I hadn't been driving that fast.

I directed my attention back to the ceremony. These life-altering moments are over in a heartbeat. Vows, blessings, the flash of gold rings in the muted light, and it was done. A new marriage begins. The moment was so moving that I felt the sting of tears in my eyes.

That would never do. I dabbed surreptitiously at my eyes, taking care not to smudge my mascara, for that wouldn't do either. The first married kiss was over. It was on to the reception.

~ * ~

"I didn't see Brent anywhere in church," Annica said, "and he isn't here. He *was* invited, wasn't he?"

Annica had been hoping she'd be able to wear her blue sleeveless dress. With the rash gone, she could wear it, then proceeded to drape a shawl around her shoulders.

"He received an invitation, I know."

"Where is he then?" she demanded.

I had no answer for her.

Of course I'd already noticed that Brent was missing from the ceremony. Something serious must have detained him.

Not trouble, I told myself. *Don't think of trouble. Think of this fantastic cake.*

It had disappeared from my plate with lightning speed. This was one of the few bridal confections that both looked and tasted delicious, but then, Camille had made it in her own kitchen and decorated it with blue forget-me-nots and pink hearts, which had been Leonora's choice.

"Do you think Brent's in trouble?" Annica asked.

"Probably not," I said. "He may have a headache after yesterday's fiasco."

She looked so distraught that I added, "He may show up later."

"He wouldn't miss a chance to eat Camille's cake, would he?" she asked.

"I wouldn't think so. Brent loves cake."

"I saw his wedding present on the table with the other gifts," she said.

Clearly she had covered all the bases. But how had Brent's present gotten to the hall without Brent? I was curious, but I didn't need another mystery.

Lucy frowned. "I feel certain he's all right, which means he probably didn't go blasting off to Ashton bent on revenge."

"Let's hope not," I said. "The last I heard, Mac was going to search the town and arrest anyone who looks suspicious."

This wasn't the first time I'd worried about Brent's whereabouts. On a few of those occasions he'd been in serious danger. But how hazardous was taking Byrony Limon out to dinner? Like Lucy, I didn't think Brent had gone back to Ashton, and the Emergency Room doctor would have warned him about the possibility of headaches. Along with Annica I had to ask, 'Where is he then?'

I tried an alternate scenario. This time Lucy was wrong. Brent was lying in his bed slowly losing consciousness because of a misdiagnosed head wound. His days were numbered...

It wouldn't happen like that.

"Here come the bride and groom," Camille announced.

Leonora and Jake were making the rounds with a basket. As they approached our table, I saw they were handing out individually wrapped slices of wedding cake. Jake placed one in front of each of us.

"We want to make sure everyone has cake to take home," Jake said.

Leonora sent Camille a special smile. "This is the most amazing cake. We keep cutting it, and it keeps growing."

"I used a secret ingredient," Camille said, and Gilbert laughed.

"It's sugar," he said.

Everyone at the table laughed, but I didn't get the joke. I must be losing my sense of humor.

Leonora glanced at the empty seat next to me. "Where's Crane?"

"He was talking to that deputy who works with Jake."

Telling him about the ghost town? Perhaps, now that it was no longer a secret.

"We'd like to see him before we leave on our honeymoon," Jake said.

I knew my husband. "He's around somewhere. He'll be back for his cake."

It didn't do to hover. Still, I wished Crane would find his way back to me.

Leonora and Jake moved on with their basket, and I broke a forget-me-not off the top of my cake with a fork, wishing I could embellish my own cakes as artistically as Camille did, wishing the evening would never end, and at the same time, wishing it would.

I was suddenly, unaccountably tired.

This quiet, elegant evening had driven home to me how I'd been pushing myself to solve the mystery of the ghost town. I resolved to use the remaining days of my summer vacation to rest up for school, to walk in the sun, and savor the joys of my home.

What a good idea, I thought. *If you don't, you'll need another vacation. Now do it.*

Forty-eight

In the early morning, the spirit of romance tried hard to maintain its golden glow amidst the clatter of pans and dishes and the fussing of the collies. In my estimation, it succeeded.

The wedding had been perfection, the night better still. Crane looked fresh and bright and handsome in his uniform with its gleaming badge, and, thanks to the lingering sentimentality borne of the wedding, I felt as if I were a new bride.

I had sailed through breakfast-making with the poignant melody of *Pachelbel's Canon* playing softly in my head. The sun hadn't risen yet, but I had a feeling it was going to be a spectacular day. Yes, one of those never-failing feelings.

Being loved by the world's most wonderful man had that effect on me.

Crane drizzled maple syrup on the stack of pancakes I'd set on his plate. "What are you going to do today, honey?" he asked.

"Rest," I said. "I may work in the garden if I feel inspired."

I glanced through the kitchen window, although it was still too dark to see the yellow Victorian and Camille's marvelous garden. No matter what I did, my flowers never looked as healthy and showy as Camille's, even when she gave me some of her plants.

You were a natural gardener or you planted seeds and hoped for the best. I fell somewhere in between, a bit closer to the seed planter.

"Or maybe I'll skip the garden," I said. "It's looking pretty tired these days. Oh, and I'll walk the dogs."

Walk the dogs.

My crew heard that but could only concentrate on one pleasure at a time. At the moment, it was a pancake breakfast.

I refilled Crane's glass with fresh grapefruit juice. My plan for the day sounded a bit dull. Let's see what I could do about that. I'd walk the dogs up to Sue's horse farm and see if anyone had found Echo. That sounded a bit livelier. If Echo were still missing, I'd help Sue come up with another plan to find her.

Crane smiled. "You should be safe doing nothing. I just talked to Mac on the phone upstairs," he added. "They went out to Ashton yesterday. There's nobody there."

"The people in the town are good at hiding."

"And Mac and his men are good at searching. Not only was the town deserted but they didn't find any empty pop bottles or pizza boxes, nothing to suggest that anyone was living there recently."

I wondered what they did with their trash.

"They cleared everything out then," I said.

Including the bottles of elixir? Perhaps they'd never discovered them to begin with.

He nodded. "They didn't leave anything behind."

"Where could they have gone?"

"Probably to one of the towns."

"I can't think of any towns near Ashton. Maybe they're camping out in the woods until it's safe to go back."

"They went somewhere."

For some reason, I thought the people might have moved out of Ashton as a group. At one time I had suggested to Brent that they might be a cult. If that were the case, they would be together in a new place, in which case, they'd be certain to attract attention.

I had so many questions and no possibility of answers.

"I wonder how they knew to leave Ashton at that particular time," I said. "It's like they had a warning."

"They're psychic?"

"Could be. How about Brent?"

"No one's seen him. Mac hasn't heard from him since he made his report. But no one's looking."

"That isn't good."

"No, well, it's Brent. He'll be around. Bake one of those fancy pies he likes for dinner tonight. I'll bet he'll turn up."

I intended to do that in any event.

"He must have had a good reason to miss the wedding," I said.

"Didn't you say he left a gift?"

"That's what Annica said. But he didn't necessarily have to come to the hall to deliver it. No one saw him. He has several young workers at the barn who run errands for him."

"That's what must have happened then. Don't worry about him."

"The last time Brent went missing, he traveled back in time."

"That didn't happen last night."

"We don't know that."

"You're not serious."

"All right," I said. "It isn't likely. His last destination that I know of was a restaurant. I wish I knew which one. Maybe the Hunt Club Inn, but he took Byrony there before. Byrony was the last person to see him. I have no idea how to contact her."

"Brent will get in touch with one of us, maybe today," Crane said. "He doesn't like anyone tracking him down."

"He'd like it if he were in trouble."

"What happened to resting and working in the garden?" Crane asked.

"It fell by the wayside." Before he could offer a comment, I said, "More pancakes?"

"Please. Two more."

Candy followed me to the stove. I turned the heat on and spooned batter into the frying pan.

"Back," I said. "You'll get burned."

She didn't move. Misty padded up to stand beside her.

There was enough batter left to make small individual pancakes for the dogs.

I'm a servant and a cook for dogs, I thought.

I might as well spoil them. They'd have a rude awakening when school started.

a~ * ~

We were the only ones abroad this morning, Gemmy, Star, Misty, and I. A light fog hung over the lane, drenching the countryside in white magic. There was a strangeness in the damp air, an unaccustomed silence.

I listened to the clip-clop of a dozen paws on gravel. Why was it so quiet? Why weren't the birds chirping?

It was as if the world held its breath.

Something was going to happen.

Walk faster. Leave the ruins behind.

I hurried my girls past the abandoned development, past temptation. Misty veered to the left, as usual responding to a wild call I could never hear.

Gemmy tried to turn with Misty, but Star stayed on the lane. Honestly, Misty was growing as obstinate and strong as Candy. I hoped I'd be able to handle her as she grew stronger still.

"Heel!" I said to encourage my little white rebel. Star, who was heeling, flattened her ears. Holding my breath, I passed the outer limits of the ruins and travelled a good three yards beyond.

Safe.

Into the fog.

Was it getting thicker?

No, and it was still silent.

I was glad when we reached Squill Lane. Misty, single-minded, still wanted to turn left. In that direction, she'd find nothing but an uninhabited yellow Victorian cottage and a realistic scarecrow in a cornfield. I'd taken her that way once before, and she'd been afraid of the flapping collection of old clothes on a pole.

"Let's visit Sue," I said. "Let's see the horses. Horses!"

I lead my trio toward the farm, happy to see that the mist was thinner this way.

We heard the dogs barking before we could see Sue's ranch house properly. Were Bluebell and Icy making enough racket for three dogs, or had Sue added a rescue? Or was there a chance that...?

We turned in the drive, and they came running up to meet us, Bluebell, Icy, and a collie who looked like Echo... because she was Echo.

Step aside for one day, and everything changes.

Sue was outside with her new foal. She waved. Echo dashed up to us and doubled back to Sue, the picture of collie jubilation.

"Where did you find her?" I asked.

"On my porch this morning. The dogs were barking, then I heard scratching at the door, and there was Echo wagging her tail."

"Good Echo. You came home."

It wasn't that simple.

"But I don't understand," I said.

"That makes two of us. She had a note pinned to her collar. Three words, unsigned. It said: *Sorry Wrong Dog.*

We sat on the top step of the porch with the collies sniffing and play-bowing and yipping around us while I tried to assimilate the bizarre message.

"That doesn't make any sense," I said. "Someone steals your key and lets himself into your house. He steals the wrong dog, then returns her with an apology?"

"That's what happened," Sue said. "I don't know what to think. Except, how could the situation possibly get any weirder?"

Forty-nine

Six happy collies. In the morning sunlight, their coats had an ethereal shine. They were all so beautiful and so good. If Echo was the 'wrong dog,' could one of my girls be the right one? Camille's black Holly might also be in danger.

I didn't want to worry when there was no need, but it's best to be forewarned.

"Echo's coat was a mess when she came home," Sue said. "It was all over burrs. I checked her carefully for ticks. Heaven knows where they kept her."

Why did her captors neglect her? I wondered. Was it because they knew immediately that they had nabbed the wrong collie? All the time we'd been driving through Foxglove Corners and hanging 'Lost Dog' flyers, had their plan been to return Echo?

Sue reached out to pat Echo, but she danced saucily away to lap water from the dogs' drinking pail. Misty followed her example. The other collies were panting. They shouldn't stay out in the sun much longer.

"We'd better keep an eagle eye on our dogs," I said.

"I had my locks changed, and I'll never hide a key outside again. I don't know what more I can do."

"Neither do I. Maybe they'll leave you alone now." There wasn't anything to add to that subject. "Have you heard from Brent?" I asked.

"Not lately."

I told her about Brent's determination to keep his date with Byrony Limon in spite of the injury he'd received in Ashton.

"I'm waiting for him to call or drop over," I said. "He tends to keep us in the dark, or am I imagining it?"

"He really comes through for us, though. I still think the rogue league was behind Echo's disappearance."

"So do I."

With Echo's return, the sense of urgency was gone, but the mystery surrounding the rival rescue group was alive and well. More than anything I wished I would hear from Brent.

One comes home and another stays missing, I thought. *Go home and bake that pie.*

After I did that, I still had most of the day to do something just for fun. One of summer's last, lovely gifts.

"Call me if you hear from Brent," Sue said.

I promised to do so and rose, which was a signal for the dogs to cast longing looks at the beckoning road home. They were eager to return to their air-conditioned dens in our house.

~ * ~

Camille was watering her garden while Holly and Twister tried to attack the hose. They left the game to greet their canine neighbors.

"The ground is so dry," Camille said. "I'm thinking of having an irrigation system installed."

"It would save you time. You have a lot of flowerbeds to keep watered."

"I never considered it till this summer. I'd love for the grass and flowers to have a nice long drink while I sleep."

"Then you can spend more time in the kitchen," I said.

For many women that wouldn't be an incentive, but I suspected Camille was never happier than when she was whipping up a batch of muffins or a cake.

"There's rain in the forecast," I said. "I think I'll wait to water. By the way, Echo is back. The thief sent her home with a note saying, 'Sorry Wrong Dog.'"

"What on earth does that mean?"

"I don't know, but one of our collies might be next on the list. You'd better keep an eye on Holly."

"Unlike Sue, I'm usually home, and Holly and Twister are with me, but thanks for the warning."

"By the way, have you seen Brent lately?" I asked.

"Not for a while."

"He's making himself pretty scarce."

"You don't suppose he's in trouble?"

I didn't want to think that until I had no choice. "He's probably just preoccupied."

"I wish everything would settle down," she said. "It seems there's always something happening lately."

"Ever since we found the ghost town."

"And since we learned about that new rescue group."

I nodded. "We can't say it's been a dull summer."

"Sometimes dull is good," she said.

~ * ~

Three o'clock.

Two chocolate pies cooled on the counter. The dogs had been out to play and decided they'd rather nap in the house. It had turned into the kind of day that drains your energy until you feel like a rag doll whose stuffing has spilled out of the body, or like a deflated balloon.

I imagined the collies felt the same way.

I glanced through the kitchen window. While I'd been focused on not tearing my pie crust and creating high peaks in the meringue, the sky had darkened and acquired eerie yellow streaks. Once before I'd been unaware of changing weather conditions while a tornado formed and charted a course for my home. I'd vowed never to be uninformed again.

But like everyone, I'd grown complacent.

I turned on the television. There were no tornado watches or warnings, but a small thunderstorm symbol hung low on the screen. Rain would be good for the garden, but it wouldn't be prudent to go rambling around the countryside on non-essential jaunts.

With a sigh I shelved my half-formed plans for the afternoon and looked for a book to read. I found a Gothic novel, one Miss Eidt had found for me at a library sale in Spearmint Lake and read the first chapter. It wasn't especially good and soon, lulled by a lackluster plot and a gloomy afternoon, I dozed off.

Thunder rumbled overhead, sending Sky scurrying under the dining room table and Misty hurrying to my side. The other collies were oblivious.

I'd dropped the book, lost my place, but no matter. I never finish a book that puts me to sleep, never...

Another roll of thunder crashed into the silence. It didn't sound the same and seemed in the direction of Squill Lane.

Was it thunder?

What else could it be?

An explosion? Here in Foxglove Corners?

I waited for a third sound, but the silence was absolute. The sky was still ominous, but no rain fell yet.

I went outside and walked out to the lane, looking right and left, searching for some sign of smoke, which I thought would accompany an explosion. I didn't see anything that shouldn't be there and decided that I'd heard thunder, after all. Or perhaps a car backfiring.

Anyway, it was time to start dinner. I had a roast, enough to feed a dinner guest, if one appeared.

Candy and Misty watched me season the meat and lay it in the roasting pan. Now they'd begin the long wait for dinner. I wondered if all we were going to have of the storm were a few crashes of thunder.

~ * ~

As Crane had predicted, the chocolate pie drew Brent to Jonquil Lane in time for dinner.

"I told you so," he said as Brent parked the vintage Plymouth behind my Focus. "You baked a powerful pie, honey."

Brent was carrying a bouquet, the enormous kind you find in the farmers' market.

"He has flowers," I said. "I wish he didn't always bring something."

"Any other man would be suspicious."

"You aren't other men." I squeezed his hand on the way to the door.

But any other man might question the exuberance with which I greeted Brent. No one could doubt that I was overjoyed to see him.

"Where have you been?" I demanded.

"At home." He looked puzzled. "Gad. It's only been two days. These are for you... and the sheriff."

He held the bouquet high above the dogs who thought, in spite of the scents of roses and carnations, that Brent's offer was edible and intended for them.

"You missed the wedding," I pointed out, as I took the flowers and looked for a vase in the kitchen. Brent and the dogs followed me.

"Yes, I'm sorry about that. I sent Ryan with my present, but I couldn't make it."

I waited for an explanation. I knew he'd have one.

"It all caught up with me," he said.

"The attack in Ashton?" Crane asked.

"I didn't feel as good as I thought. I had a slight headache, so I took a nap, and when I woke up, it was too late to go."

Nothing sinister had derailed him, then.

I set the vase of flowers on the coffee table and stepped back to admire them.

"How did it go with Byrony Limon?"

"Byrony? Well…" He sank into the rocker and patted his knee, the traditional invitation to Misty to sit on his lap.

"I'm going to bow out of that project."

"Why?"

"It's a waste of time. Byrony isn't going to tell me anything helpful. I'm sure she knows what I'm up to."

"I thought she'd be easy to fool," I said.

"She's sharp and secretive. On top of that, she isn't very interesting. I'd just as soon eat alone."

He'd tossed the ball back into my court. I was disappointed but also determined. Somehow I'd find out what lay behind the sudden appearance of the rogue rescue league in our town.

"What I found out is stuff she didn't mind that I knew. Their money, for example. As of two days ago, they had sixteen hundred and fifty-five dollars in their account. That's all in donations."

"Very impressive," I said. "Our league doesn't have a fraction of that, and we keep spending money on our rescues."

"With them, it's all incoming, nothing outgoing. She can't tell me about a single collie they've rescued."

"Can't or won't."

"I'd say can't. Why should that be a big secret?"

"Because they haven't rescued any. Except the one whose picture was on their poster."

"I think their rescue is an elaborate scam. I wouldn't be surprised if they moved on to another town, especially since they know we're on to them."

"No," I said. "I won't let them get away with it. People will think other rescues are dishonest, too, and that might hurt us."

"What are you going to do?" Crane asked.

I didn't have any bright ideas or mediocre ones either.

"Trick them," I said.

Fifty

"Friday would be a good day to move on Byrony," Brent said. "She's going to be at Pluto's Gourmet Pet Shop selling her books."

"*Heart of Lassie.* I already bought one, but I can always go to Pluto's for treats."

"What can you do in one afternoon?" Crane asked.

"I'll have to come up with a plan."

It wouldn't be easy. First, I'd have to decide what I wanted to accomplish. I certainly couldn't accuse Byrony of running a scam without any proof. Well, I wouldn't do that in any event. I reminded myself that I was supposed to a member in good standing of the rescue league I was going to take down.

Just let her know you're on to her, I thought. *Pretend you have proof. While you're at it, suggest that she stole Echo.*

"You should take advantage of this opportunity," Brent said. "One day I'll bet they'll be gone."

"That would be good, except they'll leave with donations given in good faith."

"To fleece dog lovers in another town," Crane said.

"They sure made a bundle in Foxglove Corners," Brent pointed out. "To the tune of sixteen hundred dollars."

"At the moment, I don't have a single idea. Maybe Sue Appleton will."

I'd call her tomorrow. We might be able to take on Byrony together. But now it was time to suspend troublesome discussion and enjoy a quiet dinner together. Everything was ready.

As soon as he entered the dining room, Brent saw the pies on the credenza. "What kind are they?" he asked.

"Chocolate meringue," I said.

"Ah! Just what I was hungry for."

Crane winked at me.

I brought the roast to the table for Crane to carve, dodging collie paws and noses. I had convinced myself that Brent had met with another disaster when he'd only had a headache.

Only? I reconsidered. Headaches could be serious, especially after a blow to the head. This one had caused him to miss the wedding.

"I take it you didn't get your wallet back yet, Fowler," Crane said.

"No, and I don't think I will."

"Have you stopped your credit cards and gotten your duplicate identification together?" I asked.

"The credit cards, yes. Everything else takes time. I just wish I'd get my pocket watch back. It's a family heirloom."

He'd never mentioned having a special watch before. I was sorry he'd had to lose something he so obviously cherished.

"I hope Mac finds everything they stole, even your money," I said.

"All the cards that were in my wallet... losing that stuff is just an annoyance. The watch is most important. I had some nice pictures of the dogs, too."

I knew about the importance of heirlooms. I glanced at Rebecca Ferguson's candlesticks on the table. They were among our greatest treasures. I never let the candles burn down and thought their light cast a blessing on our lives.

"That reminds me," Brent said. "After dinner, I want to show you two something I found in my pocket. I must have picked it up in Ashton, but I can't for the life of me remember doing it."

"That sounds mysterious. What is it?"

"You'll have to see it," he said.

I noticed that Misty had left the semi-circle of collies in the doorway and slipped quietly into the dining room. She sat at Brent's feet, pretending to be invisible.

"Back." Crane had seen her too. She moved forward, further under the table, while Halley stared at her in dismay. Not to be outdone by her apprentice, Candy inched forward.

Well, Misty couldn't very well beg from there. I suspected a chunk of beef would find its way to her waiting mouth, wherever she was.

"This is a fantastic dinner, Jennet," Brent said. "How did you get so lucky, Sheriff?"

"I live right."

"So do I, but nobody cooks dinners like this for me."

"All you have to do is marry one of those ladies you take out."

I smiled at their banter. The roast and vegetables *had* turned out well, but I was eager for dinner and dessert to be over. I couldn't wait to hear about this mysterious something Brent had found in his pocket. Could it be that the Ashton story wasn't over yet?

~ * ~

After dinner, we took our pie and coffee to the living room. The dogs, ever hopeful, followed us and settled in their favorite places.

Brent pulled an object out of his pocket and laid it on the coffee table, frowning at it as if it were destined to remain a puzzle. It looked a little like Crane's badge, except for the primary illustration, a beast of some kind, perhaps a lion that had grown three horns. One yellow stone served as an eye; the other eye was missing.

"What is it?" I asked.

"A brooch. An emblem. An ornament. I guess it's meant to be worn as a pin, but it's too heavy for a shirt or suit coat."

"Is it okay if I touch it?" I asked.

"Touch away. When I first found it in my pocket, it was dirty. I cleaned it up and polished it. I thought it might be important. If I could just remember finding it."

The edges were sharp and the appearance vaguely unpleasant. The emblem could be worn on a thick coat, but it wouldn't do much to enhance it.

"I call it Yellow Eye," Brent said.

"Where did you find it?" Crane asked.

"In that house we thought could belong to the doctor… I think. I'm not sure. I thought you could help me remember, Jennet. It had to have been in that house, or I'd have showed it to you at the time."

"I'll try to help," I said. "But I don't know. I never saw it before."

While the day of the last ghost town nightmare was burned in my memory, a lion pin with a yellow eye wasn't part of it.

"Let's go back and try to remember every detail," Brent said.

"Okay. You were looking for a file cabinet. You thought the doctor might have left his files behind. I decided to check out the second floor."

He interrupted me. "Even though we'd planned on staying together. Why did we do that?"

I shrugged. "I don't know. My idea, I suppose. The one bed looked like it had been slept in. I never had a chance to tell you. That's when I heard a crash. I thought you'd dropped something. I called to you but you didn't answer."

Brent continued the story, first backtracking a little. "I didn't find any paperwork on the first floor, not even an unpaid bill. I remember going into the kitchen to check the cupboards when something heavy crashed down on my head. Prior to that, I didn't hear anything. I can't remember seeing this ugly emblem, much less putting it in my pocket.

Then I was lying on the beach. I heard your voice, saw you… I didn't look in that pocket until I was undressing for bed after I got out of Emergency."

"I'll never understand how your assailant moved you out of the house so fast. I came back downstairs as soon as I heard the crash. By the way, how's your memory lately?"

"It's good. I remember you bake the best pies in Foxglove Corners."

"You have me confused with Camille," I said, "but that's all right. We won't tell her. How about headaches? Have you had any more?"

"That was the only one. So far. Are you suggesting I just forgot picking up the emblem?"

"It's a possibility. Here's another idea. Could the person who struck you have planted it on you after stealing your watch and wallet?"

"Why would he do that?" Crane asked. "It doesn't make any sense."

"I'll admit the idea is bizarre. That blow might be more serious than the doctor led you to believe. I wish you'd go back to Emergency for a follow-up exam."

"I feel great," Brent said. "Who knows? Tomorrow I may wake up and remember picking up old Yellow Eye. Anyway, I don't have time for doctors, do I, Misty Girl?"

She wagged her tail.

"Have you gone back to Ashton since that day?" Crane asked.

"Once, but only for about a half hour. I didn't see a living soul, not even a creature or a black cloak. But the place spooked me. I don't like being there alone."

"You can't take Jennet with you," Crane said quickly.

"Or Annica or Lucy," I added. "The people in the town left before Mac could drive them out. Our ghost town adventure is over and, really, would that be so tragic?"

Brent tousled the fur on Misty's head. "Not tragic. Just unfinished."

We'll have to finish it then.

I didn't say that out loud, but I might as well have. I suspected we were all thinking it.

Fifty-one

We stood outside the window of Pluto's Gourmet Pet Shop admiring the imaginative display of canine-themed cookie jars, along with the trays of dog treats that resembled cookies and tarts for humans.

The ceramic dogs would make a charming addition to a dog lover's kitchen. My favorites were a spaniel with a scarf tied around his jaw to indicate toothache, a golden retriever in a Santa Claus hat, and a collie. Should I ask if the collie was for sale? My counter was already crowded, but I could always find room. Somewhere.

"Those cookies look good enough to eat," Sue said.

"Liver chip? I'm not that hungry."

"Our collies will be when they see them. And look at those little cakes. They look like pineapple upside down cakes."

Which they weren't, of course.

A blown-up cover of *Heart of Lassie* accompanied a poster announcing Byrony Limon's appearance in the shop. Propped up in a corner a rescue poster contained a plea for generous donations to the Foxglove Corners Collie Rescue League.

To the Rogue League, I thought wryly.

The illustration in the upper right corner, a collie with a winsome face and tulip ears, reminded me of Echo. Sue had the same thought. "Except for the blaze, she's a dead ringer for her," she said.

"I still don't have any bright ideas for waylaying Byrony," I said. "Do you?"

"We can ask her when the next fundraiser will be and volunteer to help."

"But we don't want to help. Of course that would give us another chance to mingle with them. All right. You do that. I'm going to try to come up with something more devious."

I wasn't going to demand too much of myself, however. It was unrealistic to think that I would be able to effect any change in five or ten minutes. I might not even have that long. I had an idea, though. Without knowing what use I could make of it, I had borrowed a picture of Echo from Sue, thinking something would come to me. It did.

Sue said, "I'll do my shopping first. If you were a dog, Jennet, would you like beef tarts or liver cookies?"

"Beef tarts, definitely," I said. "Unless I saw one of those pineapple cakes first."

Why did I suddenly crave a pineapple sundae at The Ice Cream Parlor?

Sue took off on her mission and I sauntered over to Byrony's table. Her green silk blouse matched the stripes on her cover, a clever touch. She gave me a bright professional smile. Copies of her books surrounded her, at least thirty of them.

She had brought along a companion, a tricolor collie. He lay at her feet gnawing a bone that looked real, but, as this was Pluto's, it was probably a clever albeit tasty fake.

I returned Byrony's smile, hoping she would think it was sincere.

"Jennet," she said. "How nice of you to come to my signing when you already bought a book."

I held on to my smile. "What's his name?" I asked.

"Name? Oh, the dog. This is Pluto."

"Cute name. He has a gorgeous thick coat."

The collie didn't look up from his bone. It was most un-collie-like not to respond to a compliment.

Since I was primed to be suspicious, I wondered if Pluto was the dog's real name, if he even belonged to Byrony. For that matter, did Byrony know the dog's name?

Collie for hire, I thought. *A little aid to selling books.*

"Are you in the market for more copies of my book?" Byrony asked, handing me an excuse to linger.

"I came to buy two more," I said, thinking quickly. "When you autograph them, one is for Jennifer and the other for Molly."

They were my young collie friends on Sagramore Lake Road. Although I hadn't read *Heart of Lassie* yet, I thought they'd like to have their own copies of Byrony's book. They shared the care of a collie, Ginger, and read everything about the breed they could find, both fiction and non-fiction.

"Have you or your members rescued any collies lately?" I asked.

Cool under fire, she took two books from the stack and opened one. "Lately? No. Thankfully all the collies have been staying close to home."

"That doesn't give you much to do."

"As you know, that can change at the drop of a hat," she said. "When it does, we'll be ready with the funds and foster homes to rescue them."

She signed her name in Jennifer's book with a flourish and opened the second one to the first page. I placed a twenty dollar bill on the table. At least I was receiving a tangible return for my money.

"I know of a collie who's gone missing," I said. "More accurately, she was stolen. Her owners would give anything to get her back."

"Are they offering a reward?"

"Two hundred dollars. She's a show dog."

I took the picture of Echo out of my shoulder bag and set it on Byrony's table, watching her expression.

As Brent said, Byrony was clever. She didn't hesitate and didn't give anything away. "What a pretty girl! Her name is Echo, you say?

Ah ha! I hadn't mentioned the lost collie's name.

I didn't give anything away either. Aware of people waiting in line behind me, I took the books and thanked Byrony for the autographs.

"I'm sure the girls will enjoy these," I said. "Now I'm going to buy some treats for my dogs."

~ * ~

"Gotcha!"

We left the shop behind, lugging several pounds of canine treats and two paperback books. "I wish I could have said that to her."

"That was brilliant, Jennet. You don't want her to know she trapped herself. Not yet anyway. Now what are we going to do with her?"

"In a perfect world, we could run her out of town on a rail."

"They don't do that anymore. Seriously, what can we do?"

"First, are you absolutely certain that none of the 'Lost Dog' flyers mentioned Echo's name?"

"They didn't. I always think it's better if whoever picks up a dog doesn't know its name. That's why I don't let my dogs wear name tags."

"Then here's what we'll do," I said. "Tell everyone who'll listen that they're not a legitimate rescue. If people don't believe us, they can ask to see their records and accounts. They can ask how many dogs they've rescued. How much they spent on vet bills for each one."

"They could always fabricate records," Sue said.

"How fast could they do that? They wouldn't expect to be challenged."

"If they're smart, they'd have falsified records ready."

"Let's hope they felt secure enough not to do that."

I trusted the grapevine, especially when it came to kennels and rescue groups. Word of unsavory doings would spread quickly. The rogue league, being new, was at a disadvantage. People trusted the Lakeville League and Sue Appleton. Over the years we had weathered a few problems, but, for the most part, had earned the respect and admiration of collie lovers in and around Foxglove Corners.

Although I firmly believed that Byrony's group was a scam, I felt there was more going on, something I couldn't know at this time but might find out if I dug deep enough. I couldn't rid myself of the idea that the formation of the group was also a personal attack on Sue Appleton.

Sue didn't think so. She had never met Byrony Limon, and none of us knew the ever-elusive Ann Clarke. At times I thought the rogue league consisted of one person—Byrony Limon. The other people, those at the meeting, for example, were borrowed for the occasion, perhaps paid a stipend for their participation.

As for Sue, she taught riding lessons to young people, rescued collies, and led the Lakeville Rescue League. She lived a quiet life in the country. What could anyone have against her?

That was for me to find out. It would take time, however, as did anything worth achieving.

Fifty-two

I was dreaming about the story again. That infernal story. Standing at the podium in my classroom, turning pages in my literature textbook, I tried desperately to find *Evening Primrose*, the subject of today's lesson. It should be there, but it wasn't.

The only explanation I could think of was that a whole chunk of my book was missing, including the pages which contained the story. The class was waiting. A few impatient whispers swelled into a cacophony of young adult voices yelling and screaming. A paper airplane landed on my desk. The principal walked by and glared through the window.

What was I going to do about the missing story?

As I rifled through the book, searching for a substitution, the dream changed.

Through the streets of Ashton I bolted, not knowing whether I was heading toward the lake or the bridge and freedom. They were behind me, hordes of sinister forms with masked faces and long cloaks.

I kept running. Pain sliced through my ribs. I could barely breathe. I would have given a year of my life to be back in my classroom, searching for the pages which were unaccountably missing from my book.

Abruptly I woke up. The dream shut itself off, but the terror of pursuit remained. I couldn't outrun them. Crane and Mac and Brent would come to Ashton, searching for me. They'd never guess that I'd been turned into one of the enormous Indians that stood sentinel outside the dime store.

Fully awake, I became aware of Misty standing by the bed, breathing heavily as if she were the one who had run through Ashton. If the beginning of school was going to inspire such ghastly nightmares, perhaps I should rethink my career.

I'd considered leaving Marston in the past, but for any number of good reasons had decided to stay.

Every teacher is apprehensive at the beginning of a new semester. I already knew my schedule, which was the same as last year's, but the computer didn't understand how a few students, even one malcontent, could affect the make-up of an entire class. Maybe it did, but being a machine, didn't care.

It flung names blithely into groups and spit out lists. I could have cooperative classes that were a joy to teach, difficult ones or— horrors—another class from hell.

Don't worry about it now.

Whatever the computer threw my way, I'd deal with, but dreams like the one I'd just had were another matter. In their grip, I was terrified. Running. Losing the race. Afraid of something outrageous waiting at the end.

Getting turned into a mannequin.

How outrageous! Still, the fear stayed with me.

What I should do was find a copy of *Evening Primrose* and read it. Strip it of the power to haunt me. And do it soon. Summer was winding down like a spent dog toy.

Make the most of each day. Walk the dogs and play with them. Get take-out dinners from Clovers and visit Annica. Bring a treat back for Camille. Top the days off with romantic evenings with Crane.

It all sounded good.

As soon as Crane left to begin his patrol, I leashed Misty, Star, and Sky, and took them walking up Jonquil Lane. I planned to visit Sue and Echo.

It had occurred to me that Byrony must be unhappy that she'd returned Echo with a cryptic note when she could have had a reward.

Except, of course, the reward was my fabrication. Byrony didn't know that. She'd know, however, that Echo was back home—if she'd returned her or ordered her return.

Misty gave a petulant little yelp. I might have known that we couldn't pass the ruins without some kind of drama. I had my easy collies with me, but Misty was rapidly growing into another category.

She sat in the middle of the lane, her brakes on, and gazed at the tangle of trees and vegetation and ruined structures as if all the wonders of her young life were contained therein.

"Misty, heel." I tried to make the command sound as enticing as 'cookie' or 'tart.'

She cast me a look of sheer deprivation. Her very life depended on turning into the ruins and running free. Did I really love her? If I did…

Collies can communicate so much with soulful eyes and pitiable whimpers.

Not that I considered letting Misty have her way. Not for a second.

Sky and Star lay down, waiting for my decision.

"Misty, come!" I gave the leash a gentle tug.

She countered by pretending I'd choked her.

"We are *not* going that way," I said.

For any one of a dozen reasons, along with a new one. The site looked especially forbidding today. Although the sun shone brightly on the lane, it barely reached the outskirts of the development. It appeared that more pieces of the mansions had crumbled since my last visit, which hadn't been that long ago. More trees had fallen, new saplings had sprung up, and vines had grown longer.

An illusion, surely, borne of my negative feelings about the place. Still, there was something… Something different about it today. I couldn't name or describe it, but it called more incessantly than usual to Misty.

Illusion. Imagination.

I wanted to be on our way.

"Who's the mistress here?" I demanded and gave Misty's leash another tug, a little less gently.

Finally convinced that I was, she padded beside me to Squill Lane. It looked to me as if she were pouting.

~ * ~

The rewards for being obedient were the biscuits Sue kept on the porch and also seeing her beautiful horses from a distance.

Her three collies were chasing one another around the ranch house, stopping every now and then to lap water and solicit pats from the guest. Misty indicated by every means available to her that she wanted to join them, but Star and Sky were content to lie in the small patch of shade they'd found.

Sue said, "I'm afraid Byrony is going to strike again."

"She's not likely to snatch Echo a second time."

"She'll do something else then. She knows you're up to something. You've challenged her, and she doesn't like to lose."

"We'll wait for her next move," I said. "In the meantime, relax."

"I wish I could. We may never be able to take Byrony and her group down."

"At this point, I'll be happy if we can drive her out of Foxglove Corners."

"Well, if people stop showering her with money, that may happen. I called everyone in the League to alert them to the situation, everyone except Leonora. Let's hope the grapevine is functioning."

"Leonora is still on her honeymoon," I reminded Sue. "I'll fill her in when she gets back."

"Your Misty would really, really like to run free, especially when she sees other dogs off their leads."

"She isn't going to."

I could see Misty, let off her leash, high tailing it back to her beloved ruins. She had two sides. One the gallant white collie who had shared my strangest adventures, and the other the wild young adolescent whose fascination with the ruins had reached new heights.

I loved them both but didn't quite trust the wild one.

What if Misty is the next to go? I thought.

Go where?

Byrony wouldn't dare steal her.

But she or her minion had grabbed the wrong dog before, if the author of the note were to be believed.

Did Byrony even know I had seven collies? I'd revealed this once at a meeting, but I didn't think anyone was listening to me.

There was no telling what Byrony might do. I'd better not take a chance.

~ * ~

To reach our house, we had to walk past the ruins again. When we reached them, Misty acted in the same annoying way, putting on her brakes, trying every trick in her repertoire to entice me into detouring into the heart of the development.

She was out of luck.

Raven left her house and dashed up the lane to meet us. When I opened the side door, she was the first one in. This appeared to be one of the rare times she wanted to spend a little time in the house.

I was happy to let her. After leaving Sue I'd been tormented by the thought of Byrony stealing our dogs. My next stop was Clovers, and I'd be more at ease if my entire brood was safe inside during my absence.

Byrony wouldn't have to concern herself with keys to take Raven. But I was reckoning without Raven, who could hold her own against most woodland creatures and occasional two-legged intruders.

Still, I believed that any dog could be stolen if the thief used the right method.

It wasn't the happiest thought I'd ever had.

Fifty-three

I strolled past Clovers' dessert carousel, surprised to see ice cream confections sharing space with pie and cake. A chocolate soda topped with whipped cream, an ice cream puff drenched in hot fudge, a pineapple sundae that reminded me of the upside down cakes at Pluto's—who could resist such delights? It was cool in the little restaurant but not so cool that ice cream desserts should remain as fresh as if they had just been made.

Annica, who was arranging slices of strawberry pie on the middle tier, noted my fascination.

"Why aren't they melting?" I asked.

"Because they aren't real. Everybody asks that. Sundaes are half price this week. This is Mary Jeanne's idea for advertising the sale."

"They look good enough to eat."

"You wouldn't want to bite into one." She twirled her earrings, miniature cones with mint ice cream scoops that set off her red-gold hair. I was happy to see her wearing a sleeveless green sheath. The rash on her arms was definitely gone.

"I can't pass up a bargain," I said. "I'll have a pineapple sundae and iced tea. I've been thinking about pineapple ever since seeing the upside down cakes at Pluto's."

"The pet shop? You'll find our pineapple is more appetizing."

"I hope so."

The booth with the best view of the Crispian woods was empty. Quickly I claimed it.

"What's new?" I asked.

"You just missed Brent by about fifteen minutes. He told me someone broke into his house."

"With all his dogs?"

"He was at the barn at the time, and the dogs were with him."

Poor Brent. He'd already lost his wallet, his heirloom watch, what most people would consider an enormous amount of money, and now he was a victim again.

"What did they steal?" I asked.

"More money. Apparently he leaves cash lying around out in the open. That's asking for trouble."

"It should be safe in your own house," I said. "He should leave Napoleon at home on guard duty."

Napoleon was one of Brent's rescues, a dog of formidable size and sharp white teeth.

"Yes, well, Brent likes to keep his dogs close."

I wondered if the burglary was an attempt to nab one of Brent's pets, perhaps his rescue collie. But that was a stretch. Besides, Byrony wouldn't know that the dogs weren't in the house.

"Is there anything new about Ashton?" Annica asked.

"I understand all the people left a few hours before Mac and his men arrived. It really is a ghost town now."

"Weren't the authorities going to take it over?"

"The property authorities?" I couldn't keep the sarcasm out of my voice. "I thought so, but they haven't yet. We were the only ones who cared about Ashton and what happened there."

"Now I only have one mystery left," she said. "The violet."

I'd forgotten about the mysterious flower that some of us connected with Violet Randall who had once lived in the pink Victorian house on Huron Court.

"Is it still growing?" I asked.

"It's multiplying. We have about eight or ten of them now, all in bloom."

"Then it's acting like a regular wildflower," I said. "We just have to identify it."

"If you're right, there goes my last mystery."

"You can help us shine a spotlight on the rogue collie rescue," I said. "We want everyone to know they're running a scam."

"How can I help?"

"By telling people that all the money they collect goes into their own pockets. Look for people who are likely to be sympathetic."

"That doesn't sound like anything a waitress should do," she said.

"No, but it's safe," I said. "Well, relatively, and you can choose who you talk to."

"I guess so." She rose. "I'll get your sundae. Are you going to order take-out today?"

"I'll have two stuffed cabbage dinners," I said. "This is one of those too-hot-to-cook days."

~ * ~

It was the kind of day in which conditions were perfect for thunderstorms to develop. I took Halley and Gemmy for a short walk down the lane, keeping an eye on the dark clouds amassing in the sky. By the time we reached the elegant white Queen Anne Victorian, the crown jewel of Jonquil Lane, the first raindrops began to fall, and we hurried home.

Later, with dinner in the oven keeping warm, I looked for a book to read. I remembered my intention of looking for *Evening Primrose*, and I'd never even opened Byrony Limon's *Heart of Lassie*. So, choose a story that haunted me fairly close to bedtime or familiarize myself with Byrony's book?

Heart of Lassie, I decided, and found the copy I'd bought from Byrony at the fair.

Lassie was a sable and white collie with a blaze, as the reader knew from the cover. This was her story, told in the first person, from her earliest days as a puppy, one of a litter of six sable females born on a farm in Harrisville, Michigan.

Her first days were filled with the wonder of green grass, a soft, loving mother, litter mates to play with, and marvelous toys. Eventually the scene changed. Green grass in a different place replaced her little family and familiar toys. She acquired a mistress, a young girl named Helena, who played with her and loved her and took her for long walks and to obedience school. Life was the series of happy days every puppy deserves.

Jennifer and Molly would love the book because it was about a collie. But they had cut their reading teeth on the meaty works of Lucy Hazen. They would ask more of a book than a chronicle of sentimental doggy vignettes.

I read to the end of the second chapter, then looked up from the page. To rest my eyes, I told myself, but also to wonder if anything was going to happen. It had to. Byrony's story couldn't sustain itself without a plot.

Seeing I was momentarily distracted, Misty tossed her Frisbee at me and fixed me with a look that clearly said, *Play with me.*

"In a while, pup," I said.

I should check the cabbages. I almost got up until I remembered that they were simply staying warm in the oven, not cooking.

Back to the book. I turned to the end, something I never allowed myself do with my Gothic novels. Byrony's book had one hundred and thirty-nine pages. It was a novelette, really, a genre I tended to avoid, but the illustrations were charming black and white sketches of a fluffy puppy turning into a stunning adult.

Misty yelped imperviously. I threw her Frisbee. When she didn't bring it back, I kept reading and eventually came to ripple in Lassie's smooth life. A new man came into Helena's life. He didn't like dogs, but Helena, who was besotted, made excuses for him. Before Lassie was a year old, she found herself secretly transported to a new location away from everything she had come to love. This new place had a name: the Lakelawn Rescue.

Did I really want to read this? Maybe not.

Thinking *Evening Primrose* would have been a better choice, I applied my speed reading techniques to *Heart of Lassie* and learned that Byrony's canine heroine went from the Lakelawn Rescue to a series of new homes. Her heart belonged to Helena whom she never saw again, hence the title.

Oh, for heaven's sake.

I closed the book. A dog story should have a happy ending. Real life often ended in heartbreak, but fiction didn't have to. Storybook dogs should live forever. Byrony could have written a heartwarming scene in which Lassie and Helena were reunited and the perfidious suitor came to an inglorious end. That was what I would have done.

Something tugged at me. A sense of *déjà vu*. Had I read a story similar to *Heart of Lassie*?

I sat back and tried to figure out what it was. Something about a woman whose boyfriend had given her collie to a shelter or rescue without her knowledge.

That had happened to our rescue. I remembered now. The Lakeville Rescue League had almost been involved in a lawsuit when a collie had been surrendered and placed in a forever home without the knowledge of the owner. In the end, the lawsuit hadn't happened, but I couldn't recall any further details.

Lakeville... Lakelawn...

Sue would know.

Byrony might have heard a similar story and used it in her book, as writers often do. On the other hand, maybe there was more to the incident... for example, a personal experience.

The matter was worth looking into.

Fifty-four

Four-thirty.

By now Sue should be finished with her riding lessons. Having made a tenuous connection between Byrony Limon and the Lakeville Rescue, I was anxious to see if Sue remembered the near-lawsuit.

As I reached for my cell phone, chaos erupted around me. Candy and Misty barreled into me in their race to the dining room window. From other parts of the first floor, the other collies added their voices to their clamor. I steadied myself on the edge of the credenza.

What had set them off? And why wasn't Raven barking? She was our first line of defense.

I pushed in between Candy and Misty and stood at the window just in time to see...

An image that disintegrated in the blink of an eye. What was out there? Shadows, a twisted, blowing branch that seemed to have human features, a large, dark bird flitting by?

None of the above. A face framed with stringy hair had stared back at me with burning eyes. Then it was gone so fast I wasn't sure I'd seen anything at all except a moment of nature whipped into a fury.

Nothing was there, but the dogs didn't believe it. They dashed back and forth between the window and the kitchen door, barking furiously, demanding to be let out. The enemy lurked on the other side of the glass.

We need to protect you!

Halley and Gemmy joined in the fray while Sky melted under the table, alarmed at the disruption in her peaceful routine, and Star pressed her body against my legs. Thank heavens for Sky and Star, the quiet ones.

"You're not going out," I said. "None of you."

I moved the candlesticks from the credenza to the table and began to set the table for dinner. As I arranged silverware around the dishes, I wondered if I'd really seen a face. I wasn't sure. If I were going to imagine a face in the window, I might as well have set the stage for weirdness by reading *Evening Primrose*.

In any event, there was no face outside the window now, no body attached to a face. Nothing. Regardless of what the dogs thought.

You saw a bird. Here for a fraction of a second, then gone. Or—maybe—a woman.

Show me a bird that looks like a woman, a woman with long, stringy hair and piercing eyes.

Byrony? It was natural that I'd think of her as she'd been so much on my mind. But Byrony took care with her coiffeur and her eyes were normal. I couldn't recall their color.

All right. If I didn't see a face, from what dark corner had I dredged up those details?

It was time to assemble a few facts stripped of emotional color. First, people didn't travel around Foxglove Corners on foot. Second, there were no cars in the lane. Third, Raven should have emerged from her house, barking at least as fiercely as Misty and Candy at an intrusion in her territory.

I opened the door and managed to slip outside without a canine at my heel.

The storm clouds were dark and full and low. I didn't see a single creature on our property or in the lane. Not even a bird, large or small.

Raven wasn't lying in front of her house, which wasn't cause for alarm. Often she took off on a run through the woods. She would be home for her dinner. She always was.

I went back inside, keeping the collies contained in the house. They were still agitated.

"Everyone, calm down," I said. "It's gone, whatever it was."

I'd been about to call Sue. I'd better do it now before Crane came home and before something else happened to prevent it.

~ * ~

Sue remembered the incident only too well.

"That was my first mistake as president," Sue said, "and it was major. It could have sunk the Lakeville Rescue League."

"Can you refresh my memory?"

"A man, Alex, surrendered a collie named Sparrow to the League, and I found a wonderful home for her. But it turned out that Sparrow belonged to his estranged girlfriend, Deanna, who had entrusted him with her care while she was in the hospital. Deanna is the one who threatened to sue us for giving away her dog.

"Then Sparrow was stolen from her new owners' yard and dumped in a high kill shelter. Deanna took matters into her own hands. She tracked Sparrow down and refused to part with her."

It all came back to me, the impossible dilemma and Sue's request for my help.

"Later Alex was killed, shot to death, in an unrelated incident," I said.

I recalled wondering at the time if Deanna had killed Alex in retaliation for what he had done to Sparrow. She swore she hadn't.

"Believe me, I never made a mistake like that again," Sue said. "Before we accept a dog, I check its papers and double check, then check again. Why do you ask?"

"Did you read *Heart of Lassie* yet?"

"No, I haven't had time."

"In the book, Lassie has an experience like that. If something similar happened to Byrony, it might explain her desire for revenge."

"But Byrony wasn't involved in Sparrow's story."

She had a point. I was certain I'd never heard of Byrony Limon until we had attended the rogue rescue's fair.

"How often is a dog surrendered to a shelter out of spite?" I asked.

"I suppose it's been known to happen. It would be the ideal way for a person to hurt someone he hated. What happened in the end of Byrony's book?"

"Nothing good. Lassie was never reunited with Helena."

"Well, our real life story had a happy ending. I think any similarity between the two is a coincidence."

"It's worth considering," I said. "Anyway, it's all we have."

Sue disagreed. "*Heart of Lassie* is pure fiction. I don't know how it could possibly tie in with our situation."

"I don't either, at the moment, but I'm going to delve into it. Did you save any notes on the Sparrow incident?"

"I have a file, I'm sure," Sue said. "I'll set it aside for you."

Having alerted Sue, who hadn't reacted with the enthusiasm I'd hoped for, I ended the call and became immediately aware that my surroundings were still unsettled. Misty and Cindy were pacing back and forth and panting as heavily as they did in hot, humid weather. The other collies were unduly restless. Halley had nudged Star away from my side.

"What's wrong?" I asked.

In reply Misty began a high-pitched keening that bordered on a howl.

I looked out the window to be certain the face hadn't returned. This time darkness stared back at me. Any moment it would rain, and I couldn't see anything unless deer had ventured too close to the house and vanished back into the woods.

But I'd better make a more thorough check. With protection.

My first choice of a canine companion would be Candy, but I couldn't take a chance that she would get away from me. Misty then. Leashing her, I squeezed through the door and circled the house, walking through the fading gardens, searching for the source of the disturbance.

Misty caught me off guard, pulling me out to Jonquil Lane. She headed straight for her favorite place in the world, the abandoned development.

I decided to trust her. We'd walk a little way. Then Misty would be satisfied, and I'd be sure that the owner of the intrusive face was gone.

If she had been there in the first place.

Fifty-five

We walked into the wind. Misty pulled on her leash, desperate for me to match her pace. I tried to keep up with her, but she seemed to have acquired super powers. All I could do was stay upright.

I didn't intend to venture much farther along the windswept lane. Bits and pieces of debris torn from the woods blew in my face. With my left hand I brushed them away.

This was madness. We'd better turn back.

Ahead a splash of black along the side of the lane caught my attention. A moment later I realized that it was an animal...

And in another moment realized that it was a black dog. I had found Raven. My beautiful collie lay at the entrance to the abandoned development like a black cloak that had been tossed aside.

Oh, Raven... No!

As I reached her, she looked up at me, trusting me to undo the damage, to make it better.

She was alive.

But she was hurt. Blood pooled under her right leg and formed a red trail to the lane's edge. Her leg... Crossed the way she held it when she slept.

Tears scalded my eyes. I saw but hardly registered the deep groves worn in the brush by tires. A car had hit her. The fiend behind the wheel had driven away.

There's no time for tears. Raven needs you.

"It's going to be all right," I whispered.

Misty nudged Raven's head. Licked her face. Lay next to her. Whimpered softly. She had known. All the collies had known, and Misty had done her part. Like Raven, she trusted me to make this horror better.

I reached in my pocket for my cell phone…

Not there. Of course not. I'd only meant to leave the house for a few minutes.

Then I had to… My mind froze. I willed it to thaw.

My frantic thoughts stilled long enough to form themselves into a plan. Take Misty. Go back to the house… Come back in the car… Doctor Foster could help. Was Crane home? Camille?

I gave Raven a kiss on the head, grabbed Misty's leash, and we ran back home, now propelled by the wind.

~ * ~

Crane wasn't home yet. It was too early. The dogs were in a high state of agitation, milling around, barking. Even Star and Sky. I took Misty's leash off and gave her a gentle shove into the pack. I didn't trust myself to speak to them.

My gaze fell on the kitchen towels hanging on a rack. I grabbed two of them and my shoulder bag with my driver's license and keys and dashed outside.

Now to see if Camille was home.

She was in her garden, dropping tools in the bucket she used for weeding, obviously finished with her gardening for the day.

"What's the matter, Jennet?" she called across the lane.

"You have to help me," I cried. "It's Raven. Up the lane. She was hit by a car."

The rake fell out of her hand.

"Is she… She isn't dead, is she?"

"Not yet. We have to get her to Doctor Foster."

"Just give me a minute to get my purse and lock the house," she said.

I couldn't begrudge her that minute, but it seemed like an hour. When she came back, I had the car turned around and the passenger door open.

"Thank God I was home," she said. "I almost went out. Are you sure it was a car? I haven't seen any traffic on Jonquil Lane in days."

"I saw the tire tracks. It's her leg."

Let her be alive. I prayed all the way to the ruins. Such a short distance to seem so long. So unending.

Finally I was there. I brought the car to a stop in the lane.

God, please let Raven live. She's always been such a good dog.

She hadn't moved. As I approached, her eyes fluttered open.

Camille's voice trembled. "Poor girl. We're here now."

"It'll be okay, baby." I touched Raven's head lightly, doubled the towels and gently wrapped them around her damaged leg.

Between the two of us, we managed to lift her and settle her in the back seat of the car, the bad leg facing the car's roof. She was so quiet. Was that good or bad? I couldn't think straight.

Camille scooted into the back and began applying light pressure to her leg. "I've done this before," she murmured. "And the dog was fine."

"Wait," I said. "I have a blanket in the trunk."

I spent precious minutes getting the blanket and settling it over Raven.

"Now, let's go," I said.

I'd forgotten Crane. Well, there was no time to write a note, but I had my cell phone.

"She closed her eyes," Camille said softly.

"That's good. I think."

Out to the lane. One road at a time. Drive as fast as possible. To the Foxglove Corners Animal Hospital where Doctor Foster had been known to work miracles.

A new prayer played in my mind. *Let Alice be there. Let her be able to help Raven. Please.*

~ * ~

This is your fault.

My inner voice had no sympathy to spare for me while I sat beside Camille in the waiting room of the Foxglove Corners Animal Hospital waiting for Alice to tell us that Raven was going to be all right. It continued to berate me.

You should never have let her run free. This was bound to happen.

Camille said, "I'm just glad you found her when you did. What made you go out with a storm on the way?"

The rain had arrived, a full blooded storm with crashing thunder and sheets of rain compensating for a hot, dry summer. It pounded on the high windows and sent many of the other furred patients looking for shelter, if only under their owners' chairs.

"The dogs knew something was wrong," I said. "They wouldn't settle down."

I'd forgotten about the face in the window. No need to mention it. Imaginary faces were irrelevant.

"If you hadn't gone out when you did, Raven might still be lying there," Camille pointed out.

The voice spoke again:

What if she liked to live outside in her house and run free through the woods? You're the human. You knew the dangers. You should have trained her to walk on a leash and sleep inside.

"I'll make her live in the house from now on," I said aloud. "She was used to running free when she came to us."

"What?" Camille asked, looking puzzled, not having heard the reproach. "Oh, yes, dear. That's a good idea. Keep her in the house. If you can do it."

Do it or prepare to lose her the next time, the voice warned.

"Jennet?"

Finally Alice appeared in the doorway. The young veterinarian looked like a college student with her long blonde hair worn long and loose over her shoulders. But I'd known her as long as I'd been in Foxglove Corners. She had skill and compassion and, best of all, experience. I couldn't have asked for a better doctor for Raven.

"The fibia of her leg is broken, and her ribs are bruised," Alice said. "She's going to pull through, but if a car mowed into her, it could have been much worse. I set her leg and will put a cast on it," she added. "Your girl will have to learn keep away from water and stay off it until it heals."

Camille wiped her eyes. "I don't know how anyone could hit a dog and just leave her lying in the road. It's criminal."

"Unfortunately it happens all the time in the country," Alice said. "People drive way too fast. They don't expect dogs to cross their paths."

"Is she suffering?" I asked.

"We gave her medication for the pain."

"May I see her?"

"Certainly, but she's sedated. I'm keeping her overnight. Call me in the morning, and we'll take it from there."

Now that Alice had worked her magic once again, now that the crisis was passed, I felt like crying.

Think about something else. Thank God for hearing your prayers.

Camille squeezed my hand. Alice had gone, and Raven didn't need me to be strong and brave for her at the moment.

"Maybe we can bring her home tomorrow," Camille said.

Home, I thought.

I had other collies at home to feed and take care of. And Crane. I'd left a voice mail for him, but he must be home by now. Raven and I were alive, and all I had to do suddenly overwhelmed me.

And there was something not on the list. As soon as possible, I intended to return to the abandoned development. The rain would have washed away the tire tracks, but possibly I could find a trace of the driver who had left my collie for dead in the lane.

Fifty-six

I stood knee-deep in the high grasses of the forsaken ruins attempting to recreate the accident. It seemed to me that the car had left the lane and swerved in Raven's direction, intending to crash into her. Along the way it had crushed a sapling, a patch of blue wildflowers, and Queen Anne's lace.

I assumed the impact had hurled Raven into the underbrush. Or... in another reconstruction of the events, she was already in the ruins, minding her own business when the driver aimed the vehicle at her. If that were the case, this was no accident.

There was the trail of mashed vegetation to consider. If Raven had been walking in the lane when the car crashed into her, could she have attempted to hobble on three good legs to the safety of the shadowed vegetation and collapsed where we'd found her?

I didn't want to believe that any human who possessed a heart could run a dog down on purpose. Not even Byrony Limon.

But someone had done this. Byrony?

I knew that I was demonizing her, blaming her for everything that went wrong, but I didn't care. I wasn't accusing her in a court of law, and it was less painful to blame Byrony than myself for Raven's misfortune.

Possible scenarios chased themselves around in my mind until my head began to ache.

I should have accepted Camille's offer to accompany me. She would have told me if I was too far in left field in believing that Raven had been deliberately targeted. When I'd declined her invitation, however, she'd left for a delayed trip to the store.

I glanced at my watch. Crane would be home soon. Interpreting clues in wreckage was part of his job, as part of mine was to have his dinner ready on time.

There was no reason for me to stay here in the wilderness speculating. Chances were I'd never know who had struck Raven and left her injured and alone.

Go on home, I told myself.

I had no love for these bits and pieces of would-be mansions flung far and wide. Glass fragments lurking in overgrown grass, entire collapsed walls, boards riddled with lethal nails—one wrong step could lead to disaster.

In the best of times, the ruins were gloomy and vaguely threatening, a place of death and decay. A bastion of evil. At present, these acres seemed particularly dangerous, although I couldn't have explained why. Maybe it was the heavy silence that hung over the area like thickening fog.

I didn't need to linger here any longer while my ever-robust imagination conjured demons. Anyway it felt like rain again.

Why are you still here then?

As I forced my gaze away from the tracks, I noticed a streak of orange a few feet away. It lay alongside a plant with monstrous green leaves larger than any leaf I'd ever seen. I went closer and saw that the orange object was a carrot lying on its side.

Straight from the carrot patch, still covered with particles of soil. Camille had a new vegetable garden. The bunch of carrots she'd given me for my last pot roast resembled this one. I recalled she'd been complaining recently about a bird or something—or someone—helping themselves to her harvest.

"It isn't the deer," she'd said. "I'll swear it's a person. But who on earth could it be? People on the lane have their own gardens."

A few feet beyond the carrot was a large tomato, not yet ripened, and an ear of corn. Then I found three small pickling cucumbers, the kind that tastes so good you can eat them like candy. I might have been looking at a trail of vegetables.

In fact, it appeared as if the fallen chateaux parts had been cast roughly aside to create a rough trail through the wilderness.

And how strange was that?

But the ruins attracted vagrants. Periodically Mac raided them, hoping to flush out ne'er-do-wells and even criminals.

I recalled the last time I'd ventured into the ruins. I'd discovered one structure, built far back from the others, that was in better shape than its fellows. To be sure, it lacked all four walls and a section of roof, not to mention the occasional window, but it was slightly habitable—for one who was desperate for shelter.

Desperate enough to plunder another's garden for lunch.

I told myself that these discarded vegetables needn't concern me. That, speaking or rather thinking of vegetables, I had to get those stuffed cabbages out of the oven. It seemed as if they'd been there keeping warm all day. Also I wanted to call Alice tonight to see if there'd been any change in Raven's condition.

But Raven was in good hands, and the fallen vegetables had captured my fancy. They seemed to form an arrow to that slightly habitable structure.

It wasn't too far away, a five-minute walk, if that. I knew I wouldn't rest until I determined whether or not another squatter had taken up residence in the ill-fated development.

Leaving the carrot behind, I set out in the remembered direction, making my way through tangled jungle-like growth, ever mindful of avoiding hidden glass. Eventually I came to the mansion that had defied the odds and remained somewhat intact while those around it had slowly come apart at the seams.

Again I became aware of the deep silence in the ruins. It reminded me of the silence in the ghost town when the very creatures of the woods appeared to have departed the earth.

Silence isn't always good.

The house looked the same as it had when I'd come this way before, a bit more wind-torn, perhaps. Gingerly I stepped through the opening that had been cut for a door and moved quickly through unfinished rooms on the first floor. Dust and debris drifted in from the surrounding woods made the floor slippery, and a pungent odor that I couldn't identify pushed its way through the stale air.

Presumably the staircase was in the same fair condition as the last time I'd navigated it. Planning to view the entire area from the second floor, I climbed the stairs, wishing the builder had added a banister.

Where was the best viewing window?

Most likely the largest room on the second story, the master bedroom. I found the window I sought—and something else. A threadbare brown blanket was spread on the floor next to an upturned cardboard box that held a paper cup. The cup was filled with murky water. Bed, nightstand, and carafe.

Someone had been squatting here, which wasn't a surprise. No doubt it was the person who had carried and spilled the purloined vegetables intended for a makeshift dinner.

In a place where there was no water to wash them, no electricity, and no stove, not to mention a pot or pan.

Well, desperate people have to make do with what they have.

I'd really better get out of here before the squatter returned. When I reached home, I'd call Mac, and he could make another one of his sweeps.

As I turned to go, I saw the off-white tiles. Affixed to the wall, each one bore a letter. Together they read: *Hilla's Room.*

Hilla. I remembered that unusual name and these tiles. When I'd last seen them, they'd been in a room in a house in Ashton. At the time I'd thought they were a little girl's way of claiming ownership of her bedroom before she had to evacuate the town.

Subsequent events had pushed the memory out of my mind.

Seeing them in this spooky, unfinished mansion, I didn't know what to think. Well, I did, but was it believable?

I stepped into the hall, anxious to get home and do everything I needed to do.

A rumbling cough, followed by footsteps on the first floor, told me I'd waited too long to leave. The footsteps moved slowly, heavily, up the stairs and came to a sudden stop at the top of the staircase.

The woman stood in front me, surprise etched into her wrinkled features. The black folds of her dress-like garment hung limply around her. Her hair looked like strings of yarn sewn into an unruly wig, and a straw hat with a wide brim topped her hair. A pin with a yellow stone added the only color to the unrelieved expanse of black. Brent's badge, Yellow Eye.

It was the owner of the face in the window, the face with stringy black hair and piercing hazel eyes with flecks of yellow. She must be the one who had burglarized Brent's house. And the black-cloaked figure who moved like a wraith through the streets of Ashton. The thief who stole vegetables from Camille's garden.

We stared at each other for a moment that seemed to go on and on.

Then she coughed again and swiped her hand across her mouth.

"You can't stay here—Hilla." I inched forward slightly.

She was blocking the stairs, cutting off my exit. But she was elderly and looked fragile. I could push her aside, overpower her. Possibly.

Fury flashed in those strange yellow-flecked eyes, but she didn't speak.

"You're trespassing on private property." I added a white lie for good measure. "I own this land and everything on it."

She didn't speak but looked over my shoulder.

The attack came from behind, came without a warning, without even a disturbance in the air. Pain exploded on top of my head. I felt myself falling, and darkness fell around me.

Fifty-seven

It was raining.

My head hurt. Dear God, how it hurt! I'd never had a headache so severe, and I was lying on a hard, cold surface which didn't offer any comfort.

I listened to the rain beating its hypnotic rhythm on the window. It was a soothing sound. I wondered if I should take a pain pill or just rest.

I couldn't go to school today; that was certain. I didn't feel strong enough to get out of bed. So I would lie still and let the sound of falling water sooth me. Maybe I could sleep the pain away.

~ * ~

Someone was calling my name. A familiar voice. I should know it, but it seemed to originate in a faraway place. It sounded like the ocean heard in a seashell. No, that wasn't quite right. It sounded like an echo then?

Gradually the voice faded. I turned on the pillow and looked through wet windows at a depressing gray sky. I felt ill or possibly hungry. Or both. And the pain in my head hadn't lessened, as I'd hoped.

I closed my eyes. The pain couldn't find me if I was asleep.

~ * ~

"How do you feel, honey?"

I knew that voice. Crane leaned over the bed. He was in his

uniform, wearing his badge. For a moment I thought it was embellished with a yellow stone, but that was ridiculous. A deputy sheriff doesn't wear a jeweled badge, even if he is the foremost deputy in Foxglove Corners.

"Any better?" he asked.

I grasped his hand. Felt its strength and warmth. Felt anchored.

"Terrible," I said. "Where am I?"

"In the hospital."

For a moment, I almost remembered. Green vegetation closing in on me, a smell of decay, tumbling down, rotting boards. A searing pain. Darkness.

I touched my temple. It felt tender, but the awful headache had abated. A little.

"What do you remember?" he asked.

Images danced crazily through my head. The line between reality and feverish imagination was blurred.

"A walking scarecrow coming to life," I said. "A crone, although I guess that isn't a polite word. An elderly woman. Anyway, she couldn't talk."

He kissed me, smoothed my hair back from my forehead.

"It'll all come back to you," he said. "Give it time. I love you. Go back to sleep."

~ * ~

Crane was right. He was almost always right. The next time I awoke I remembered. My trek to the abandoned development to view the tire tracks, the trail of spilled vegetables, my notion to explore the unfinished mansion, the living scarecrow climbing the stairs, staring at me, and the debilitating pain on top of my head—it all came back in a rush.

Why on earth had I thought it was a good idea to follow a carrot, cucumbers, and... other garden vegetables? I couldn't even recall what they were.

I let the restless images settle and recalled the tiles on the wall of the master bedroom in the crumbling mansion. *Hilla's Room.*

Hilla, the refuge from the ghost town. She must have been one of the original inhabitants of Ashton, one who hadn't left but still survived.

How strange. In all our visits to Ashton we had never seen her. Not fully. She'd been a black cloak rounding a corner, a hushed footfall beyond our peripheral vision, an entity moving in silence.

But there had been someone besides Hilla in the mansion, someone standing behind me.

"That woman must have come from Ashton," I said. "But why did she move to Foxglove Corners of all places?

I planned to ask Crane, but he was gone.

~ * ~

The next time I woke, it was dark. My dinner of fish and mashed potatoes lay untouched, and Crane was dozing in a chair by my bedside. Finally past events were clear, and I remembered the incident closest to my heart.

"Where's Raven?" I asked.

Crane jolted into wakefulness.

"Raven is home, honey. She's recuperating, but she isn't very happy. I think she'll do better when she sees you."

Anger welled up in me. A would-be killer had run Raven down and left her lying in the lane… or had steered the car into her path.

"Is she staying in the house?" I asked.

"That's why she isn't happy. And she doesn't like keeping her cast dry and not walking."

"We can't let her run free again. I don't know how we'll manage, but it has to be done."

Apparently Crane didn't know either, but our top priority was to keep Raven alive.

"Camille bought her a new bed and new toys," Crane said. "Misty stays near her. She brought Raven her toy goat."

Misty's treasured goat that she'd loved since she was a puppy.

I felt like crying. Or raging. The gown they'd given me was ugly. Dingy white with its stupid aqua and pink pattern that resembled twisted stars. I wanted to wear my own clothes.

"I should be with her," I said.

"You will be."

I was afraid to ask him when, lest it be longer than a day. Instead I said, "How did you know where to find me?"

"Camille remembered you were going to check out tire tracks. When you weren't there, I scoured the ruins. I remember you told me once about that house that wasn't entirely decrepit."

I told him everything that had happened up to the confrontation with the scarecrow woman who'd never uttered a word. After that my mind was a blank.

"Did they find the person who hit me?"

"Yes. By accident. It was a man who calls himself Slash. Mac stopped an old rattletrap going under the speed limit on the freeway. There were four people inside. None of them had a driver's license or identification. He has them in lock-up for assault."

"For attempted murder," I countered. "I could have died."

"I wasn't going to let that happen."

"Those people in the car, they were from the ghost town," I said. "When they left Ashton, they came to Jonquil Lane. I wonder why."

"We think because of you and Brent. Then that accursed site was a godsend for them. They had everything they needed to survive until you came along."

"I don't understand," I said. "Why were they following Brent and me? Just because we discovered their secret town?"

"Believe it or not, because of the badge the old woman wore. According to Slash, she's their leader. It gives her control over the others. They're like a clan," he added, "and there are more of them in other secret places. After they left Ashton, they split up. Brent still doesn't remember picking the badge up, but the woman suspected he had it."

The burglary. Brent would miss his money even though he left it lying around the house, but he probably never gave Yellow Eye another thought after he showed it to us.

"So she stole it back from Brent. That makes sense. But why attack me?"

"My guess is because you found their new home."

"And I told her to leave. I said she was trespassing on my property."

In retrospect, I could have said something less threatening, something that didn't include a lie.

"It's funny how things happen," I said. "All because someone had hit Raven and I returned to study the scene of the crime. And it *was* a crime. In ordinary circumstances, I would never have gone three yards into the ruins, never have seen the vegetables or thought of the one mansion that was still relatively intact."

One event led to another, and these thoughts brought me to a new suspicion. Could the vagrants' rattletrap have been the car that had struck my collie? Maybe now that the group was in custody, I'd have a chance to know.

~ * ~

It was a blessing to be in my own home with a clean bill of health. But everywhere I looked I saw hanging threads that begged to be tied up.

The scarecrow, Hilla, who refused to reveal her surname, couldn't or wouldn't talk. If only she could be persuaded to speak to me. Here was the witness I'd longed to meet. I didn't doubt that Hilla had been a child when the sickness had come to Ashton. What tales she could have told.

But she remained silent. Well, I hadn't exactly befriended her.

Slash knew some of the story. Mac had extracted details from him during a friendly interrogation. Slash had discovered Ashton one year while seeking for a safe place to spend the winter. He was overjoyed. He could choose whichever house appealed to him for his own and have a shelter and a bed. There was no warmth, of course, but in those early days it was possible to find cans of stew and salmon, beans, and fruit juice in abandoned cupboards.

Nothing he ate or drank in Ashton had killed him. Best of all there were no police to drive him out of town.

One day he discovered Hilla, who claimed that Ashton belonged to her, and she allowed him to stay. Over the years, others came and the group banded together, developing skills for making themselves invisible on the rare occasions when someone from the 'real world' intruded on their sanctuary.

Mac said, "The woman you call Hilla won't talk to us, Jennet. She threw a royal fit when they took that badge. You may have to wait forever to hear your history of Ashton."

"I can wait," I said.

In the meantime, I had my hands full keeping Raven amused, taking care of the other dogs, and obeying Crane's edict to rest so I would be in good shape when I went back to school.

"There'll be no more accidents or incidents," he decreed.

About the rogue rescue league, I could only continue to speculate.

~ * ~

I couldn't stop thinking about Hilla. The incident was over, the former transients of Ashton were in custody, and there was no reason I should spare them a thought.

Still, Hilla kept invading my thoughts. In my mind, she looked as I'd last seen her, dressed in scarecrow rags. And she still didn't talk. She was as silent as she'd been when I informed her that she would have to leave the ruins, that she was trespassing on my property.

In my defense, I was fearful, and justifiably so. However, I didn't have to speak so unkindly to her, and in truth, I didn't own the land the ill-fated chateaux were built on.

I also thought about her in another way: as a young girl living in a doomed town, arranging tiles to spell 'Hilla's Room.' Perhaps her family had perished. Or they could have left her behind when they fled Ashton. Whatever the cause, she had grown older in the ghost town and in later years became the leader of the band of homeless people.

What would happen to her now?

"She isn't your problem," Mac Dalby said when I asked him.

"Is it all right if I visit her?" I asked.

"Why do you want to do that?

"For closure," I said. "For her."

"That's idiotic, but if you insist, if it's all right with your husband…"

"Crane has nothing to do with this," I said.

He looked doubtful but agreed to let me see her for fifteen minutes. No more. Our meeting would take place on the following day, which gave me time to do something I had vowed never to do again.

As soon as I received his permission, I went home, leashed Misty, and hurried back to the gloomy, shadowy ruins. We tramped through thick, hostile vegetation until we reached the least deteriorated mansion, the scene of my latest confrontation.

Misty, who had been overjoyed at being led into her favorite place, balked as we entered the manor.

I hesitated. Could one of the vagrants have drifted back to the former sanctuary? I didn't think so. Mac had checked and assured me the people were gone. I believed that was true, if only because of the unearthly quiet that surrounded me.

Misty must have sensed my apprehension or perhaps the echo of the conflict that had taken place here.

"It's okay," I told her. "We won't be long. Just a few minutes…"

I retraced the route I'd followed earlier to the second story bedroom in which I'd seen the tiles. Quickly I removed them from the wall, which wasn't easy as their backs held the remnants of a sticky substance.

At home, I wrapped them in tissue paper. Tomorrow I'd take them to Hilla, along with a box of doughnuts from the Hometown Bakery. The doughnuts were a last-minute inspiration. Perhaps she'd think of them as a gesture of goodwill.

~ * ~

She didn't say anything but watched me as I removed the string and opened the box. The dozen doughnuts, cream and jelly filled, some with chocolate frosting, worked their magic.

She grabbed a chocolate doughnut and took a mammoth bite out of it.

I handed her the tiles. "For your new room."

Wherever that might be.

While the people who prowled through Ashton had scattered, finding new places to stay, I thought Hilla would go back to the ghost town, especially as the unknown powers that be appeared to have lost interest in it.

I knew I wouldn't be returning to Ashton, nor would any of my friends.

Lucy had seen Ashton some years in the future in which nothing had changed. Perhaps Hilla could live in peace in her own house, in Hilla's Room. And who knew? In time other homeless wanderers might discover the sanctuary town and form another family of sorts.

Ignoring the stack of napkins the bakery clerk had added to the box, Hilla grabbed another doughnut. She would probably eat them all. They had to be better than anything Mac could give her. I only hoped she wouldn't make herself sick.

"I have to go now," I said, aware of Mac hovering outside the cell, looking at his watch.

"Good luck," I added.

"All done?" Mac asked.

"Yes, and thanks, Mac."

I was ready to leave. By rights, I should feel happy. I'd accomplished what I'd set out to do. But I didn't. I felt only depression as I walked back outside into the sweet summer air.

Fifty-eight

In a week Leonora and I would be in our classrooms beginning another school year. I felt far from rested. In many ways, my summer vacation had been as trying as a ten-month stint of teaching English to teenagers who, for the most part, resisted learning.

I should have spent the summer lazing on a sunny beach. Oh, well. At this point all I could do was make the most of every remaining hour of freedom.

Unfortunately my summer was ending on an unfinished note, or rather, notes.

I still didn't know who had run Raven down or stolen Echo, then returned her with that cryptic message. And had Byrony Limon formed the rogue collie rescue solely as a scam or did she have an ulterior motive?

You'll never know, I told myself.

The fiend who had broken Raven's leg had driven away from the damage he'd caused, most likely without a further thought. Echo was safe at home with Sue. As for Byrony, I would need another entire summer to untangle the web she'd spun.

That evening, Brent came over to celebrate the end of the ghost town mystery with two pounds of human chocolate for Crane and me and two pounds of liver bonbons for the collies. Mac had returned his heirloom watch. The man called Slash had it.

"More good news," he announced. "They're gone."

"The vagrants?" I said. "Did Mac release them?"

"I'm talking about Byrony and her cohorts. When I couldn't reach her on her cell phone, I drove out to that house where she held the meeting. It's closed up with a 'For Rent' sign in the yard. Then I stopped at Pluto's Gourmet Pet Shop. Somebody took their poster down."

"Who?"

"The manager didn't know. Something weird is going on. I'm thinking that if I tracked down that *Banner* with the story of the group, it wouldn't be there."

Although he couldn't have meant that literally, I felt a momentary chill. "This *is* Foxglove Corners, but we didn't imagine them."

"Hell, no. I'm not saying we did. I didn't take a ghost lady out on a date."

He dropped in his favorite rocker, still holding the boxes, and the dogs gathered around him, lured by the sweet smell of liver.

"Byrony knew you were on to her, Jennet," Crane said. "She wrapped up her operation and skipped out of town before you could go any further."

"I was hoping she'd have to pay for running the scam."

"I don't think there were many people in that rogue group," Brent said. "Those women at the meeting could have been hired actresses. They didn't seem committed."

"The same goes for the girl at the fair with the sheltie that she claimed was a collie. The whole booth could have been a set-up."

"Byrony went to a lot of trouble to deceive us," I said.

"It paid off. That so-called rogue group is hundreds of dollars richer."

"And I'll bet Byrony never rescued a single collie," I added.

Brent yielded to collective canine pressure and opened the box of bonbons, scattering treats on the rug. He saved a handful and carried them to Raven who lay quietly in her new bed. "So we're through with them."

"Let's hope so," I said.

I couldn't be too happy, though. I hated to see a loose string dangling in mid-air.

"There's something I learned from Mac about the vagrants, but I don't know if I should tell you," Crane said.

"Tell me."

"The day Raven was injured, Slash was behind the wheel. He lost control of that old car the people had."

"So it wasn't deliberate?"

"He says it wasn't."

I couldn't say 'That's okay, then' because it wasn't. But I could stop wondering and obsessing about it.

~ * ~

"Oh, good," Sue Appleton said. "School didn't start yet. Have you recovered from your little setback?"

A blow on the head, a concussion, a monster headache? I'd call them major.

"Pretty much," I said. "Thanks for the flowers. Those rainbow carnations were lovely."

"I need a favor, Jennet," she said. "Desperately."

I wished I'd ignored the melodious voice of my cell phone. A call that began this way never ended well. Still I asked, "What is it?"

"I wouldn't ask you if there was any other way."

This wasn't going to be good. I waited.

"Okay. I'll just come out and say it. I need someone to drive up to Harrisville tomorrow to pick up a rescue. Bonny is a little sable female, three years old. She lost her home through no fault of her own, and it so happens that I have an application from a wonderful family. They're looking for an older dog. They lost their collie last week."

"This is where I came in," I said, remembering the day we drove north to pick up Echo, the thunderstorm, and the dark beyond the bridge. "Can't you go, Sue?"

"I'm getting ready to leave with some of my students for a horse show. I can't desert them."

"What about Emma Brock? Or someone else in the group?"

"I've called everyone, even Leonora. She just came back from her honeymoon, but she says she'll go if you will. It'll be just a few hours out of your life, and the weather will be ideal for a short trip."

"Foxglove Corners to Harrisville and home again. I wouldn't call that short."

"Well it isn't long. You'll be home before dark. You can drop Bonny off and have plenty of time to enjoy your evening."

"Leonora said she'd go?" I asked.

"She did."

I found that hard to believe. Leonora had just come back from her honeymoon and hadn't even called me yet. Sue wouldn't lie. She might exaggerate, though.

"I guess I can," I said. "But I'll have to check with Crane."

He might veto the idea. But should I let Crane dictate to me? And this was my last chance for a short getaway until... Next summer?

"Oh thank you, Jennet," she said. "Thank you. We'll find a way to reward you."

"Well," I said, "give me some time to think of a good one. By the way, if you're going out of town with your riding students, who'll be there to welcome Bonny?"

"My niece will. She's taking care of the dogs. Are we all set, then?"

"As set as we'll ever be."

~ * ~

We set out early the next morning with a case of bottled water, peaches and plums, and my map of Michigan, which we didn't need as Sue's directions were crystal clear.

We stayed on the freeway, made no detours, and, hence, made no marvelous discoveries on the way.

"Jake is an exceptionally understanding man, being willing to part with his bride so soon after the honeymoon," I said.

"He's going to be gone on sheriff's business for two days," Leonora informed me. "But, yes, he's every bit as wonderful as I dreamed."

She seemed ready to launch on an exposition of Jake's perfections. Had I ever been that rapturous about Crane? Surely not.

"Our contact, Judith Prine, is a retired teacher and collie breeder," I said. "She founded the North Country Collie Rescue. She lived near Lakeville, so we should know many of the same people."

As we covered the many miles to Harrisville, a plan took shape in my mind. Judith and Sue knew each other. Was it possible that Judith also knew Byrony Limon—or Ann Clarke? By the time we sighted Lake Huron, I was counting on it.

Judith lived in an old white farmhouse on an acre of land. As we slowed down, even before we came to a stop, about twenty collies, all colors and sizes, rushed to the fence. They pushed one another out of the way to be the first to greet the newcomers and solicit pats.

Judith came out to greet us, a plump woman in jeans with dark brown hair and an engaging smile.

"Welcome, Jennet and Leonora," she said. "Did you have a good trip up?"

I thought of thunderstorms and ghost towns. "It was uneventful."

"Which one is Bonny?" Leonora asked.

"The small sable, third from the left."

The girl who held her tail between her legs and her ears flat against her head. My heart went out to her. If we could win her confidence and give her a happy new home, I'd have a better reward than any Sue could give me.

"Bonny's owner passed away unexpectedly," Judith said. "She's a little timid. I'll bring her inside, and we'll sit and have a cold drink... or lemonade, whatever you like. She'll get used to you and you can have a brief rest before starting the drive downstate."

We sat around her dining room table with tall glasses of lemonade while Bonny lay close to a wing chair, her front paws crossed, her dark eyes regarding us gravely. Judith busied herself gathering Bonny's papers.

The clock in the living room chimed twice. We weren't going to have unlimited time to visit, so I'd better not waste any of it.

"Did you ever hear of Byrony Limon?" I asked.

She frowned. "I don't think so. That's such an unusual name. Did she have another one? A married name, maybe?"

"How about Clarke? Ann Clarke?"

"Ann," she said the way one would say 'spider' or 'toad.' "Oh, yes, I had the misfortune to know her well. But she called herself Ann Clarkston when she lived in Harrisville. Why do you ask?"

I told her about Byrony Limon, the organization that had set itself up to compete with our Lakeville rescue league, and the scam.

"Ann did that here," Judith said. "Ran a scam, I mean. She went around buying collie puppies from the farmers. Then no one ever heard of those babies again. Do you think she's the same woman as this Byrony Limon?"

"It's possible. I thought at one time she was just a name."

"If Ann has resurfaced, you're in trouble," Judith said. "I had no idea she was still in business."

"I think she's moved on to another town."

"With all that money. That's criminal."

"Yes, it is. One of Sue's rescues was stolen and returned with an odd message: *Sorry, wrong dog.* I wondered if Byrony was behind that."

"It sounds like her. She used to love to play weird, hurtful pranks. She really had it in for Sue Appleton. Sue refused to let her adopt a pair of rescues one time. Her phony application must have raised a number of red flags. Ann didn't like anyone to cross her."

Why couldn't Sue have remembered this? Possibly Ann/Byrony had used a third alias or they'd only communicated by phone.

Well, if it sounded like Ann, it *was* Ann. I didn't have proof, but I would always believe that Ann had taken Echo and taunted Sue with the cryptic message.

Leonora glanced from the clock to her watch. "We should start back, Jennet. It's a long drive."

I drained my glass and rose. "Thank you for everything, Judith. You've been a great help."

Leonora took Bonny's papers, and I approached our dignified little rescue.

"Will you come with me, Bonny?" I asked. "I'm going to take you to a wonderful place where you'll be the top dog."

The little collie got up and stretched. Once again her tail disappeared between her legs.

Well, what else could I expect? We had several hours to win her over, and we were going to do it.

~ * ~

Four hours later we reached Foxglove Corners. Our little rescue had been carsick, then slept through the rest of the trip.

"All's well that ends well." Leonora gathered up the dish we'd used for Bonny's water. "I'm going to go home and do my baking for the week now. I want to have good desserts for Jake every night just like you do for Crane. Pretty soon, we'll be busy with meetings and schoolwork."

"Sometimes I cheat and buy them at Clovers, but you know that."

"Oh, I'd never do that," she said.

"Ha!"

I dropped Leonora off at her house and a sleepy collie girl at Sue's farmhouse where Sue's niece made an elaborate fuss over her. My thoughts then turned to home. Crane was waiting for me with my own dogs. Raven must be figuratively climbing the walls. The evening was young, and this was my life, as glorious and new as that of a bride. I couldn't wait to start living it again.

With a light heart I turned the Focus around and headed back down the lane.

Meet Dorothy Bodoin

Dorothy lives in Royal Oak, Michigan, with her Wolf Manor collie, Kinder Brightstar. Royal Oak is an hour's drive from the town that serves as a setting for her Foxglove Corners cozy mystery series.

Dorothy graduated from Oakland University in Rochester Michigan with Bachelor's and Master's degrees in English and taught secondary English for several years until leaving education to write full time. She has written one Gothic romance and six novels of romantic suspense, along with the Foxglove Corners series.

Other Works From The Pen Of

Dorothy Bodoin

Treasure at Trail's End (Gothic romance) - The House at Trail's End seemed to beckon to Mara Marsden, promising the happy future she longed for. But could she discover its secret without forfeiting her life?

Ghost across the Water (romantic suspense) - Water falling from an invisible force and a ghostly man who appears across Spearmint Lake draw Joanna Larne into a haunting twenty-year-old mystery.

Darkness at Foxglove Corners - Foxglove Corners offers tornado survivor Jennet Greenway country peace and romance, but the secret of the yellow Victorian house across the lane holds a threat to her new life. (#1)

Winter's Tale - On her first winter in Foxglove Corners Jennet Greenway battles dognappers, investigates the murder of the town's beloved veterinarian, and tries to outwit a dangerous enemy. (#3)

A Shortcut through the Shadows - Jennet Greenway's search for the missing owner of her rescue collie, Winter, sets her on a collision course with an unknown killer. (#4)

Cry for the Fox - In Foxglove Corners, the fox runs from the hunters, the animal activists target the Hunt Club, and a killer stalks human prey on the fox trail. (#2)

The Witches of Foxglove Corners - With a haunting in the library, a demented prankster who invades her home, and a murder in Foxglove Corners, Halloween turns deadly for Jennet Greenway. (#5)

The Snow Dogs of Lost Lake - A ghostly white collie and a lost locket lead Jennet Greenway to a body in the woods and a dangerous new mystery. (#6)

The Collie Connection - As Jennet Greenway's wedding to Crane Ferguson approaches, her happiness is shattered when a Good Samaritan deed leaves her without her beloved black collie, Halley, and ultimately in grave danger. (#7)

A Time of Storms - When a stranger threatens her collie and she hears a cry for help in a vacant house, Jennet Ferguson suspects that her first summer as a wife may be tumultuous. (#8)

The Dog from the Sky - Jennet's life takes a dangerous turn when she rescues an abused collie. Soon afterward, a girl vanishes without a trace. Ironically she had also rescued an abused collie. Is there a connection between the two incidents? (#9)

Spirit of the Season - Mystery mixes with holiday cheer as a phantom ice skater returns to the lake where she died, and a collie is accused of plotting her owner's fatal accident. (#10)

Another Part of the Forest - Danger rides the air when a kidnapper whisks his victims away in a hot air balloon, and a false friend puts a curses on a collie breeder's first litter. (#11)

Where Have All the Dogs Gone? - An animal activist frees the shelter dogs in and around Foxglove Corners to save them from being destroyed. Running wild in the countryside, they face an equally distressing fate and post a risk to those who come in contact with them. (#12)

The Secret Room of Eidt House - A rabid dog that should have died months ago from the dread disease runs free in the woods of Foxglove Corners, and the library's long-kept secret unleashes a series of other strange events. (#13)

Follow a Shadow - A shadowy intruder haunts Jennet's woods by night, and a woman who can't accept the death of her collie asks Jennet to help her find Rainbow Bridge where she believes her dog waits for her. (#14)

The Snow Queen's Collie - A white collie puppy appears on the porch of the Ferguson farmhouse during a Christmas Eve snowstorm. In another part of Foxglove Corners a collie breeder's show prospect disappears. Meanwhile, the painting Jennet's sister gave her for Christmas begins to exhibit strange qualities. (#15)

The Door in the Fog - A wounded dog disappears in the fog. A blue door on the side of a barn vanishes. Strange wildflowers and a sound of weeping haunt a meadow. The woods keep their secret, and a curse refuses to die. (#16)

Dreams and Bones - At Brent Fowler's newly purchased Spirit Lamp Inn, a renovation turns up human bones buried in the inn's backyard, rekindling interest in the case of a young woman who disappeared from the inn several decades ago. As Jennet tries to solve this mystery, she doesn't realize it may be her last. (#17)

A Ghost of Gunfire - Months after gunfire erupted in her classroom at Marston High School, leaving one student dead and one seriously wounded, Jennet begins to hear a sound of gunshots inaudible to anyone else. Meanwhile, she resolves to find the demented person who is tying dogs to trees and leaving them to die. (#18)

The Silver Sleigh - Rosalyn Everett was missing and presumed dead. Her collies had been rescued, and her house was abandoned. But a blue merle collie haunts her woods and a figure in bridal white traverses the property. (#19)

The Stone Collie - Jennet's discovery of a collie puppy chained in the yard of a vacant house sets her on a search for a man whose activities may threaten Foxglove Corners' security. Meanwhile, horror story novelist Lucy Hazen is mystified when scenes from her work-in-progress are duplicated in real life. (#20)

The Mists of Huron Court - The house was beautiful, a vintage pink Victorian in a picturesque but lonely country setting, and the girl playing ball with her dog in the yard was friendly, suggesting that she and Jennet walk their dogs together some time. Jennet thinks she has made a new friend until she returns to the house and finds a tumbling down ruin where the Victorian once stood and no sign that the girl and dog have ever been there. ((#21)

Down a Dark Path - What hold does the pink Victorian on Huron Court have on Brent Fowler who is determined to re-create the home of long-dead Violet Randall? When he disappears, could he have been cast adrift in time?

Shadow of the Ghost Dog - An invisible dog grieves inside the house chosen as a setting for a movie based on Lucy Hazen's book, *Devilwish,* and a landscaper unearths a human skeleton in the backyard while planting shrubs.

44626977R00176